Praise for D.R. Meredith's John Lloyd Branson Mysteries

MURDER BY IMPULSE

"D.R. Meredith's High Plains mysteries started great and got better. MURDER BY IMPULSE is the best yet—delightful characters in a dandy story. If you haven't read D.R. Meredith, here's the book to begin with."

Tony Hillerman

"The crime is imaginative, the characters memorable, the West Texas locale evocative, and the story hair-raising. In four increasingly suspenseful novels.... Meredith has developed into a fresh, snappy voice of crime fiction."

Newsday

MURDER BY DECEPTION

"The first mystery I've seen in which the truth is more frightening than fiction, the only mystery I have ever read in which I felt that *I* might be one of the ultimate victims."

Sharyn McCrumb

"Meredith again demonstrates that sinister criminals and horrifying crime do not require London fog or New York streets to be exciting.... Branson and his lovely assistant keep the action and the humor flowing as the horror dances around the edges of the tale."

Fort Worth Star-Telegram

Also by D.R. Meredith
Published by Ballantine Books:

MURDER BY IMPULSE
MURDER BY DECEPTION

MURDER BY MASQUERADE

D.R. Meredith

BALLANTINE BOOKS • NEW YORK

Library of Congress Catalog Card Number: 90-93283

ISBN 0-345-35986-0

Manufactured in the United States of America

First Edition: January 1991

To the victims:
Mary Ann Nichols
Annie Chapman
Elizabeth Stride
Catherine Eddowes
Mary Jane Kelly
Lest we forget them in our fascination
with him who murdered them.

Amarillo, Texas—August 31

FEAR WALKED BESIDE PURPLE RAIN.

She heard his footsteps as a hollow echo inside her head, smelled his sour breath as the acrid stench of her own flesh. She didn't bother glancing around or cringing in the nearest doorway. After five years of walking Amarillo Boulevard, she recognized him. Any of the girls who walked the Boulevard where it sliced through the north part of the city between Grand and Hughes streets recognized Fear. He was as familiar as their own slick faces in the summer when the work day started at four in the afternoon and the sun boiled your skin to the shade of a red-hot candy; as familiar as bare, purple legs in the winter when the wind dropped the chill factor to below zero.

Fear was dependable, too, she thought, scanning the passing cars for one whose driver looked at her with something more than a sneer in his eyes. He was always there, like an extra gland. Or a patron saint for hookers. Maybe Fear made a lousy saint, but she lived in a lousy world, and Fear was the only thing nobody could take away.

Fear accompanied her to the police station when the cops

1

busted her for prostitution, waiting with her until Jo-Jo arrived with bail money. Fear witnessed her beatings when Jo-Jo accused her of slacking, or of being too ugly or lazy or stupid. Fear laughed when she was too cold or too hot or too tired, or when a john knocked her around just to hear the soft thud of his fists on her flesh, or when Jo-Jo was late making his drug connection and her world took on sharp edges. Fear laughed hardest when, stinking of sweat and too many men, she returned to the squalid motel room and dreamed of being someone else tomorrow.

She stopped in the middle of the sidewalk and laughed. It was pretty damn funny at that. Whores don't have tomorrows. They don't have yesterdays either. They only have today. The Cowgirl said that. She was always making pronouncements like that, things you remembered even when you were floating high and outside on some drug-tinted cloud, looking down on yourself and seeing someone that maybe wasn't so lost after all.

She walked on, her feet sweating in the cheap vinyl pumps. Her whole world was a six-block length of Amarillo Boulevard. Back and forth, like a dog with a chain through its collar and the other end fastened to a clothesline. The Cowgirl was right. Purple Rain didn't have a tomorrow. Her fairy godmother was a pimp waving a line of coke instead of a magic wand, and any Prince Charming she might meet damn sure wouldn't be holding a glass slipper. She was Purple Rain, not Cinderella.

She licked the sweat from her upper lip, its salty flavor tainted with the dirty taste of yesterday's makeup. Names. She had so many of them. Streetwalker, prostitute, hooker, slut, whore, depending on who was doing the name-calling, and none of them the one she was born with. Jo-Jo got rid of her real name a long time ago.

"You gonna be born again, girl," he had said. "You gonna be Purple Rain, and don't call yourself nothin' else." He had grinned, the diamond mounted in his gold front tooth flashing. The Cowgirl called him a stereotypical pimp, but not where he could hear her, not after he had beaten her so badly she spat blood for a week.

She shrugged her shoulders and hurried down the block

to the next streetlight. It didn't matter, not anymore. What the hell was a name anyway? Just another hook for the cops to hang you on, track you from city to city like you were some endangered species with a radio transmitter planted under your skin.

She laughed again and coughed, a hacking sound from too many cigarettes, too much dry, Texas Panhandle air. Endangered species! That was another fucking laugh. Whores were endangered, but not of becoming extinct. They were in danger from pimps and johns and drugs, from disease and other jealous whores and growing old, and from funny little invitations made up of letters cut from newspapers, invitations like the one in the scarred vinyl purse slung over her shoulder.

CHAPTER ONE

SERGEANT LARRY JENNER HAD A BELLYACHE CREATED IN equal parts by the chief of the Amarillo Police Department; his lieutenant; the entire vice squad including its head, Lieutenant Roger "the Bean" Green; the hot-as-hell-for-September weather; the patrol car's nonfunctional air-conditioning; and the special he'd just eaten at Lu Chee's Chinese Emporium. He belched and fumbled two chalky tablets out of his uniform pocket. Lu Chee offered a choice of fortune cookies or so-called digestive aids with the special. A smart man, being anybody who had previously eaten at the establishment, picked the digestive aids. The fortune cookies were only good for hammering nails.

Not that he was such a smart man, Jenner thought as he chewed. A smart man didn't sneeze when the chief asked for volunteers, then argue with his lieutenant about it afterward. A smart man didn't work Vice wearing a uniform and driving the only car on the lot whose air-conditioning didn't work just because Roger "the Bean" Green wanted to show "a presence" on the Boulevard. A smart man didn't eat in Lu Chee's Chinese Emporium. A smart man wasn't a cop, but *if* a smart man just happened to be a cop, he didn't lose a witness.

4

"Now tell me again how you managed to fuck up this one, Jenner."

Lieutenant Roger Green had small feet, a small head, spindly legs, narrow shoulders, and a round little potbelly that bulged against his shirt. Put a green stem on top of his head and he would look exactly like a bean pod. He also had mean eyes. In Jenner's experience, bean pods didn't ordinarily have mean eyes.

The mean eyes blinked. "I'm waiting, Sergeant."

Jenner pulled his sodden uniform collar away from his neck. "Four A.M. and it's still hot as hell," he said, following the observation with a chuckle. When a cop's just screwed up and his superior is about to castrate him, a little levity defuses the situation.

"I didn't ask for the time and temperature."

Obviously this superior didn't appreciate levity. Jenner began again. "I had just taken my dinner break down at Lu Chee's. You ought to try it, Lieutenant. Good food, plenty of it, and . . ."

"When I want a restaurant report, I'll read the paper," Green interrupted, taking a deep breath that stretched his shirt tighter over his bean belly. "Now get to the point before I put you in charge of body searches at the city jail."

Jenner swallowed, visions of dirty, bug-infested, nude bodies dancing in his head like spoiled sugarplums. There were three indisputable laws of nature regarding body searches: one, no one to be searched had bathed in the previous three weeks; two, seventy percent had vomited just before being searched; and three, the remaining thirty percent vomited *while* being searched.

"I was heading west down Amarillo Boulevard when this hooker ran out in front of the car, waving her arms and screaming at me. Scared the crap out of me, Lieutenant. There I was, minding my own business, checking the passing scene for anyone that looked suspicious or out of place, like maybe somebody in a store when the store was closed, or . . ."

"You weren't looking for hookers?" asked Green softly. "Like you were supposed to."

"Look for them! Hell, I didn't have to look for them. They

were all up and down the sidewalks like an Easter parade. What I wasn't expecting was to find one in the middle of the Boulevard breathing on my radiator. Looking through your windshield to see a woman wearing nothing but a leather vest and miniskirt looking back at you isn't my idea of a relaxing time. In fact, it was a downright stimulating experience. I slammed on the brakes, did a doughnut, and stopped by that streetlight.''

"You didn't stop *by* that streetlight; you stopped *on* it.''

Jenner felt his face turn even redder as he looked over Green's shoulder at his patrol car, its radiator resting comfortably on either side of the streetlight. "Damn it, you didn't expect me to hit the girl, did you?''

Green expelled a loud breath, then took another, and Jenner decided the older man's buttons were sewn on with elastic. It was the only explanation why they hadn't popped off with the velocity of speeding bullets. "What happened next, Sergeant?''

Jenner cleared his throat. "The girl leaned against the car door and yelled that somebody butchered Purple Rain. I told her to stay put and I tried to get out of the car.'' He stopped and took a breath. This was where things got a little complicated. "The door was, uh, stuck, jammed against the frame, from the impact, I guess. Anyway, the girl took off like a running back for the Dallas Cowboys as I, uh, climbed out my window. I chased after her, but she was gone. I came back to the car and that's when I found the bloody handprints on the door.'' Jenner nodded his head toward the car. Maybe Green would be excited enough about those prints to forget he'd lost the hooker.

Green wasn't. "Sergeant, did you think maybe she was a Sunday-school teacher reporting some kid for stealing from the collection plate?''

"No, sir.''

"You thought she was a hooker, is that right?''

"Yes, sir.''

Green sighed. "In your experience, Sergeant, are hookers reliable, responsible, well-meaning citizens ready to help the police?''

"No, sir.''

"Then why in the hell didn't you grab her wrists and slap the cuffs on her when she leaned in your window? Did you think she was going to wait around like some Brownie scout until you got out of the car?"

"Things were happening pretty fast, Lieutenant. Besides, I didn't have any cause to cuff her. Even whores have rights. *sir*," he added when the lieutenant's face turned an interesting shade of puce.

"No cause to cuff her? A whore whose hands just happen to be dripping blood tells you another whore has been murdered, and you don't think you've got probable cause?"

Jenner pulled at his collar again. He felt knee-high to a year-old steer already, and his next admission ought to leave him feeling lower than an ant's belly. "I didn't see her hands."

Green assumed a long-suffering expression. "Somehow that doesn't surprise me. You couldn't see a pile of dog shit ten feet high if you stepped in it."

"That's not fair!" exclaimed Jenner, feeling a little long-suffering himself. "I'm a good cop. I just had a touch of bad luck, that's all."

"That's not fair," mimicked Green. "Jesus Christ! Tell it to the ACLU. Did you at least secure the crime scene, Jenner, or did you give guided tours to all these good folks?" the lieutenant asked, waving his arm toward the Boulevard denizens who padded around outside the narrow beams of Jenner's patrol car like scavengers sniffing after spoiled meat.

Good folks, my ass, thought Jenner. The good folks deserted the Boulevard by six o'clock every evening after locking and barring their businesses tighter than the American Embassy in Beirut. After sundown, the pimps, hookers, winos, gamblers, pickpockets, bookies, pushers, dealers, and creatures of indeterminate sex and occupation crept, crawled, slithered, sneaked, slinked, sidled, minced, scuttled, flounced, stalked, strutted, swaggered, or tottered out from whatever rocks they lived under during the day. Like cockroaches and vampires, they avoided the sunlight. Jenner ground his teeth together when he heard a snicker from the crowd. It was bad enough to be chewed out without Green's doing it in front of every piece of shit on the Boulevard.

He gathered what was left of his dignity, squared his shoulders, and pushed his chin forward belligerently. Bloody, but unbowed, that was him. "No one has gone near the crime scene after I ascertained the victim was a D.R.T., dead right there."

Green rubbed his chin. "I guess even you could tell a slit throat from a red ribbon. And you called for the Special Crimes Unit?"

"Yes, sir," Jenner replied, swallowing hard. Jesus, but he wished Green weren't so graphic. The victim's throat did appear to have a red ribbon around it, but that was because the wound gaped open at least a thumb's width. There were massive wounds on the body, too, but he hadn't looked too closely at those. It was enough to know that no one could live through having her throat cut to the backbone.

"That's two things you did right, Jenner," said Green, looking pensively toward the slack, white body lying a few feet inside an unpaved alley.

"What was the other thing, Lieutenant?" Jenner asked, trying to think of anything he'd done since birth for which Green hadn't chewed his butt.

Green drew another deep breath. A button popped off his shirt and rolled under the patrol car. "You said whores had rights. They do. They've got the right not to be beaten by their pimps, not to be worked or drugged to death, not to cater to every whim of some sick bastard with a hard-on. Most of all, Jenner, they got the right not to die like a butchered hog."

Jenner almost liked him. "You sound like you feel sorry for them."

Green shook his head. "They're a piss poor lot, most of them, but there's worse people. The pimps, for example. They're maggots." He turned his head to look west up the Boulevard. "Here comes Special Crimes. Took them long enough to get their butts in gear."

He looked back at Jenner. "You stick around to answer any questions, then head home. You're off this detail. The Boulevard's gonna heat up over this murder like Old Faithful ready to erupt, and I don't need a fumble-butt like you around."

"I'm *not* a fumble-butt. It's like I told you, I had some bad luck."

"Don't give me hard luck, Sergeant. I hear that from every asshole I arrest. I don't need it from you. Just stand over there by your car and try not to fuck anything else up." Green walked away to meet the Special Crimes personnel, scratching his hairless belly where it was exposed by the missing button.

"Goddamn it!" said Jenner, slamming his fist on his bumper. The patrol car give a wet hiss from its radiator and settled more comfortably against the light post. He looked balefully at it and kicked the right front tire that promptly flattened against the asphalt with a tired whoosh. In ten years of being a cop, he'd never been booted off an investigation. Of course, he'd never wrecked a black and white before, and he'd never lost a witness either.

He turned as the large, cream-colored van with POTTER-RANDALL COUNTY SPECIAL CRIMES UNIT printed on its side spewed out white-clad figures from all four doors. Since the unit was in charge of investigating all suspicious deaths, and since suspicious deaths usually involved blood leaking from one or more artificially created orifices in the victim's body, all the Special Crimes investigators resembled workers checking for radiation leaks after an atomic bomb test. Better to waddle around in hot, uncomfortable, disposable clothing than risk contacting AIDS from infected blood.

Jenner felt as if he had some life-threatening disease of his own. Even his own men, his traffic cops, who had been arriving by ones and twos during Green's tirade to direct traffic and to keep the predatory spectators at bay, were avoiding him. He couldn't blame them. A good rule of thumb for cops was to stay out of the way and look busy when another cop was getting his ass chewed. That way they protected their own asses if the chewer was in a feeding frenzy and one victim was insufficient to satisfy his appetite.

Jenner shifted his feet and looked around. Time to Band-Aid his bite marks and get back in the game. Otherwise, he might as well kiss the police department goodbye. A sergeant who looks ridiculous soon loses his authority and his self-respect. And right now he, Sergeant Larry Jenner, had about as much authority and self-respect as a pimp in a Volkswagen.

He straightened his collar, tucked his shirt in, checked to see that his fly was zipped, and took several deep breaths. No point in talking to Green again. Green wouldn't let him back on the Boulevard if he were the only one-eyed cop in a department of blind men. But the figure standing next to Green would. No doubt about it. That figure, looking like a square Frosty the Snowman in his protective clothing, was Sergeant Larry Jenner's ticket back into the game.

"Schroder," he said, walking up to the two men.

Lieutenant Green jerked his head around. "I thought I told you to keep your butt back by the car," he said, standing nose to nose with Jenner.

"Schroder, I gotta talk to you," repeated Jenner, sidestepping out of range of Green's bad breath.

Sergeant Ed Schroder of Special Crimes turned around and all resemblance to Frosty the Snowman ended. There was nothing jovial about Schroder's face. From thinning sandy hair, bushy eyebrows like caterpillars overhanging faded blue eyes, and square jaw, to the unfiltered cigarette clamped in one side of his mouth, Schroder looked like a cop who expected the worst and generally wasn't disappointed.

"You catch this squeal, Jenner?" asked Schroder, expelling a cloud of tobacco smoke.

"Yeah," replied Jenner, thinking that the investigator had the most mobile half a mouth he'd ever seen. Schroder could talk, eat, and, for all Jenner knew, kiss the ladies, without removing his cigarette.

"Probably another mistake on his part," said Green in what Jenner classified as a pissed-off tone.

A rumbling sound that passed for laughter issued from Schroder's barrel-shaped chest. "Jenner would rather catch herpes than a murder squeal."

"Schroder, I want to talk to you about that," Jenner began.

"Hold on, son," interrupted Schroder, stubbing out the last half inch of his cigarette. "The flashbulbs are dying down. That means either the photographer's taken pictures of everything that'll stand still, or he ran out of film. Let's examine the body while he decides which.''

"I'm not your son, damn it, and I've seen the body," protested Jenner.

Schroder wrapped a meaty hand around Jenner's arm. "You might've missed something."

Jenner had. He'd missed the extent of damage to the girl's torso. He wished he'd missed Lu Chee's special. The combination of the two threatened to send him running to the gutter. Schroder objected to anyone vomiting on the crime scene.

Jenner concentrated instead on Schroder's motionless figure squatting by the body. People shaped like Schroder didn't kneel; they squatted. Jenner thought it had something to do with the leg length in proportion to the sum of the right angles of the torso. In Schroder's case, that meant a square with no identifiable waist resting on two rectangular blocks.

"Recognize her, Green?" asked Schroder as he rose, clutching a plastic bag containing a piece of paper in one hand.

"The other hooker called her Purple Rain," answered Jenner.

"Your name Green?" demanded the lieutenant, glaring at Jenner.

"What other hooker?" asked Schroder, stepping away from the body and toward the street.

"The one that told me about the body," answered Jenner, following him. "The one that jumped in front of me and caused that." He waved his arm toward the wrecked patrol car.

"The one *he* let get away," said Green, jerking his thumb in Jenner's direction.

"But I got her fingerprints on my car. In *blood*," he added, with a glance at Green.

Schroder glanced from Jenner to the patrol car and back again, then stuck another unfiltered cigarette in the corner of his mouth and lit it. As the smoke curled around his face like a noxious fog, he snapped his fingers at another figure dressed in protective clothing. "Dust Jenner's car," he grunted. Jenner supposed it wasn't actually possible to grunt words, but the investigator came close.

"What'd she look like?" asked Schroder, rolling his cigarette to the other corner of his mouth.

Jenner felt his sweat glands go into overdrive. When Schroder asked for a description, he expected every detail down to how many fillings and in which teeth. "Uh, it was quick, and I didn't expect her, so I might have missed a few minor details."

"Like what?" asked Schroder, again with that grunt in his voice.

"Uh, her hair was long . . ."

"Jesus Christ," said Green. "That fits about ninety percent of the hookers on the Boulevard."

". . . and she wore a leather vest and miniskirt."

"That sure cuts it down, Jenner," said Green. "To maybe about fifty percent. A lot of johns like the leather look. Makes 'em feel naughty."

Schroder didn't say anything at all for several seconds, or maybe hours. Jenner couldn't tell which. Time spent with Schroder always seemed long. It was a gift he had. "Quit fartin' around, Jenner," the burly investigator finally said. "Tell me what you saw that scared you into acting like a candy-assed rookie."

Jenner rubbed his wet palms up and down the stripe on the side seam of his uniform trousers. "I was driving with the low beam on, so her face should have been shadowed when she jumped in front of the car. It wasn't, Schroder. Maybe for a second she was close enough for even the low beam to light up her face, but I don't think so. If she had been, I would've hit her. Even putting the car in a spin I don't think I could've missed her."

"Wait a minute!" shouted Green, scratching his exposed belly vigorously. "Just wait a damn minute. What about the crap you gave me about that hooker breathing on your radiator? You made it sound like she was fixing to climb through the windshield. Now you're saying she was too far away for you to get a good look at her face but that you did anyway. Which is it, Jenner?"

"I saw her face," Jenner said desperately, feeling more

like a fool every minute. "It was so white, her eyes looked like two holes burned in a sheet; so white, it damn near glowed in the dark. It was—eerie."

"Was she still *eerie* when she leaned in your window?" asked Green sarcastically.

"I never said she leaned in the window; you did. I said she leaned on the car. I never saw her face after that one time."

He heard Green utter a particularly colorful profanity and figured he'd just moved up to the number-one place on the lieutenant's shit list, but he couldn't worry about it now. "I'll know her again, Schroder. Transfer me to Special Crimes so I can work this case, and I'll find her."

"You're not going to let this fuckup work a homicide, are you, Schroder?" demanded Green. "Besides, I just kicked his butt back on traffic. He ain't safe on the Boulevard."

"Sergeant Jenner has worked two homicides with me," said Schroder softly with a bland expression in his eyes. "He's like a bloodhound on the scent, can't wait to start tracking down another dangerous murderer."

In a pig's eye, thought Jenner. If he had any other choice, he'd run like hell as far away from a murder case as he could, and furthermore, Schroder knew it. The bastard had him by the short hairs, and Schroder knew that, too.

"That's me, Lieutenant, a bloodhound," agreed Jenner, trying not to gag over the words.

"If he's a bloodhound, I'm a horse's ass," said Green.

Jenner decided not to argue that point.

"Who was her pimp?" Schroder asked Green.

"Piece of scum named Jules 'Jo-Jo' Jefferson. High visibility pimp, drives a white Lincoln with a TV antenna on the roof. He's got a rap sheet so long it takes a forklift to pick it up: drugs, pimping, gambling, assault, murder. You name it, and he's been charged with it. Not that it does much good to pick him up. We charge him, the D.A. tries him, and he walks. Witnesses leave town, develop amnesia, or turn up in an alley with busted kneecaps and heads. A busted kneecap's no incentive to perform your civic duty."

"How bad did he knock around his girls?" asked Schroder.

Green shrugged his shoulders. "He never killed one that we know of."

"Think he'd cut one up like this?"

The lieutenant scratched the cowlick on top of his head. "I could see Jo-Jo beating one of them to death if she crossed him, but to tell you the truth, Schroder, I can't see him doing this. He's a badass and crazy, but I don't think even Jo-Jo Jefferson's crazy enough to gut a woman."

Schroder looked at the plastic bag in his hand. "And he sure as hell wouldn't warn her first."

"Warn her? You're talking like he's a rattlesnake. The only warning Jo-Jo ever gives that he's pissed off is that first busted kneecap." Green snickered.

"We found an invitation to join a heavenly choir clenched in the victim's hand."

Jenner felt a chill start at the top of his head and work down his spine. "Jesus, that's sick."

Green peered at the plastic-sealed piece of paper. "That's the third thing you've got right, Jenner. It's sick, but it ain't Jo-Jo. All the words are spelled right."

"Hey, Schroder." The fingerprint expert interrupted, squinting at the sergeant with a perplexed expression. Jenner had noticed that all print men squinted. Must have something to do with staring at whorls and arches all day. "I dusted those bloodstains on Jenner's car, and you ain't ever gonna guess what I found."

"I'm not in the mood to play Twenty Questions, Patterson," said the investigator, shifting his attention from Green to Jenner. Jenner wished to hell he'd find someone else to look at. Preferably someone in the next county.

Patterson shook his head. "I didn't find anything, Schroder. No prints, no fibers from gloves, just two hand-shaped bloodstains."

"Holy shit," exclaimed Green. "A whore with rubber gloves? What do you think about that, Schroder? You think your bloodhound let a murderer run off?"

Schroder looked back at the body, a stark, white figure with one scarlet ribbon around her throat and another between her breasts, down her belly, and disappearing into the dark pubic hair. "I think Sergeant Jenner's not safe on the Boulevard."

CHAPTER
TWO

Canadian, Texas—September 1

"DEAN JOHNSON, THIS IS LYDIA ANN FAIRCHILD."

"Is the old bastard dying?"

"What? Who?" Lydia exclaimed, squeezing the telephone receiver and feeling it slide against her wet palms.

"John Lloyd, of course," answered the dean impatiently. "That is whom this conversation is about, isn't it? I presume you're not calling me at home on a Saturday morning because you want to hear my melodious voice."

"No. I mean, of course I don't mind hearing your voice," said Lydia, feeling her throat tighten.

The dean's sigh whistled over the line. "Miss Fairchild, students don't like to hear my voice. I'm always asking questions they don't want to answer, or making statements they don't want to hear. Which is it?"

"Which is what?" asked Lydia, swallowing to loosen her vocal cords.

"Did I ask you a question you don't want to answer or make a statement you don't want to hear? To repeat, is John Lloyd dying?"

"No! I mean, it's a possibility." In fifty years or so, she

16

thought, and wondered if her prevarication counted as a full lie or only a half lie in whatever eternal record book God kept on law students who worked part-time for lawyers like John Lloyd Branson.

"Had a sudden relapse, did he?" asked the dean.

"Relapse?"

"I've been reading the papers, young lady. John Lloyd may live four hundred miles away in a town with fewer people than the average college campus, but he's still good copy. Eccentrics always are. There was an article in the *Dallas Morning News* about him and a corpse in a corn field."

"Wheat field," said Lydia.

"What?"

"The corpse was found in a wheat field."

"I knew it was some edible crop. Held the tottering old fool's hand while he fought for truth and justice, did you, Miss Fairchild?"

"John Lloyd's not old!"

"I doubt that he's tottering either."

"Of course not!" said Lydia, then realized how indignant she sounded and continued more cautiously. "But the case was exhausting. After Mrs. Dinwittie called you last week— you know, John Lloyd's secretary . . ."

"I know Mrs. Dinwittie," interrupted the dean. "She dismembered her husband in lieu of a divorce."

"According to John Lloyd . . ."

". . . it was self-defense," said the dean, finishing her sentence. "A reaction to Mr. Dinwittie's habit of firing a revolver around the house. Mostly at her. I believe John Lloyd called her behavior a temporary aberration. The jury believed it. I'm not sure I do. At any rate, I'm damn uncomfortable around that woman when she has a sharp object in her hand. Aberrations can be a lot like malaria; you never know when an attack is coming. You were saying, Miss Fairchild?"

Lydia tried to backtrack through the conversation. Talking with the dean was like being lost in a maze; you were always looking for a point of reference.

"After Mrs. Dinwittie called me," prompted the dean.

"Oh, yes. Well, you excused me from class, and I drove

right up. You thought that since I clerked for John Lloyd this past summer I might be able to help. You'll never believe what I found, Dean Johnson. John Lloyd was"—she searched for a word—"undone."

"You're right, Miss Fairchild. I don't believe it. John Lloyd Branson's buttoned tighter than any man I know."

"Well, he was tired. There were complex issues involved in his client's defense, long hours of researching case law, preparing briefs . . ."

"Miss Fairchild, did John Lloyd ever mention that he has a photographic memory?"

"Uh, no."

"Son of a bitch remembers everything he's ever read, and that includes damn near every law book published since Gutenberg invented movable type. He doesn't spend hours researching; he spends a few minutes marking passages for whatever judge has the audacity to argue with him over a point of law. Do you know why I'm the dean of Southern Methodist University School of Law instead of John Lloyd?"

"Uh, no."

The dean chuckled. "He didn't want the job, so I took it. Now I spend my time arguing with the regents for a bigger budget and cooking gourmet faculty dinners which the faculty surreptitiously slip to my wife's five poodles when they think I'm not looking. And John Lloyd? Well, John Lloyd practices law."

"It's about his law practice," began Lydia desperately.

"What about it? Is he still defending lowlifes and freeloaders for nothing? Don't worry about it. He can afford it, but it makes the rest of the profession look bad."

"Dean Johnson," interrupted Lydia, "I'm trying to tell you that I need to miss a few more classes. John Lloyd needs help with another case and . . ."

"Miss Fairchild, is John Lloyd really sick, or is this just an excuse to miss Professor McCoy's contracts class?"

Lydia glanced at John Lloyd's closed office door then cupped her hand around the receiver. "Uh, his leg has been bothering him a lot."

"Always has. Ever since that old reprobate shot him,"

said the dean, but with the first real concern in his voice Lydia had heard.

"Shot him? John Lloyd was shot?" cried Lydia, nearly dropping the receiver.

"Didn't tell you, did he? Well, I'm not going to tell you either. Being shot is a personal thing. However, we can't let the man suffer without a good woman to wipe his brow. Take a few days, Miss Fairchild. Hell, take a few weeks. I sat in on your contracts class Friday, or rather I slept through it. Professor McCoy didn't give a very good lecture when I first heard him ten years ago, and he hasn't changed a word since, so you're not missing much."

"Thank you, Dean Johnson," said Lydia, feeling as though she'd received a reprieve from a date with the firing squad. "I'll be back as soon as John Lloyd is feeling better."

There was another chuckle. "Just tell John Lloyd to recover in time for you to take midterm exams. Goodbye, Miss Fairchild. I've got a pan of plum sauce burning on the stove. I think I'll serve it at the next faculty dinner. My wife's poodles love plum sauce."

Lydia hung up the phone and looked at Mrs. Dinwittie. John Lloyd's secretary looked like an aging Kewpie doll, spoke in clichés, and wore heart-shaped glasses with pink lenses. She was also loyal to John Lloyd down to her last aberration. The chances of her discussing his secrets were somewhere between slim and none, but Lydia decided to ask anyway. "Mrs. Dinwittie, who shot John Lloyd?"

Mrs. Dinwittie patted her varnished black waves and blinked her eyes behind the pink lenses. "Oh, my, Miss Fairchild. You know I'm as close as a clam about Mr. Branson's business."

Lydia resisted the urge to ask how close a clam was. "But it's my business, too. John Lloyd asked me to join the firm as a full partner after I graduate in June. How can I be law partners with a man who keeps a secret like that? We're not talking about a stubbed toe; John Lloyd was the victim of a crime."

Mrs. Dinwittie shook her head. "Let the past bury the past, I always say."

Maybe Mrs. Dinwittie had buried her past in the form of

Mr. Dinwittie, or pieces of him anyway, but Lydia doubted that John Lloyd had. Otherwise, why was he so sensitive about his leg? The whole subject was festering inside him waiting to be lanced and she just happened to have a scalpel.

"I'm going to ask him," she said abruptly, and grabbed the doorknob.

"Miss Fairchild, please don't. Remember, least said, soonest mended," pleaded Mrs. Dinwittie.

"Whoever said that had no curiosity," retorted Lydia, and opened John Lloyd's office door.

She marched through the sitting area with its Victorian furnishings, under the arched wall that separated it from the office proper. "John Lloyd," she said to the tall, thin figure seated in the swivel chair with his back to her.

"It is none of your business, Miss Fairchild," he said as he whirled his chair around and faced her. His voice was several degrees colder than an Antarctic iceberg.

Lydia felt pierced—no, skewered—by his black eyes and frozen by his voice. "You—you were listening on the extension," she stuttered.

"When you fail to moderate your voice, Miss Fairchild, eavesdropping is unnecessary. To borrow one of Mrs. Dinwittie's clichés, you were yelling like a banshee."

"I was not!" John Lloyd Branson arched one blond eyebrow, a feat that never failed to exasperate Lydia. No human being should have that much control over his own body. "Besides, I don't know what a banshee is," she finished.

"Then might I suggest that you direct your insatiable curiosity toward a study of Celtic culture, rather than concerning yourself with a subject I have no intention of discussing. In short, Miss Fairchild, you are invading my privacy."

"But I care about you. I want to help you. I don't think you've ever reconciled yourself to what happened, and that's why you get so angry whenever anyone mentions your leg." She gulped when she saw his expression grow increasingly frigid, but she decided to finish what she had to say. He couldn't freeze her out any more than he already was. "If you just talked about it to someone who's really concerned, I'm sure you'd feel better."

"Might I suggest you direct your passionate concern toward a more worthy cause—such as saving the whales. Sometimes, Miss Fairchild, confession is *not* good for the soul. I have frequently seen it lead to divorce or a long prison sentence. Remember that when you counsel your future clients.'' He pulled a watch from his vest pocket and glanced at it. "I trust you are packed."

"Packed? Where are we going?" She groped for the edge of the library table that stood perpendicular to John Lloyd's rolltop and served as her desk. She needed something to hang on to. Between John Lloyd's chilly tone and his change of subject, she felt a little dizzy.

"*We* are not going anywhere. *You* are returning to Dallas. You have classes to attend, Miss Fairchild. Graduation is a prerequisite to a partnership, and you can hardly expect to gain the knowledge required to graduate without regular class attendance."

"But the dean excused me," Lydia protested.

John Lloyd waved his hand through the air as though batting her words aside. "The dean is much too lenient with you, Miss Fairchild."

His slow drawl contrasted with the sharp, clipped tone of a moment before, and Lydia gritted her teeth. He always assumed that slow, down-home, good-old-boy drawl when he thought he was getting his way. "It was your idea that I stay longer, John Lloyd, and don't deny it. I was going to help you with the Case of the Notorious Note." She noticed his pained grimace and shrugged. So much for the Perry Mason analogy. "You remember, the letter that stank so badly of perfume, you needed a gas mask to read it. Now you're trying to get rid of me, and I don't intend to leave until I know why."

John Lloyd handed her a newspaper and pointed to a small article. "I believe this explains the situation, Miss Fairchild."

Lydia read aloud: "The mutilated body of Grace Lynette Morrison, better known as Purple Rain, was discovered before dawn this morning in an alley just off Amarillo Boulevard. Sergeant Ed Schroder of Special Crimes has refused comment about the nature or extent of the victim's injuries."

She dropped the paper in John Lloyd's lap. "Would you care to explain why you wanted me to read this?"

"But of course, Miss Fairchild. I always answer pertinent questions; just not impertinent ones." He reached out to touch her forehead. "Are you feverish? Your face is definitely flushed."

"Just explain," said Lydia, her jaws clenched.

John Lloyd inclined his head in an imperial gesture that made Lydia clench her jaws more tightly. "Grace Lynette Morrison, often called Purple Rain," he began, "was a young woman of no fixed abode, and whose employer, one Jules 'Jo-Jo' Jefferson, was not believed to be paying his share of Ms. Morrison's withholding and Social Security taxes."

"That's enough! That is enough!" Lydia repeated, standing over John Lloyd and feeling an aberration coming on, one involving lifting his blond scalp and gagging him with it. "The IRS may be interested in Mr. Jefferson's tax arrangements, but I am not. My God, don't you ever get to the point? What does that newspaper article have to do with my going back to law school?"

Lydia caught just a hint of a disapproving expression in the depths of his obsidian eyes. His voice held more than just a hint. "Miss Fairchild, I find that remark flippant as well as revealing of your decidedly declining powers of generalization. Ms. Morrison was the lady of ill repute who received the ominous invitation and wrote asking for my help. With her death, I find myself without a client or a case. Thus, there is no need for you to neglect your studies."

Lydia opened her mouth to suggest a location where he might put his opinions of her intellectual prowess when Mrs. Dinwittie knocked, then tottered into the office on her spike heels. Lydia always felt as if she ought to follow Mrs. Dinwittie around with a net to break her fall when the older lady toppled off her shoes.

"What is it, Mrs. Dinwittie?" asked John Lloyd, rising as he always did whenever his secretary entered the room. Lydia realized he hadn't bothered to rise when *she* had entered.

Mrs. Dinwittie marched—or perhaps goose-stepped,

thought Lydia, given the height of the secretary's heels and the fact she didn't bend her knees—to John Lloyd's desk. Grabbing the newspaper, she separated it into sheets and began spreading them over the seats of the couch and chairs in the sitting area.

"Mrs. Dinwittie," repeated John Lloyd in the more brusque tone of a man unused to being ignored. "What are you doing?" Lydia resisted the urge to snicker.

Mrs. Dinwittie dusted her hands off. "Your appointment is here, Mr. Branson, and I want to tell you I've never seen people like that in my life, not up close anyway, and I thank my maker for that. Poor old Mrs. Jennings was waiting to talk to you about changing her will, and she is just dumb-founded, and you know how much it takes to dumbfound Mrs. Jennings. I mean, she's sitting out there with her mouth open so wide you can see the gold caps on her back molars. What the druggist on the first floor will think I can't imagine. People will talk. You mark my words, Mr. Branson, people will talk."

John Lloyd held up his hand. "Please, Mrs. Dinwittie, I hardly think you mean that the druggist and the populace will be scandalized by Mrs. Jennings's gold caps. You are distraught. Compose yourself and explain."

"I'm not distraught; Mrs. Jennings is! As soon as I show these creatures in, I'm calling your insurance company. I want to know if you are liable in case Mrs. Jennings has an angina attack while sitting in your reception area. Then I intend to call the exterminator. I want him standing by to fumigate just as soon as those—those whatever leave."

"Mrs. Dinwittie!"

Lydia decided John Lloyd's eruption qualified as either a roar or a bellow. At any rate, it silenced Mrs. Dinwittie.

"Thank you," he said, lowering his voice to a quiet drawl and inclining his head. In Lydia's opinion, the perspiration beading his forehead spoiled the pose of a feudal lord ac-knowledging the obedience of his serfs. It was nice to know that somebody could make John Lloyd sweat.

"Exactly who is here for an appointment, Mrs. Dinwittie? Please be specific."

"Purple Rain, of course."

"Purple Rain is deceased, Mrs. Dinwittie."

The secretary didn't look surprised. Lydia assumed not much surprised a woman who'd chopped up her husband. "No one told them they're dead. And even if someone did, no respectable cemetery would bury them. I'll let them in now, Mr. Branson, but make them sit on the papers. The man who shampoos the upholstery drives all the way from Amarillo, and he charges the moon and the stars."

She teetered toward the door like an acrobat on stilts and flung it open. "Mr. Branson will see you now," she said, then ducked back as if she were afraid the clients were carrying some terminal disease transmitted by touch.

"My God," whispered Lydia when the first person paused in the doorway, his head moving like an animal's checking for spoor. "What is it?"

"A panderer, Miss Fairchild, a procurer; otherwise described as a pimp. A particularly loathsome subspecies of latent Homo sapiens. Mrs. Dinwittie is wise to provide papers. One is never sure of the extent of a pimp's social graces."

"You the lawyer?" asked the pimp, sauntering through the door followed by three women.

Lydia closed her eyes. Surely she just imagined seeing a diamond set in one of his gold front teeth. She opened her eyes. She hadn't. She hadn't imagined the feather-garnished fedora, the turquoise silk shirt, the white suit, and those horrible shoes with the pointed toes, either. The black man was a drunken casting director's idea of a pimp. He was a walking stereotype, the bogeyman that mothers warned their children not to take candy from. Lydia noticed one other detail about him: his eyes were as cold and hard as the diamond in his tooth.

"I am John Lloyd Branson, attorney at law," John Lloyd finally replied.

"You just the man I came to see. The name's Jules Jefferson, and entertainment management's my game."

Lydia felt rather than saw John Lloyd stiffen at the pimp's name. "I am familiar with your reputation, Mr. Jefferson. You receive extensive media attention as a result of frequent court appearances."

Jefferson tipped his panama a little to one side and flicked at his lapels. "Them reporters," he said, shaking his head. "They's down on me, treatin' me like I was some kind of dis-ease instead of just common folks."

"I am certain you are common, Mr. Jefferson," agreed John Lloyd.

Other than an almost imperceptible tightening of the up-turned corners of his mouth, Jefferson didn't acknowledge John Lloyd's comment. "I run a little business in Amarillo, kind of an escort service and lonely hearts club. A business-man comes to town, don't want to eat dinner or go to the movie by hisself, so he calls me, and I fixes him up with female companionship for a small ree-numeration. These are three of my girls here," he said, waving his hand at the women. The pimp's diamond and his eyes flashed with the same cold light.

Lydia decided three things at a single glance. In the first place, none of the women fit her definition of girlhood. Not that they *looked* all that old, but there was something about them that *felt* old, like a late-model car with a hundred thou-sand miles on it. In the second place, all of them looked not exactly dirty, but not clean either, as if the filth of a thousand street corners and doorways had seeped through the pores to form a layer just below the skin. In the third place, the first two places didn't matter because Lydia realized that while there were three female bodies other than her own in the room, hers was the only one occupied. The other women, in some way she couldn't explain, were not at home. They breathed—she could see their chests rising and falling—and they moved, but looking into their eyes was like looking into the empty sockets of a broken doll.

She shivered and hugged herself, and wished she'd fol-lowed John Lloyd's advice. Even Professor McCoy's con-tracts class was easier to take than the pimp's cold eyes and the prostitutes' dead ones.

John Lloyd raised his silver-headed cane and pointed to one of the armchairs. "You may sit there."

The pimp looked at the paper-lined chair, then back at John Lloyd. "You treating me like I was some alley cat that ain't house-broke?"

"On the contrary, I have always held that breed of feline in the highest regard."

"You trying to insult me?" the pimp demanded.

John Lloyd leaned on his cane and contemplated his questioner. Rather like a biologist studying a new species of stink bug, thought Lydia. "Is it possible to insult an object which, by its nature, is already an insult? You have posed an interesting philosophical question. Unintentionally, I am sure." He bowed to the three women who stood fidgeting in front of the couch. "Ladies, please sit."

The pimp snapped his fingers. "Sit, bitches."

"W-what did you say?" stammered Lydia, watching the women drop onto the couch like three grubby Barbie dolls.

"Who's that?" the pimp asked, nodding his head in Lydia's direction.

"Miss Fairchild, please," said John Lloyd. "I will handle the interview."

She turned her head to look at him. "But didn't you hear what he called those women, John Lloyd?" She heard her voice quiver and bit down on her lower lip.

"I heard," said John Lloyd as he turned his attention back to Jefferson. "This is my partner, Miss Fairchild, a woman of strong convictions who is unfamiliar with the vernacular of your particular profession. Since I prefer that she remain in that condition, I must ask you to refrain from further lapses into obscene street language."

"Say what?" asked Jefferson with a blank expression on his face.

She took a step forward and felt John Lloyd clasp her arm and firmly pull her backward. "Do not do it, Miss Fairchild," he whispered.

"Do what?" she hissed out of one side of her mouth.

"Assault Mr. Jefferson," he replied, tightening his grip.

"I wasn't," she protested. "I was just going to go sit by those women as a gesture of feminine solidarity."

"This is not the occasion to rally to another of your causes, Miss Fairchild. Your interference has already endangered those women. Look at them."

Lydia glanced at the three women huddled on the couch and felt nauseated. Two of them, the light-skinned black girl and the tiny one with Oriental features, no longer looked like dolls with empty eyes. She wished they did, because she could live with that, even feel indignant that women could be so robbed of self-esteem. But the fear in their eyes, fear so deep she knew she'd never felt anything resembling it, fear directed at *her*, at what she might say, sickened her. She swallowed and tasted bile.

"Say what?" repeated Jefferson, furrows climbing from his eyebrows to disappear under his hat brim. Lydia guessed pimping didn't prepare one to decipher John Lloyd's convoluted sentences.

"He doesn't like the way you talk, Jo-Jo," explained the last prostitute, a white girl dressed in a leather vest and skirt, and with the most improbable orange hair Lydia had ever seen.

"Don't like the way I talk?"

"Bitches," said the prostitute, looking at Lydia. "She don't like it."

Jo-Jo Jefferson's expression of puzzlement changed to one of enlightenment. In Lydia's opinion, the transformation was comparable to turning on a ten-watt bulb in a dark closet. "That don't mean nothing, just a nickname. Don't get the girls mad, does it?" he demanded, stepping closer to the couch until he loomed over the women. "Ain't that right, Honey Bran?" he asked the black girl.

Honey Bran swallowed convulsively and rhythmically stroked a scuffed leather purse. Her fingernails were bitten to the quick and dabbed with a yellowish polish the color of a corpse's flesh. "That's right," she agreed, her voice as empty of expression as her eyes.

"China Doll?" asked Jo-Jo, staring down at the second woman's bowed head. Lydia decided the name was appropriate. Although the prostitute was more likely Laotian or Vietnamese than Chinese, since Amarillo had large communities of both ethnic groups, she definitely wore a doll's painted features. Washed clean of makeup, her face would be as blank as a doll's.

"You gonna answer me?" demanded Jo-Jo, nudging the woman.

"She agrees with you, Jo-Jo," said the last prostitute,

smoothing her orange hair. "You know she doesn't talk much."

"Shut your mouth, Cowgirl," said the pimp with the closest sound to a snarl Lydia had ever heard in a human voice.

"She's sick, Jo-Jo; got up this morning not feeling good," continued Cowgirl, her voice just missing sounding defiant.

"I said shut your mouth," said Jo-Jo, raising a hand toward Cowgirl.

"Stop!" commanded John Lloyd, releasing Lydia's arm and darting forward. Hooking his cane around Jo-Jo's wrist, he jerked, and Jo-Jo tumbled backward into the armchair. "You have twenty seconds to state why you appropriated Purple Rain's appointment," he said over the sound of rustling newspaper and Jo-Jo's steady cursing. Retrieving his cane, he poked it in the pimp's chest. "You may begin, and please avoid your former circumlocution of the truth. You are a pimp, a modern-day dealer in female slaves, as well as in other dangerous and most certainly illegal commodities. Do not insult my intelligence by assuming I believe otherwise."

"Purple Rain's dead!" cried Jo-Jo, his eyes expressing enough hatred to bury John Lloyd. Oddly enough, Lydia thought she also saw respect in those black, cold eyes.

John Lloyd's own eyes expressed contempt without the respect. "Fifteen seconds."

"She was one of my bitches. The cops are going to be on my ass 'cause of that, and I need a criminal lawyer. Mr. J. W. Hargreves handles my business affairs, but he ain't up to this heavy stuff. He says you the best money can buy."

John Lloyd straightened to his full six feet four inches. Pale red suffused his thin, ascetic face then faded to smudges on his high cheekbones. "While my personal and legal code of ethics has always held that every man, no matter how despicable, is entitled to an attorney and an adequate defense, I am prepared to suspend my ethics in your case. I will, however, provide you a list of attorneys of sufficiently low character to accept you as a client."

Lifting his cane from Jo-Jo's chest, he turned and bowed to the prostitutes. "I will represent you ladies should you ever require my services. Whatever your transgressions against society, they cannot equal the transgressions against you by Mr. Jefferson. Call me, and I will come.''

Jo-Jo struggled out of the chair. ''They ain't calling you no where, no how. On your feet, bitches; we just gonna make it back to the Boulevard in time to catch the late lunchers.''

''You don't have to go with him,'' said Lydia, following the three women to the door. ''Haven't you ever heard of the Civil War? The Emancipation Proclamation? Slavery's illegal!''

Cowgirl turned around. ''The Civil War wasn't fought over us, and Abe Lincoln never mentioned hookers in his Proclamation.''

''You're educated!'' exclaimed Lydia.

''Yeah, and it don't mean a thing on the Boulevard. Might even get a girl in trouble. You don't know anything about it, little girl. You're so dumb, you're gonna hurt yourself one of these days.'' She looked over Lydia's shoulder at John Lloyd, self-loathing giving her face animation. ''Thanks, mister, but you know we're not gonna call you. We've been lost so long, we couldn't find our way back with a road map, and most of us don't want to.''

Lydia stood looking at the closed door for a moment, then whirled around to watch John Lloyd gathering up the newspapers from the furniture.

''What is she talking about, John Lloyd? She's not saying they want to live like that, is she? And why do they let that subhuman speak to them that way?''

John Lloyd crumpled the newspapers and deposited them in a wastebasket. ''I doubt that any normally stable woman wants to be degraded to the level of a prostitute.''

''Then why?''

''They are addicts, Miss Fairchild, as are most prostitutes. Jo-Jo Jefferson is their supplier, and they are his chattel as surely as if he held a legal bill of sale for each. They live a life of masquerades. They are slaves who pass as free, hiding their identities behind tawdry street names and trading their bodies for drugs, the ultimate masquerade which allows them to hide from themselves. They would not appreciate your interference.''

Lydia swallowed and took several shallow breaths in an

effort to ease the tightness in her chest. "But one wanted out, or at least asked for help."

John Lloyd nodded. "Yes, and she must have been a woman of extraordinary strength to have reached outside her world."

"Well, what are you going to do about Purple Rain?"

John Lloyd looked astonished, an emotion Lydia didn't know he was acquainted with. "Miss Fairchild, I am not the police, or, God forbid, a private investigator; I am an attorney with no client."

She wiped away the tears she felt running down her cheeks. "What kind of an attorney, what kind of a *man*, would allow his client to be knocked off by some psychopath without lifting a finger to do anything about it?"

"You are distraught, Miss Fairchild," he said, handing her his handkerchief.

"Oh, tell it to Mrs. Dinwittie!" she cried, wadding up his handkerchief and throwing it back at him.

CHAPTER THREE

Amarillo, Texas—September 8

SERGEANT LARRY JENNER HIT THE SIREN, STOMPED THE ACcelerator, and skidded out of the police parking lot onto Buchanan Street heading north. He had another bellyache, but this one didn't have anything to do with Lu Chee's Chinese Emporium. The honors for this pain in his gut belonged to Lieutenant Roger "the Bean" Green. Well, maybe not entirely, he thought. That son of a bitch Schroder held part interest. On second thought, Schroder deserved fifty percent of the credit.

All his life Jenner had wanted to be a cop. Even when cops weren't popular, he'd still aspired to be one. He'd wanted to defend the weak and helpless, protect the widow's mite as well as the millionaire's mansion. He'd wanted to be fair and honest and just. He'd wanted to be one of the good guys. He'd wanted his parents, his wife, his children, even his beagle, to be proud of him.

He *did not* want to be called Sergeant Screwup.

Jenner made a wide turn by the ice-cream shop and headed west on Amarillo Boulevard, zigzagging through the traffic to the right lane. Ten years on the force, and all he'd achieved was an unfair nickname and a bellyache that had him nipping at a bottle of Maalox like it was seven-year-old Bourbon. The more he thought about his bellyache, the more he decided that maybe Schroder deserved the majority of the blame—say, seventy percent. Damn it, the detective knew he had a hot lead in the person of Sergeant Larry Jenner, and he brushed it off. Usually Schroder treated an eyewitness like a sponge, wringing every bit of information out of him until the poor guy was dehydrated. Schroder hadn't even given him a good squeeze.

Jenner stood on his brakes and stopped his black and white next to a mobile unit from one of the TV stations. A few cars away was a rival station's van, and beyond that, still another van with the third station's logo on its side. Parked across the street in the hospital parking lot were cars belonging to three radio stations and the newspaper. The press could smell a crime faster than a hound dog could smell a rabbit. Jenner always thought the narcs ought to use reporters instead of dogs to smell out drugs. Promise a reporter an exclusive, and he'd sniff his way nonstop to Colombia with nothing but a canteen of beer and a change of underwear.

Climbing out of the car, Jenner pushed his way through the crowd of those off work, out of work, or consciously unemployed—all of whom seemed to materialize out of the air like a bunch of damn ghouls whenever there was a murder. And there was very definitely a murder. Approximately thirty feet down the unpaved alley that separated the convenience store (busily selling coffee and doughnuts to the crowd) from the Rest Easy Motel (best known for renting its rooms by the hour), in a tiny ten-by-ten-foot paved cul-de-sac, lay the mutilated body of another prostitute. Where there was a body, there was Schroder.

Jenner didn't particularly want to see either the victim *or* Schroder, but damn it, he felt responsible. He climbed over the police barricade and trotted up the alley. He turned the corner into the little cul-de-sac formed by the convenience store's cinder-block wall on the south, a chain-link fence overgrown with weeds and ivy on the east, and a tall cedar fence on the north, and crowded by the white-clad Special Crimes boys huddled around the victim. If he hadn't screwed up, or if Schroder had let him on the case, there might not be some girl lying in a filthy alley with her . . .

"Holy shit!" screamed Jenner, stumbled backward around the corner, tripped over a man crouched down on the ground, and sat down hard in a puddle of glutinous liquid, the exact source of which he wasn't too interested in speculating on.

The crouching man looked up, and Jenner recognized Frank Clifford, North Amarillo's black justice of the peace. Clifford had first run for office before anybody ever thought of Freedom Riders and registering blacks to vote. He'd campaigned in neighborhoods where a black man was never seen unless it was to mow a lawn. The old-line politicians said he would lose, but when the election was over, Frank Clifford had triumphed. The commentators had volumes to say about block voting and demographics, but Jenner had always figured that Clifford's neighbors, black *and* white, had decided color, like beauty, was skin-deep, but honesty went all the way to the bones. Whatever the reason, Clifford had been reelected seven times. He was the antithesis of Jo-Jo Jefferson and proved what Jenner had always believed: don't judge a race by its sons of bitches.

Clifford wiped his mouth and crawled over to Jenner, his black skin tinged with gray. "Holy shit don't cover this situation. I've been pronouncing people corpus delicti in this part of town for thirty years, and I ain't never seen anything so revolting. Law says I got to come to the scene to do my pronouncing, but damn if I don't wish I'd done this one over the phone."

"Clifford." Schroder stood over the old justice of the peace, and Jenner thought even he looked a little off-color. "You through? Can I send the body to the morgue for an autopsy, or you want another look?"

Clifford pushed himself to his feet, his old man's joints creaking at every move. "Hell, no, I don't want another look, and yes, you can take the body. I don't know what the pathologist is going to have left to do, though. The bastard who killed her already did an autopsy. Those were her guts lying on her shoulder, weren't they?"

Jenner closed his eyes and swallowed hard. Several times.

"Yeah, they were," said Schroder. "Go on home, Frank. Have some breakfast."

Jenner opened his eyes in time to see the justice of the peace give the homicide detective a reproachful look. "Maybe you can eat after looking at something like that, but I can't. I'm gonna take one of my wife's Valium and go to bed instead. Next time you call me to look at a body like that, you warn me beforehand so I can take *two* Valium first."

Schroder watched the old man wander toward his car, then looked down at Jenner. "Get up. You're sitting in dog shit and you look like a fool. What are doing down here anyway?"

"Son of a bitch!" Jenner leapt up, grabbed his handkerchief, and wiped the seat of his trousers. The smell wasn't helping his bellyache. "Goddamn it, Schroder, some of this is your fault. If you'd given me a temporary assignment to Special Crimes last week when the first hooker was killed, maybe this wouldn't have happened. Maybe I could've found that missing prostitute. Maybe she'd be in jail. Maybe . . ."

"Maybe you'd be dead, too," interrupted Schroder, lighting one of his unfiltered cigarettes.

"Huh?"

"This isn't a woman's crime, son. This is a genuine serial killer, one of those sociopaths all the psychiatrists like to talk about, and they're usually white, over thirty, and male. Unless you saw somebody in drag, your witness isn't male, and if she'd been over thirty, you'd have known it. Any hooker that age looks like she ought to be standing over a cauldron in *Macbeth*. I guess she musta been white, or maybe you'd have noticed. Or maybe you wouldn't. You ain't exactly covered yourself in glory on this case."

"I know it, Schroder, but damn it, what's all this got to do with somebody killing me? I'm not a hooker."

Schroder puffed on his cigarette and an inch-long ash broke off the end and rolled down the front of his disposable suit. " 'Cause our boy thinks the prostitutes down here on the Boulevard are his own special game preserve, and if you go sticking your nose in, he just might chop it off. He probably wouldn't bother sending you one of his invitations either;

you'd just wake up dead and missing some of your vitals without any warning.''

Jenner dropped his handkerchief in the convenience store's Dempster Dumpster. ''So isn't that what's going to happen to that hooker if I don't find her before he does? Did you ever think of that, Schroder?''

''Why do you think you've been guest of honor at all those lineups this week? You think we're having a beauty contest and you're the judge? Special Crimes's hunting for that hooker, son; Lieutenant Green's men are hunting.''

''Why do you think the Bean's men can find her?'' Jenner heard himself shout and consciously tried to lower his voice. ''They didn't see her; I did.''

Schroder snorted. ''Green's men fit in down here. They don't look like cops; they look like something you'd find in the gutter after a rainstorm. You look like every mother's son. Hell, you even got freckles across your nose. You think anybody'd believe you were scum? If we were trying to bust a gambling ring, you'd be my man. You look like a damn mark. But we're trying to trace a whore, and we can't use you to do it. Your hooker'd recognize that face and run so fast in the other direction, we wouldn't see her for her dust.''

''Why wouldn't she run to me? Did you ever think of that? Why wouldn't she want protection? She's got to be scared shitless. Maybe she won't go to one of Green's men because they *don't* look like cops.''

Schroder squinted one eye and looked at Jenner. ''I think I'm the only one doing any thinking around here. If your hooker saw something, and I'm not convinced she did, and you blunder around looking for her, you might just lead the killer right to her. You stay out of this case and off the Boulevard, son. You couldn't disguise that face with a hockey mask. I got enough problems without worrying about you. This whole side of town's like a fucking army surplus store. Everybody's buying a gun, legally or illegally. There are more arms dealers in North Amarillo than in the Persian Gulf. You can buy anything but a Stinger missile and I'm not sure you can't pick up one of those if you know the right number to call. We've already had four shootings this week, and it won't stop there because every bastard who just bought himself a Saturday night special will want to try it out.''

Jenner felt a shiver race up his spine to the middle of his back and stop. Every cop on the Boulevard was feeling that same icy spot, like a damn bull's-eye, and wondering when some hophead with a brand-new gun would attempt a little target practice. He heard Schroder curse.

"Goddamn it! What does that horse's ass want?''

Jenner looked toward the mouth of the alley. There stood William Elliot, self-styled defender of North Amarillo's reputation and a candidate for mayor. Jenner figured Elliot wasn't much good at either job, but judging by the number of minicams and microphones poking at him from every angle, the press didn't care. Bill Elliot, all six feet four inches of redheaded, barrel-chested, bombastic blowhard, was news.

"I have asked our present mayor, I have asked our chief of police, I have asked our Potter County sheriff what measures are being taken to protect the lives of those living in the shadow of death. I have offered to sit down with those individuals to help them work out a campaign to catch this beast. And what is their answer?'' Elliot paused dramatically. "That law enforcement is a job for professionals.'' He pointed down the alley. "See what the professionals have wrought!''

The side of Schroder's lip not curled around his cigarette turned up to reveal a nicotine-stained cuspid. Jenner decided he resembled a pit bull in the early stages of pissed-off. "Damn bastard sounds like a preacher in some offshoot Baptist church that can't afford anybody decent,'' said Schroder, lip still curled up. "Know what the fool wanted? He wanted the chief to deputize all those idiots who trail along after him—Elliot's Extras he wanted to call them. Chief told him the police department didn't have deputies and sent him over to the old courthouse to see the sheriff.''

"What did the sheriff do?'' asked Jenner.

"Passed the buck to the mayor who decided it was a good time to tour sewage treatment plants around the Panhandle. Said something about how looking at raw sewage was better than listening to it.'' An odd noise somewhere between a belch and a wheeze issued from the investigator's mouth. Jenner decided the sound might pass for a snicker.

"You! Sergeant Schroder!" called Elliot, pointing his finger at the detective.

"I didn't know Elliot was a fan of yours," said Jenner with a snicker of his own. He choked back an additional pithy comment when he saw Bill Elliot charge through the police barricade and march up the alley followed by his entourage of Extras. One young blonde TV reporter followed, which marked her as a woman new to Amarillo. The rest of the journalists knew better; the Pulitzer Prize wasn't worth risking stepping on Sergeant Ed Schroder's crime scene. Jennor propped one arm on the Dempster Dumpster lid and prepared to watch. He suddenly realized his stomach didn't hurt any more.

"Sergeant Schroder," said Elliot, stopping in the middle of the alley and tilting his chin up and slightly to one side for a better camera angle. "As a resident of North Amarillo and as a candidate for mayor, I demand action from Special Crimes."

The investigator shrugged his shoulders. "Suits me. Sergeant Jenner, arrest him."

"What?" exclaimed Jenner, jerking his arm off the Dumpster and rapping his funny bone in the process.

Elliot's mouth dropped open, displaying his double chin to the TV camera. "What?" he blustered.

Schroder lumbered down the alley with the deliberation of a hungry grizzly. "You broke through a lawfully erected police barricade to trespass on a crime scene under investigation." He took two more steps.

Elliot's mouth opened and shut a few times, like an algae eater in a clean fish tank, before he synchronized his brain and his vocal cords. "What?" he repeated. In Jenner's opinion, the synchronization wasn't worth the effort.

"You endangered the integrity of the evidence," continued Schroder, moving inexorably forward, the grizzly intent on a meal.

"I—I," began Elliot.

"Interfered with an officer, namely me, in pursuit of his

duty.'' The grizzly was closer now, within snapping distance.

Elliot did a backward broad jump, all two-hundred-sixty-five pounds and size fourteen high-heeled cowboy boots making a safe landing on the toe of one of his followers. The follower promptly howled, and Elliot did a fancy sidestep onto the TV reporter's foot, which happened to be hanging out the end of an open-toed pump. The lady journalist demonstrated that her command of certain Anglo-Saxon aphorisms was equal to any male's. Jenner rubbed his elbow and watched the show.

''. . . All of you are under arrest for obstructing justice,'' finished Schroder. The sounds of thudding feet running toward the barricade punctuated his sentence.

''The chief will hear about this,'' yelled Elliot, following the limping reporter out of the alley.

Schroder dusted his hands and walked back up the alley toward the body without answering. ''Disrespectful bastard,'' he muttered as he stopped beside Jenner.

''I wouldn't exactly use that word,'' remarked Jenner, gently touching his elbow and wondering if he'd broken the damn thing. It felt a little swollen.

Schroder looked at him. ''I would. We got a dead woman over there. Maybe a crime scene isn't as sacred as a church. Maybe the victim wasn't somebody we'd want to take home to Mama. Maybe she was just plain trash who died in a goddamn stinking alley. But that doesn't give an asshole like Elliot the right to host a press conference damn near on top of her body. I tell you something, Jenner. That poor woman probably never got a dime's worth of respect her whole life, not from anybody, and she died like nobody ought to die, but by God, her body's going to be treated like she was somebody important.''

For years, Jenner had heard a rumor that after a funeral was over and the cemetery was empty, Schroder always personally laid a wreath on a murder victim's grave. He believed it now.

CHAPTER FOUR

BOULEVARD BUTCHER CLAIMS
ANOTHER VICTIM
by Louis Bryant

AMARILLO, TEXAS—The murderer dubbed "The Boulevard Butcher" has claimed another victim. The mutilated body of Elizabeth Ann Green, 20, was discovered early this morning in an alley behind the U-Tote-Um convenience store on Amarillo Boulevard. Earl Brothers, a clerk at U-Tote-Um, stated that he "nearly tripped over the body" when he was taking out the garbage.

Green, known to the police as Honey Bran, is described by a source close to the investigation as "a garden-variety prostitute with a long arrest record." A friend of Ms. Green's who asked to remain anonymous described the victim as "a misunderstood girl just trying to make a living."

Sergeant Ed Schroder, investigator for the Special Crimes Unit, refused to speculate on the connection between Green's murder and that of Grace Lynette Morrison, another Boulevard prostitute. Sergeant Schroder stated that "investigations are continuing in both cases."

When asked if Special Crimes had any leads, the sergeant had no comment.

William Elliot, North Amarillo businessman and perennial candidate for mayor, has filed charges of police brutality against Sergeant Schroder following an incident at the crime scene. "Some of my fellow citizens and I have volunteered to walk a beat on Amarillo Boulevard, and I was attempting to talk to Schroder about it when he ordered an officer to arrest me and my supporters. I was slightly injured in the ensuing scuffle. This country is in sorry shape when police officers spend their time threatening honest citizens instead of chasing killers."

Sergeant Schroder had no comment about the charges, but did say he welcomed help from citizens "who had no personal ax to grind." Schroder said that those who believe they might have information about the murders should contact the Potter-Randall County Special Crimes Unit.

He decided to write the letter after all. Much better than typing it or using the word processor. Particularly for this letter. He wanted to give it a personal touch, let the words flow from his head to his fingers, feel his muscles contract to squeeze the pen and form the words. Better yet, dip his finger in blood and draw the letters in viscous crimson strokes.

But that was impossible.

He laid down his pen, a common red ballpoint unique only because he owned it, and flexed his hands, feeling the coarse fibers of the heavy work gloves rub against his skin. Bad enough to wear gloves to guard against leaving fingerprints on his very special stationery, but to wear them while dipping his hands in blood, not to feel it stain the creases and cuticles of his fingers, was impersonal, unthinkable.

Writing in blood, like murder, was an act of intimacy, best done barehanded.

He sighed, a rush of air that disturbed the deadly quiet in the room, a quiet he had insured by installing acoustical tiles over dirty plaster walls and ceiling. He wasn't sure, but he might need a soundproof room. His finale would be very intimate indeed. He picked up his pen and pulled a strip of paper closer. But first there was the original theme to follow with his own unique variations, a maniacal Gregorian chant with each victim a separate canto.

He wondered how long his adversary would remain confused as to the theme and variations. Surely not too long. Schroder was clever, but on the other hand, he was tone deaf. How unfortunate the sergeant was the best Special Crimes had to offer. He wanted an adversary of subtle intellect, a man of monkish purity, a titan to battle, not a broken-down champion dedicated to the proposition that all women were created equal.

As he wrote his salutation in cramped letters so unlike his own, he wondered how long before Schroder identified the stationery as butcher paper.

CHAPTER
FIVE

Dallas, Texas—September 9

LYDIA ATE ANOTHER PIECE OF HOT BRATWURST, THEN FOL-
lowed the sausage with a mouthful of kosher dill. Lifting a
tankard of Coke, she took several swallows and managed to
transform a healthy belch into a more polite hiccup. God,
but she had always loved Sunday lunches at the little German
delicatessen across the street from the Southern Methodist
University campus. She loved its wooden benches and smell
of sausage and strudel and hot German potato salad. She had
always felt like a burgomaster at a village feast: filled to
bursting with well-being and cholesterol.

Until this Sunday morning.

This Sunday morning all she felt was stuffed and queasy;
stuffed because she had eaten too much trying to fill up that
cold empty spot masquerading as her stomach, and queasy
because she kept recalling Honey Bran's jagged, bitten nails
covered with that hideous yellow polish. But queasy was
better than actually vomiting, which was exactly what she
had done after first reading Louis Bryant's article. She wished
she had never found that little newsstand that sold the *Amarillo Globe-News*.

She wished she could talk to John Lloyd, wished he would tell her it was all a mistake, a misprint of some kind. There was no murder, no pitiful mutilated body lying discarded in an alley. Nothing ugly was happening on the Boulevard, no butcher prowled its sidewalks.

But that was impossible.

There *was* a body, and a butcher did stalk the Boulevard, seeking his prey among the most vulnerable, most degraded citizens.

Even if she called John Lloyd, the conversation would evolve into a shouting match, a one-sided match since John Lloyd never shouted. At most he would drop his drawl, and his voice would grow colder and colder until she developed frostbite. That is, provided he talked to her at all. He had made his position very clear last week—just after she had thrown his handkerchief back in his face, and just before she walked out the door.

"I never interfere with a police investigation, Miss Fairchild," he drawled, catching his handkerchief in midair.

"The hell you say!" she shouted.

John Lloyd frowned in disapproval. *"Profanity is unbecoming, not to mention unprofessional."*

"Oh, no, you don't," said Lydia, shaking her head. *"You're not going to have the last word this time. I'm not letting you put me on the defensive. The fact is, John Lloyd, that you interfere all the time. I've watched you. What else do you call conniving with a defendant to help a witness skip town without testifying like you did in that case involving the nuclear waste dump?"*

"Skip town? Miss Fairchild, your vocabulary is deplorable. And I never connive, *another word with disreputable connotations, I might add. However, in answer to your question, I am not responsible for any information my client may pass along to another party. Besides, that witness's testimony was unnecessary."*

"That's for the police and the D.A.'s office to decide, not you."

"My behavior was within legal boundaries."

"Was it? What about your behavior now?" Lydia demanded.

"I presume you will explain that accusation."

"You're interfering now, John Lloyd. Remember the letter, the one from Purple Rain, the letter in which she describes her invitation to join a heavenly choir? Have you turned it over to Sergeant Schroder? It's evidence, you know. It's proof that Purple Rain wasn't a random victim, that she knew her murderer."

John Lloyd folded his handkerchief and tucked it back in his breast pocket.

"Well, what do you have to say? Anything? No defense to the charges?" asked Lydia, folding her arms in triumph.

He looked at her, his black eyes mesmerizing. "You are drawing a conclusion based on a false assumption, Miss Fairchild, something you have a lamentable habit of doing. The infamous invitation to which Purple Rain referred was found tucked in her handbag, a fact I ascertained by speaking to Sergeant Schroder this morning. There is as yet no proof whether the invitation list was short or if it included every prostitute's name."

"A form letter mailed to occupant?" suggested Lydia. "Meet me on such-and-such a corner at midnight, and I'll insure you a solo part in a choir I'm forming? No training necessary, since all the parts are silent because the dead have such quiet voices, but I'm working on that problem. . . ."

"That is enough, Miss Fairchild. This is not the occasion for your humorous quips," interrupted John Lloyd.

Lydia winced at the expression of anger in his eyes, but she felt some anger of her own. "I wasn't being humorous; I was being ludicrous so you would see how ridiculous the idea of a mass mailing is. Purple Rain knew her murderer, John Lloyd. It's only logical. That's why she was afraid. That's why she wrote you. And you accepted her as a client by granting her an appointment. You have a contract with her, an unwritten one maybe, but still a contract."

"A contract with the dead is a literary device, Miss Fairchild, and has no place in this discussion. In reality a contract between two individuals is generally void if one of the parties dies," he said impatiently, his drawl completely gone.

"But we did have a contract, John Lloyd, a moral one. Doesn't that make us morally obligated to at least go to the Boulevard and question her friends and associates?"

"No! Absolutely out of the question, Miss Fairchild."

Lydia considered his look of horror. "If you think it's beneath your dignity, I'll go. The women would probably feel safer talking to me anyway. In their profession I don't imagine they think too highly of men."

John Lloyd's fingers turned white from grasping his cane so tightly. "They will not speak to you either. Your very physical appearance, your hopes and aspirations, the fact you have a future while they have none, is a reproach to them The whore with the heart of gold is a myth, Miss Fairchild. They will not respond to your goodness. They will perceive you as an interloper, a troublemaker, and they already have enough troubles for a lifetime."

Lydia felt a moment's hesitation. "But I'm not trying to convert them, just question them."

Another expression momentarily overshadowed the anger in John Lloyd's eyes, but faded before Lydia could identify it. "There are two boulevards, Miss Fairchild. One is the mundane respectable business district that exists during the daylight hours, and the other is a world of unspeakable vice that exists after dark. Two parallel universes occupying the same space, each the moral opposite of the other. A study in abstracts, good versus evil. No one visits the Boulevard when evil is ascendant and leaves unmarked."

Lydia felt the fine hair on the back of her neck stiffen. "I'm not afraid."

John Lloyd sighed and limped over to the window to look down at the brick streets and Victorian houses half-hidden by giant cottonwoods. "Go back to school, Miss Fairchild. Do not push this subject any further."

"I don't intend to leave in the middle of an argument. Don't you understand, John Lloyd, we can't just not do anything. We must help those women." Lydia was disgusted to hear her voice quiver.

John Lloyd turned around. His features looked sharper, as though his skin had shrank, and his eyes held an expression of regret. "I have endeavored to spare you this humili-

*ation. Indeed, I have given you every opportunity to regain
your professional rationality, but I see it is impossible. This
morning has taught me that your impulsiveness makes it impossible for us to work together. Your emotions blind your
logic; your obstinacy deafens your voice of reason.*" He drew
a breath and squared his shoulders. "*Go home, Miss Fairchild. Your services are no longer required.*"

Lydia wiped her eyes with her napkin. Damn it, but she
would *not* cry, at least not in a restaurant where she would
humiliate herself further. She blew her nose and slowly
counted to ten. She had not cried when she said goodbye to
Mrs. Dinwittie, nor when she packed up the rest of her clothes
and drove away from Canadian and its whispering cottonwoods for the last time. She had not even cried when she sat
alone at night in her apartment on the top floor of the old
house across from the law school, listening to the dripping
bathroom faucet and contemplating her future.

Why was she crying now?

She sniffed and considered the question. Was it because
she missed John Lloyd? Of course not. How could she miss
someone who fired her, cut her off the payroll and out of his
life as impersonally as if she were a stranger? Logically she
couldn't. Logically being fired was a positive development.
She had liked John Lloyd far too much, had even entertained
some very prurient thoughts about him, when their relationship was strictly business.

So why in the hell was she crying? Because her feelings
were hurt? Because she was disillusioned? Or because she
was disgusted with herself? She had daydreamed about going to bed with a man who would stand aside while women
died. If John Lloyd had interfered, maybe Honey Bran
wouldn't be in the morgue. In all fairness, maybe she would
be, but he could have at least tried.

"You are eating the flesh of another living creature, a
mammal not unlike yourself."

Lydia blinked away tears and images of John Lloyd and
took a moment to orient herself. "No, I'm not; I don't like
raw meat. I'm eating the *corpse* of a mammal not unlike
myself."

She popped another slice of bratwurst into her mouth and grinned at the look of revulsion on Cindy Spencer's earnest face. It wasn't that she didn't like Cindy. Exactly. But she had an aversion to anybody's equating bratwurst consumption to cannibalism. Besides, she was damn tired of being criticized.

"You're disgusting!"

"No, I'm carnivorous." Lydia felt her queasiness increase as the spicy sausage hit bottom. "What do you want, Cindy, other than to stand around and insult my dietary habits?"

Cindy slid onto the bench across from Lydia. "There are meat substitutes made from soybean."

"I'm allergic to soybean. It makes my face swell until I look like a chipmunk with a winter's supply of nuts in his cheeks."

Cindy's long, pointed nose twitched. "With your face, I'll bet you still look good."

"If you like blonde chipmunks," replied Lydia, shrugging off the backhanded compliment. Besides being a fanatic on the subject of vegetarianism, Cindy was also envious of everyone not possessed of a long, pointed nose, pointed chin, and narrow face. Sometimes, when she was peering through a frowzy curtain of straight black hair, as she was doing now, she reminded Lydia of the witch in *Hansel and Gretel*. Except, of course, Cindy didn't believe in cannibalism.

"Does this place serve herbal tea?"

Lydia shuddered. She would forever associate herbal teas with her Great-grandmother Fairchild's potions. The old lady brewed them at the first hint of fever, stomachache, rashes, chills, and the worst of all conceivable illnesses to her generation: irregularity. "Don't you ever drink anything else? What about beer? It's brewed from grain."

"Grain should be used to make bread."

"I thought you'd say that," said Lydia, taking a sip of Coke and wishing it were a full keg of beer. Cindy Spencer embraced every cause from A to W, anti-apartheid to whales, not to mention such initials as the AIM, ERA, IRA, and PLO. Unhampered by logic or consistency, she could argue in favor of two opposing viewpoints, often simultaneously. Theoretically she was a master politician in embryo. Practically her personality would have made St. Francis turn to poisoning pigeons and setting snares.

"Do you know how many hungry children you are depriving of bread by drinking just one beer?" asked Cindy with a look of disapproval that reminded Lydia of John Lloyd.

Lydia slammed her mug on the table. "Do you know how many people are murdered by friends and relatives?"

Cindy looked startled. "How would I know that?"

"If you don't put a sock in it, you're going to have some personal knowledge on the subject," snapped Lydia, feeling depression settle in for the duration of Cindy's visit. "You're going to be a statistic."

"Are you threatening me?"

"Yes! No!" Lydia wiped her hand over her face, feeling her taut features, and took a deep breath. "Just say whatever you came to say and leave me alone, Cindy. I want to finish my mammal, then go buy a six-pack without worrying about how I'm contributing to world hunger."

"You *are* threatening me," said Cindy, nodding her head with as much satisfaction as though she had just deciphered the Rosetta Stone, provided she had known what it was, which Lydia doubted. "You're so predictable, Lydia. A knee-jerk Texan. You're always taking things personally."

"And what kind of Texan are you, Cindy? A plain jerk?"

"There you go again, taking it personally. I'm using you as a symbol of this whole rugged-individualist-mindset crap, the always-ready-to-defend-the-homestead mentality."

"Defending the homestead beat the hell out of having it burned down around your ears," said Lydia, squeezing her knife and fork so she wouldn't be tempted to squeeze Cindy's throat.

"I've outgrown the narrow view, Lydia. Take world hunger, for instance. You would probably jump on a plane to Ethiopia with a sack of flour under each arm . . ."

"That's the first thing you've said I've agreed with since you sat down."

". . . the rugged individualist again."

"That's me: Johanna Wayne," agreed Lydia, laying down her knife. Considering how close she was to succumbing to an irresistible urge to kill, it might be unwise to be holding a weapon.

"No, Little Red Riding Hood taking cookies to Grandmother. Individual to individual. That's very inefficient. You have to take the overview, plan strategy to save a region, or a country, or even a continent. You can't worry about individuals."

"I don't see why not. People starve individually."

Cindy clapped her hands. "Oh, that's wonderful, all that anger, that righteous indignation. Now you just need to control yourself until the right time."

"The right time?"

Cindy nodded her head again. "Next Saturday."

"Where and over what am I supposed to lose control?"

Cindy sighed, a long-suffering sound Lydia decided was calculated to stimulate whatever guilt feelings a listener might have. "If you'd attended the organizational meeting yesterday like you were supposed to, you'd know."

"I didn't know about it."

"I left a message on your machine."

"I didn't play it back," said Lydia. She hadn't played it back for a week because there might be a message from John Lloyd. She sighed. Actually, she hadn't listened to the tape because there might *not* be a message from John Lloyd.

"Then why have an answering machine?"

"So I can return obscene phone calls?" guessed Lydia.

"Are you being flippant?" Cindy tucked her hair behind her ears for an unrestricted field of vision.

Lydia sighed again. She had forgotten that among Cindy's other personality quirks, she had the sense of humor of an earthworm. "For God's sake, why do you think I have a machine? So I won't miss any important calls."

"You missed mine."

"Exactly." Lydia looked at her watch. "You have thirty seconds."

"Until what?"

"Until I get up and leave you with the bill," replied Lydia. "Twenty-five seconds and counting." She glanced at Cindy. "Better start talking."

"We're going to picket the Lone Star Brewery . . ."

"What!"

". . . in support of our position that we're wasting precious foodstuffs needed to feed the hungry in order to make a beverage directly responsible for alcoholism. Think of it, Lydia, a two-pronged attack on two different but interrelated social issues. It's a natural for TV."

"Maybe on *Saturday Night Live*," said Lydia with a weary sense of recognition. A year ago she'd have embraced Cindy's cause with all its illogical rhetoric and strutted before the TV cameras while big-eyed children with swollen bellies died. Today—well, today she sat in a booth in a German delicatessen and whined because John Lloyd Branson hadn't played John Wayne and headed off a murderer at the pass. Not a lot of difference between strutting and whining; neither one saved a child from hunger or a prostitute from death.

"Cindy," she said, wadding up her napkin and tossing it on the table. "I've decided to lose control."

The other woman looked startled, then suspicious. "You have? I mean, I'm glad, but you understand I can't condone any unbridled individualism."

"Don't worry, Cindy; I'm not going to handcuff myself to a beer vat . . ."

"That wouldn't be an effective tactic unless we all do it as a group action . . ."

"Because I'm not going to your demonstration," continued Lydia smoothly. "I'm going to take a walk down a boulevard."

CHAPTER SIX

Amarillo—September 10

JENNER HATED MONDAYS.

Mondays were always god-awful. Mondays were Murphy's Law incarnate. If he woke up sick on a Monday, his doctor was out of town. If he dropped the morning paper, his beagle pup performed a basic function on the sports page. If he drank a cup of coffee, he burned his tongue. If he shaved, he went to work speckled with bits of toilet paper to stop the bleeding and some smart-mouth cop would ask if he didn't know which end to wipe.

There was no way to win on Monday.

This Monday was no exception; in fact, on a scale of ten, it rated an eleven. All because of those damn lineups. It was bad enough to be forced to look at a bunch of prostitutes on a Monday morning without having to hear them referred to as Jenner's hooker parade.

What was infinitely worse, what he couldn't stomach, didn't *intend* to stomach, was the refrain that greeted him whenever he walked into a room.

Hooker, hooker,
Who's got the hooker?

If he ever found out which cop started it, and *if* that cop was one of his traffic boys, he'd assign the peckerwood to a patrol area so far out in the city sticks that he'd need a road map to find his way back to civilization.

But for now he had his sights on another peckerwood.

"Schroder," he said as he marched into the eight-by-eight, smoke-filled room the investigator called an office.

"Well, if it ain't the littlest Hardy boy."

Lieutenant Roger Green lounged in the only extra chair in Schroder's Special Crimes office, his hands crossed over his hard little paunch. Jenner wasn't surprised to see him. It was Monday after all. What else could he expect but to be caught in the same room with two king cobras, both of them looking like they wanted to bite somebody and he happened to be handy?

Jenner plunged ahead. "Schroder, I've looked at more hookers than the entire Seventh Fleet on a ten-day pass and none of them even comes close to being the right one." Jenner tapped the detective's desk for emphasis, leaving a perfect latent fingerprint on its dusty top.

Schroder rolled his cigarette to the other side of his mouth. "Amarillo's a mite far from the water for the Seventh Fleet."

"Sergeant Jenner's geography ain't too good, Schroder. Bet he thinks he's still out on I-40 handing out speeding tickets." Green snickered at his own joke.

Jenner ignored him but not because of his snide remark. Any man who could sit in Schroder's smoke-layered office without coughing was clearly abnormal, and Jenner had all the abnormalities he could deal with in the person of Schroder himself.

"Come on, Schroder, you know what I'm saying. This lineup business isn't working. You haven't found the right prostitute and you're not going to. She's spooked. None of the Bean's crop is going to catch her!"

"Hey, watch it, Jenner," said Green.

Schroder's mouth pinched up at the corners in what might pass for a smile on an ordinary man's face. With Schroder it might be gas. Jenner had long since given up trying to make the distinction. "Well, what are you going to do?" he demanded.

"You're right about the lineup. . . ."

"Goddamn it, Schroder!" yelled Green. "Wonder Boy can't even get his lardass out of a patrol car . . ."

"The door was jammed!" protested Jenner.

". . . and you're telling me you're listening to this fuckup?"

"Is there something you haven't been telling the press, Sergeant Schroder?" Louis Bryant, Amarillo's answer to Woodward and Bernstein, leaned against the wall to the right of Schroder's door, and Jenner wondered how he had missed seeing him. Of course, Bryant *had* been standing behind him, but the room wasn't that big. It was Bryant's damn unobtrusiveness, his *stillness*, that allowed him to be overlooked the way a mannequin is overlooked not because it appears lifelike, but because it doesn't. Medium height, medium weight, medium looks, medium-length brown hair—there was nothing striking about Louis Bryant. Except his eyes. His eyes were large and luminous, like blue fluorescent paint dabbed in a carved mask.

"Damn it, Bryant!" exclaimed Green, twisting around in his chair to look at the reporter. "Can't you clear your throat or shuffle your feet to remind a man you're there. I've seen livelier corpses than you."

Bryant shrugged his shoulders. "Think of all the fascinating conversation I wouldn't overhear. Like this one, for instance. I've heard tell of Jenner's hooker parade, but all my sources have been laughing so hard, I haven't been able to make any sense of the story."

Green slapped his leg and started laughing. "Have you heard the latest one, Bryant?

Jenner, Jenner, hooker finder,
Had a hooker and couldn't keep her.

There's another that's a variation on this little piggy went to market, but I can't recollect it. Did you hear the bail bondsmen are taking up a collection to buy Jenner a plaque of appreciation 'cause their business is so good? I hear most of them had to hire extra help to take care of the paperwork. They're putting up so many bonds to bail out Jenner's hooker parade that one of them wants to set up a branch in the hallway outside the jail.''

"I don't think any of this is very damn funny!" said Jenner. "Those verses make the whole department look like boobs, and the lineups are futile and don't even keep the hookers off the street, except an hour or so in the daytime." He'd heard about the plaque and didn't consider that was very funny either, but maybe if he didn't think about it, it would go away.

"There's only one boob in the APD, Jenner, and I'm looking at him."

"Would the missing hooker have anything to do with the Boulevard Butcher?" Bryant shifted his gaze to Schroder.

Schroder stubbed out his cigarette in an ashtray Jenner would swear hadn't been emptied since last summer; then he leaned back in his chair. He scratched under his chin and stared at the reporter. "Could," he admitted.

Bryant smiled, giving his face a boyish innocence Jenner knew was at odds with the reporter's real personality. Police reporters were tough, and they damn sure weren't innocent. Nobody involved even secondhand in criminal investigation stayed innocent.

"Come on, Sergeant," Bryant coaxed. "Off the record."

Jenner raised his eyebrows. Schroder seldom said anything *on* the record. Off the record he was about as verbose as a pet rock.

Schroder rested his elbows on his desk and stared down at a plastic-covered piece of paper.

"I brought it to you, Sergeant," said Bryant, gesturing toward the paper. "I didn't have to."

Green turned around in his chair. "We could have gotten a court order, Bryant. That's evidence."

"What's evidence? What are you talking about?" asked Jenner.

"You'd first have to prove it, Lieutenant," replied Bryant, his eyes still focused on Schroder. "Until then it remains the personal property of the newspaper, and we—I—can do what

I want with it. Be thankful I have a sense of responsibility. I could be like several of my illustrious competitors. Anything for a headline. I'm willing to cooperate, but I'm not willing to give something for nothing."

"That's blackmail," said Green, slamming his fist on his chair arm.

"What's blackmail?" asked Jenner, feeling like an invisible man.

Bryant smiled again. "I never said I was altruistic, Lieutenant; merely that I was willing to cooperate. I don't want to turn this meeting into a confrontation."

"What in hell are you people talking about?" demanded Jenner.

"Hush up, Jenner," said Green. "You're interrupting."

Schroder looked up at Bryant with the expression of a man who is caught by the short hairs, knows it, acquiesces—an expression Jenner decided was as false as a prostitute's smile. God himself couldn't coerce Schroder.

"Green, have you heard anything from your informants?" the investigator asked without looking away from Bryant.

"Uh, no. Nothing that's checked out. And we haven't found Jo-Jo Jefferson yet to ask him how come his girls are the ones being hit, but we'll get him. He does too much business on the Boulevard to keep his fedora out of sight too long. Word is he's pissed, says he's being discriminated against."

"By the cops?" asked Bryant, his nose almost twitching as he scented a new story.

"Naw, by the Butcher. Says the Butcher is picking on him."

"So your informants haven't told you diddly-squat!" Schroder concluded.

"Not yet, but the word's out. We'll hear something. We got undercover cops behind every lamppost. We'll catch him. It's just a matter of time."

Schroder gave Green a look that Jenner thought should have shriveled the vice cop like a moth hitting a hot light bulb. "How much time? How many more chopped-to-hell bodies do we have to drag out of alleys? One? Ten? I don't need a psychological profile from the FBI to tell me I've got a serial killer, and ordinary police procedures don't catch serial killers. I don't know if extraordinary procedures are gonna catch this one. We don't have jackshit to work with except some hairs and fibers and they're worthless without a suspect. We don't have a witness that will admit to seeing anything. It's worse than a shooting at the Bimbo Bar where thirty witnesses say they were in a five-by-five bathroom and didn't see a thing, except this time I don't think anybody is lying. It's like the Butcher is an invisible man. He's a cute bastard, don't even try to hide his victims' bodies, just leaves them where he kills them. Even Bundy tried to hide what he did. Not this one. He kills in the open and the son of a bitch is hiding in the open, just daring us to catch him. I think your informants are worthless because the killer's not one of them. I don't think he even lives on the Boulevard. He butchers those women, then drives home like any innocent citizen. The Boulevard's just his hunting ground. And now this''— Schroder slapped the plastic-covered paper—"taunting us just like the California Zodiac Killer, and I don't need to tell you that the cops never caught him.''

"The Butcher wrote us a letter?'' asked Jenner.

"Hot damn!'' Green exclaimed. "It takes a while, but the sun does shine through your cloud cover, doesn't it, Jenner?''

"He wrote Mr. Bryant a letter with a few messages for me,'' said Schroder, his mouth screwed up as if he had just swallowed sour milk. "Or somebody wrote a letter. Could be from a crazy.'' He patted a bulging file folder. "We've already got a potful of letters from crazies, and we're up to two hundred calls a day. But this letter—this one gives me a cold feeling at the back of my neck. If this ain't from the Butcher, it's from some sicko son of a bitch who wants us to think he is!''

Jenner swallowed. He had never heard Schroder yell before—except at John Lloyd Branson. This case was sending the investigator around the bend. "Uh, what does the letter say?'' he asked.

"So what do you suggest, Schroder?'' asked Green, sounding a little subdued. In Jenner's opinion, a yelling Schroder could subdue anybody.

"I want those prostitutes warned . . ."

"Warned!" Green interrupted. "We've warned them. Hell, they all know what they're up against. The grapevine on the Boulevard beats hell out of Western Union."

". . . and I want them off the streets, particularly on the weekends. Green, sweep up any female that even looks like she makes her living on her back."

"What does the letter say?" asked Jenner again.

"Damn it, Schroder, did you ever hear about civil rights? We can't just pick somebody up because their skirt's too short or they wiggle their ass. Even members of Jenner's hooker parade had a solid charge against them. We gotta have probable cause."

"The probable cause is one of them is probably going to be dead a week from today if we don't," said Schroder, leaning forward to glare at Green. "The Butcher's killed a girl the last two weekends. If he sticks to his pattern, then hunting season opens again Friday night. I want those women too scared to wipe their noses, and if they do, I want a cop there holding a handkerchief."

Green looked up at the ceiling as though appealing to a higher authority. "We're gonna get our asses sued for harassment and false arrest."

"Is anybody going to tell me what the letter said?" demanded Jenner.

"Shut up, Jenner," said Green plaintively. "You're whining around when I've got real problems. Suing the police is a national pastime, Schroder. Comes right behind suing your doctor for malpractice."

"Just for a week or so," continued Schroder as if he hadn't heard Green's objections. And he probably hadn't, thought Jenner. Schroder never heard anything he didn't want to hear.

"What's that supposed to mean? You sure as hell ain't talking about the statute of limitations because it's a lot longer than any week or two on civil-rights violations." Green rose halfway out of his chair then slumped back again. "Jesus wept! Can't you just see it? The ACLU will take the case, and they'll say the hookers have a right to freedom of expression or some such shit. Then OSHA will probably fine us because we ain't maintaining a safe workplace for them."

"I'm talking about closing down the game preserve," said Schroder. "I'm talking about padlocking the motels for contributing to prostitution, and fining the hell out of the motel owners. Maximum Miller over in the D.A.'s office is getting the paperwork together. Without those motels, there'll be fewer prostitutes on the Boulevard, and we can protect the ones left. As for the rest, their pimps will move them to another city, Dallas or Denver, Kansas City maybe."

Green shook his head. "Then I wouldn't plan on visiting Dallas or Denver or wherever, Schroder, 'cause you're gonna be as popular with those cops as a Colombian drug lord."

"I don't give a damn," replied Schroder. "At least those cops won't be scooping some hooker's intestines back into her belly before they zip her in a body bag . . ."

Jenner gagged.

". . . because Dallas and Denver and Kansas City don't have the Butcher!" His voice ended in a shout, and Green winced. Schroder lit another cigarette. "Bryant, I want publicity."

"God Almighty, Schroder," interrupted Green, his voice high and jerky-sounding. "You're gonna let the motel owners read about getting their places closed before you ever buy the padlocks?"

"Nothing on the motels, Bryant, just stories about the Butcher, and I want them on the front page, and I want banner headlines. I want those women so scared that even a double dose of crack won't mellow them out."

"Jesus Christ, Schroder," interrupted Green again, jerking his head up to look at the investigator. "Do you think those hookers sit around reading the newspapers? Besides, I told you my men already warned them."

"They'll sooner believe Bryant," said Schroder bluntly. "And they'll read the paper—if the article's about them. How about it, Bryant?"

The reporter leaned back against the wall. "What are you giving me, Sergeant?"

Bryant didn't mention the motel closings, but Jenner didn't expect him to. Every reporter on the police beat learned to keep secrets about future operations until after they had gone down. Otherwise he found himself frozen out of any information that wasn't a matter of public record.

"I don't need your permission to interview prostitutes," continued Bryant after getting no response from Schroder. "And I'd already figured out the Butcher's pattern. I've figured out your pattern, too. You want something for nothing. Cut me a better deal or I'm walking."

Jenner stepped away from the door. No point in being in the way when Schroder booted the reporter out of his office.

Schroder tapped his finger and took a deep drag on his cigarette. The tip glowed red, then a small pillar of gray ash gently broke off and shattered on his tie. He brushed it off and got up. "All right, Bryant. Come on into the workroom and I'll show you a new wrinkle in the serial killer game. It's an invitation he always sends his victim. Print it. That way, at least the victim will know she's a target."

"Jesus, Schroder," whined Green, falling in line behind Bryant as the sergeant led the way out of the office. "I thought we were saving that to test whether a confession is valid. You're gonna blow the whole case."

Jenner barely waited until the lieutenant was out the door before he leaned over Schroder's desk and grabbed the Butcher's letter.

Dear Mr. Bryant,

I keep on hearing the police are close but they won't catch me just yet. I laughed when they look so clever and talk about being on the right track. The joke is on Sergeant Schroder. I am down on whores and I shan't quit ripping them till I do get stopped. Grand work the last job was. I gave the lady no time to squeal. How can they catch me now. I love my work and want to start again. You will soon hear of me with my funny little games. I saved some of the proper red stuff in a beer bottle over the last job to write with but it went thick like glue and I can't use it. Red ink is fit enough I hope. Ha ha. The next job I do I shall clip the lady's ears off and send to Sergeant Schroder just for fun wouldn't you. Keep this letter till I do a bit more work, then give it out straight. My knife is nice and sharp I want to get to work right away if I get a chance. Good luck.

Yours truly
Boulevard Butcher
Don't mind me giving the trade name.

"Holy shit," screamed Jenner when he felt a hand grab his wrist.

Schroder removed the letter from Jenner's numb fingers. "You're suspended, Jenner."

CHAPTER SEVEN

AN INVITATION FROM THE BUTCHER
by Louis Bryant

Amarillo, Texas—For a serial murderer, the Boulevard Butcher is a mannerly fellow. He courts his ladies with handmade invitations to their own murders. Made of newsprint pasted on cheap stationery, the invitations are not up to Hallmark's standards, but then the Butcher's parties are simple affairs held in dark alleys. The dress is casual, the society editor does not publish a guest list, and the party pictures are courtesy of the police photographer. Transportation from the party is provided for guests by the Special Crimes Unit: a one-way trip to the morgue.

Both Elizabeth Ann Green and Grace Lynette Morrison, whose mutilated bodies were discovered earlier this month, accepted the Butcher's invitations.

Thanks to the Butcher's lack of hospitality, his invitations may go begging in the future. Sergeant Ed Schroder of the Potter-Randall County Special Crimes Unit urges any woman who receives one to RSVP by calling the hot line set up by Special Crimes, then to stay indoors after dark. "We don't want any more murders," said Schroder.

Reaction to police requests were mixed. Jules "Jo-Jo" Jefferson, owner of an escort service on Amarillo Boulevard, accused the police of violating his employees' civil rights. "The young ladies who work for me are being treated like prisoners. They have to check in with the police and ain't free to walk the Boulevard."

One of the women of the Boulevard told this reporter that she "was scared," but didn't have a choice. "If I don't work, then my pimp will throw me out of my room." William "Big Bill" Elliot, Amarillo's perennial candidate for mayor, charged Sergeant Ed Schroder with botching the investigation. "Releasing the Butcher's notes to the newspaper is against all accepted police practices. He should have played his cards close to his vest," said Elliot. "Next thing we know, he'll be inviting the Butcher to come see all the evidence the police have."

Sergeant Schroder's response was to the point. "I'd rather have one hooker safe in her room than two dead ones in the alley."

The text of the infamous invitation is printed below by permission of Sergeant Ed Schroder.

> You are cordially invited
> to renounce the sins of the flesh,
> and cleanse your soul
> in the blood of the lamb.
> Once purified,
> you may join
> God's Heavenly Choir.

The Butcher paced the small room, breathing its stuffy air through his mouth and cracking the knuckles of first one hand, then the other. He heard neither his own heavy breathing nor the snapping sound of his bones and joints. Twirling around, he stared at the newspaper on the top of one of the two tiny tables in the room. Furiously he grabbed it and began ripping it into thin strips, continuing page by page until the floor around his feet was covered in newsprint confetti.

Throwing back his head, he howled, the sound muffled, flattened, absorbed by the acoustical titles. In his mind, though, his agonized screams spiraled up, slipped between the molecules that formed the ceiling, and reverberated over the city like the hungry cry of a predator.

His howls dwindled into pants as he felt the pressure start to build, felt himself expand, until he knew that soon—soon he would burst free. He felt thick blood pounding through his veins, felt hot pleasure building, felt saliva flooding his mouth, and licked his lips like an animal. The cold pure thrill of the game waited out there, on the Boulevard.

From far off he heard the cautioning voice: *wait—wait—it isn't time.*

But it is, his other voice whispered as he picked up the cracked leather case and removed a long-bladed knife with a peculiar thumb grip on its handle.

The cautioning voice, the voice of his other persona, the persona he wore as a mask while living, working outside this room, was growing weaker. *It's against the rules. Remember?*

"It's my game!" he screamed aloud, kicking the shredded newspaper at his feet. "It's still my game!"

CHAPTER
EIGHT

Amarillo Boulevard—September 15

AMARILLO BOULEVARD IS A MISNOMER. IT DOES NOT CON-
form to anyone's mental image of what the word *boulevard*
implies. No tree-filled, grassy median splits its four lanes.
Most of its buildings do not share a common wall, nor do
they jut up against one another with bare inches separating
them. A single building may squat in the middle of a block
with parking spaces or vacant lots on either side. Only occasionally is a block one continuous row of businesses.

When the Boulevard was a loop of Route 66, only the best
restaurants, the best motels, the best clubs lined its length from
east to west. It was a river of commerce through the city. With
the opening of Interstate 40 more than a mile to the south, the
Boulevard changed into a river whose waters are diverted, leaving those who lived and worked upon its banks stranded without custom. Loss of prosperity created desperation.

One industry flourishes on desperation.

Vice.

Pausing on a corner, Lydia glanced behind her. No one
was there, at least no one to account for the cold spot in the

middle of her back. A wino drinking from an almost empty bottle lolled against the barred window of a secondhand appliance store. Two younger men huddled under the streetlight waiting for a drug connection, or for a whore, or just waiting. Dense shadows hovered in locked doorways and gaping alleys waiting to gather in those whose wants and needs forced them to spurn the cold neon circles cast by the streetlights.

Lydia darted from streetlight to streetlight, her shoulders hunched against whoever—or whatever—lived in the dark.

"Hey, Blondie!"

Lydia screamed and whirled around to see the black-and-white unit stop at the curb and the passenger door swing open. Relief made her dizzy until she remembered she was supposed to be a prostitute, and prostitutes weren't ordinarily glad to see the police.

"What is it, Officer?" she asked, clutching her shoulder bag in both hands.

A tall patrolman in regulation black uniform stepped out of the car, a disbelieving grin on his face. "Officer? Hey, Ned, did you hear her call me officer?" he said to his partner who was climbing out of the other side of the car. "That's what I call polite."

"Sure beats the hell out of being called a pig," said Ned, a shorter, older man with graying hair and a suspicious expression on his weary face. "What's a nice lady like you doing on the Boulevard at night?"

"Minding my own business," said Lydia, feeling her stomach sink down to the vicinity of her knees.

"That business is going to get you killed, Blondie. Don't you know there's a crazy running around, and he ain't polite at all?"

"I'm not afraid," said Lydia, swallowing hard. But she was. She was paralyzed with fear, not of the Butcher—she didn't intend to walk down an alley with anyone wearing pants—but of the Boulevard itself, the source of that cold spot that even now was raising chill bumps up and down her spine.

"Blondie, if you're not scared, you ought to be," said the younger officer. "Hop in the car and take a ride downtown.

You can spend the night in a nice clean cell instead of picking up johns. Your pimp can bail you out in the morning.''

"I don't have a pimp," retorted Lydia. "Just because a woman is in the business of selling sexual favors doesn't mean she has to have a pimp. Pimps perpetuate a form of slavery.''

Ned walked around the front of the patrol car, shaking his head with disbelief. "An activist hooker. Jesus, now I've heard everything. Get her in the car, Tony," he said to his younger partner. "We're wasting time. Schroder wants all the whores off the Boulevard, and I'm not about to tell him I spent ten minutes listening to a lecture on the ERA.''

Tony stepped toward Lydia and she stuck her hand out. "Stop!" she said in as imperious a tone of voice as she could manage. "You can't just arrest somebody for walking on the sidewalk, even one with cracks the size of the Grand Canyon. I am not soliciting, I am not drunk, I am not a public nuisance, I am not a vagrant.''

Ned rubbed his chin. "Not a vagrant, huh. You got any identification?''

Lydia swallowed and thought of her billfold filled with driver's license, credit cards, Social Security number, library card, and return airline ticket to Dallas. End of masquerade.

"Identification?" she squeaked.

"I didn't think so. No pimp, looks cleaner than the average hooker, talks like a college professor," continued Ned. "Look, Blondie, I don't know what you're playing, but you can straighten it out with Sergeant Schroder downtown. We got orders to get you women off the streets, keep you safe whether you like it or not. Hell, I'm protecting you from the pimps, too. It's just a matter of time until one of them adds you to his stable.''

"Just let him try," said Lydia, backing away and winding the straps of her shoulder bag around her right hand.

"No trying to it, Blondie. Nobody freelances tail on the Boulevard. It's bad for business. The pimps won't allow it. You join a stable or you're dead meat. If you're gonna play this game, learn the rules. Better yet, find another profession. Life expectancy's not too good in this one and getting worse. Now get in the car like a lady. That's one of the rules, too. When you get picked up, go quietly. Don't lay yourself open for a charge of resisting arrest or assaulting a police officer. Costs your pimp more to bail you out, and it pisses us off. Tony, open the door for this lady.''

Lydia watched the younger officer open the back door of the patrol car. If she let herself be arrested, Sergeant Schroder might recognize her. He might call John Lloyd. That was too terrible to contemplate.

She wished her brain would shift into high gear and come up with some logical story as to why a law student from Dallas was walking the streets of Amarillo dressed like a five-dollar hooker. Any story would do. Except the truth, of course.

"You're making a mistake," she began, then flinched. Judging by the expression on Ned's face, she had made a very inauspicious beginning toward talking herself out of being arrested.

Ned became impatient. "Blondie, I've made so damn many mistakes, I'm used to it. The first one was being a cop in the first place. You gonna get in the car on your own, or do you need a hand?" He stepped closer and reached for her arm.

"Don't touch me!" she warned, twisting away. "You're already guilty of harassment and false arrest. Don't add police brutality to the charges I intend to have my attorney file tomorrow. Believe me, you don't want him on your back." Lydia nodded her head abruptly. There, that was much better; meet threats with threats; intimidation with intimidation. The law of the jungle or, at least, of the Boulevard.

"Get moving, Blondie," ordered Ned. "I've got so many people on my back, your attorney's gonna have to take a number and wait in line."

"Didn't you hear what I said?" asked Lydia desperately. "I'll sue you."

Ned pulled a handkerchief out of his pocket and wiped his forehead. He looked tired and Lydia felt an unwelcome surge of sympathy. "I heard you, Blondie, and to tell the truth, I'd rather try to explain to a jury why I arrested you than try to explain to Sergeant Schroder why I didn't. So go ahead and file your suit. At least I'll be put on restrictive duty, or maybe

I'll take some leave, go fishing for something besides hopeless women.''

Staring into his implacable eyes, Lydia sighed. He was a decent man, and she felt like a fraud. The least she could do was tell him she wasn't going to file suit, that the only lawyer she knew in the whole Panhandle was John Lloyd Branson, and he had fired her.

"Listen," she said, straightening her shoulders and stepping forward into a giant-sized crack in the sidewalk. Reeling drunkenly on stiletto heels, she careened into the door, slamming it shut on Tony's fingers. She flailed her arms about for balance, forgetting she was still holding her purse, and connected with the point of Ned's chin, rendering him uninterested in further conversation.

"Oh, God, I'm sorry!" cried Lydia as she finally got both feet on level ground. "Are you all right?"

"Son of a bitch!" screamed Tony, dancing around holding his fingers.

Ned, reclining unconscious in the gutter, gave no answer at all.

Lydia considered her options, and applied the law of the jungle. She ran like hell down the Boulevard.

Lydia ducked into the shabby motel lobby and sank down on a cracked vinyl chair. She felt her heart pounding in her chest and the sweat beading on her upper lip. She had never believed sweat could be cold until now. Classic anxiety reaction, she thought as she pulled off her pumps: rapid heartbeat, perspiration, trembling hands. Not to mention aching feet. Of course, her sore feet came from running down alleys and side streets, across vacant lots, through parking lots, for sixteen blocks. Not easy when wearing high-heel pumps and carrying a shoulder bag with a five-pound brick in it. She wondered if a brick could be considered a concealed weapon. She wondered if Tony the cop would believe she had tripped, and if Ned the cop would believe she wasn't in the habit of assaulting policemen. She shook her head. Very doubtful. No one would believe her. She didn't believe it herself and she knew she was telling the truth.

She wiggled her toes inside the cheap black mesh hose and

leaned her head against the back of the chair. She was a fugitive from the law, albeit an unintentional one. She was also a fool, and a clumsy fool at that. When would she ever learn to watch where she put her big feet?

She closed her eyes against the tears. It had all sounded so simple sitting in her apartment in Dallas: spend the weekends on the Boulevard pretending to be a prostitute, hunting for any information about the Butcher while persuading the real prostitutes to free themselves from their pimps. She laughed. The only simple thing in this charade was her mind.

"Hey, you!"

Lydia opened her eyes to discover the closest thing to a crone she had ever seen. Withered leathery skin, brittle gray-brown hair, nicotine-stained teeth, and dirty blue eyes filled with a malevolent expression peering out between drooping lids added up to an apparition from a nightmare. However, the old woman emitted an odor of human sweat so strong as to be nearly toxic, so Lydia decided the creature must be real. Apparitions couldn't possibly smell so bad.

"What do you want?" asked Lydia, trying not to inhale.

"Who's your man?"

"Man?"

"You ain't one of Jo-Jo's girls."

Lydia shuddered at the very thought. "I don't see that's any of your business."

The woman stood in front of Lydia, hands on hips. "I manage this motel."

Lydia looked around the tiny lobby with its dirty linoleum floor and moth-eaten furniture. She tried to imagine what kinds of people might stay there. Certainly nobody that could pass a Wassermann test. "Don't worry. I won't proposition one of your guests. I just want to sit here and relax. You can't imagine how my feet hurt."

"You ain't got no business hanging around my lobby."

"Then I'll rent a room and hang around there. I want clean sheets and no bedbugs."

The crone's laughter sounded like the cackling of a barnyard hen. "You stupid, girl? I don't do business with anybody trying to set up on their own. I make my arrangements with the pimps, and part of that arrangement is that I don't allow no strangers to rent rooms and take trade away from my legitimate customers.''

Lydia stood up. ''Are you telling me you won't rent to anybody but a prostitute whose pimp already has an arrangement with you? Are you telling me this whole motel is a brothel?''

The woman blinked, then studied Lydia. ''You're about as bright as a burned-out light bulb.''

Lydia swallowed. ''What makes you say that?''

''You ain't got no pimp, you don't know no better than to try to rent a room by yourself, and you're sitting on your butt during working hours. The best thing I can say about you is you ain't no cop. Lieutenant Green ain't smart, but he's smart enough not to send somebody out on the Boulevard who don't know how things work. Besides, I listen to the police scanner. You put two cops down just a little while ago, sent them to the hospital. You're trouble, and I don't need trouble.''

''Oh, my God, how bad are they?'' Lydia sucked in her breath at the sight of the woman's triumphant grin. ''I mean, what makes you think I'm the one?''

''Blonde, near six feet,'' said the old woman with a shrug. ''Ain't many like you on the Boulevard, none that I know of.''

''Are you going to turn me in?''

''Might, might not. Depends.''

''On what?'' asked Lydia, then stiffened as she heard the distant sound of police sirens override the ordinary noise of traffic. The old woman cocked her head to one side and grinned.

Even a burned-out light bulb could figure out what had happened, thought Lydia as she grabbed her shoes and purse. ''When did you call the cops?'' she demanded.

The crone lit a cigarette and tossed the match in a scorched metal ashtray. ''When you first come in. Never hurts to do the cops a favor as long as it don't lose me business, and one way or another somebody's gonna owe me.''

Lydia had an inkling of how a real prostitute might feel: afraid, lonely, desperate, at the mercy of pimps and other women, and with no choices to make but bad ones. But there was one very important difference: she could walk away, get in her rental car, drive to the airport, and fly back to Dallas. Let the Butcher make chopped liver out of these women. Only the simpleminded would try to interfere.

Lydia sighed. She had already decided she was simpleminded. "If you're so damn fond of money, how much to show me the back door and delay the cops?"

The crone slapped her leg and cackled. "Fifty."

Lydia reached in her purse. Her fingers closed around the brick, then a small can of Mace, a tube of lipstick (Passionate Red), a comb, some business cards, and nothing else. "My billfold's gone," she said, a hollow feeling growing in the middle of her stomach. "Oh, God, what am I going to do?"

"I ain't the Salvation Army," said the old woman, flicking ashes onto the floor.

"I'll bet you'd steal a dead man's shoes," retorted Lydia, trying to remember when she'd last seen her wallet. When Tony and Ned tried to arrest her? No, because showing her identification was the last thing she had wanted to do.

"If they fit. A dead man don't have no use for shoes, just like a whore don't have no use for a fancy watch, girlie." She pointed to Lydia's wrist.

It was in a bar, thought Lydia suddenly. She last had her billfold in a bar. She'd paid for a drink, then sat down at a table with several prostitutes and hung her purse over the back of a chair. Had there been anyone sitting at the little table behind her, close enough to lift her wallet? Maybe. She thought so, because there had been a full glass of beer on the table. Odd that she could remember the beer and not the person. She remembered something else; she remembered feeling chilled, as if cold hands were touching her.

"Did you hear me, girlie? I'll take the watch, tell the cops some story."

Lydia shivered. The old woman's eyes gave her the same chilled sensation as she'd had in the bar. "You get all your jewelry this way?" asked Lydia as she thrust her watch at the woman.

"Some." Dirty blue eyes squinted at the watch. "This pure gold?"

"Yes! Now where's the back door?"

"Down that hall by the desk and turn right." The woman pointed a gnarled finger.

"For a gold watch you ought to provide me with an armed escort," muttered Lydia, stuffing her sore feet back into shoes that felt two sizes too small.

"I'll throw in a little advice, girlie. A real hooker keeps her money in her shoe along with her rubbers."

"Rubbers? You mean condoms?"

The crone shuffled behind the desk, shaking her head. "You're too dumb to be out on the Boulevard by yourself."

Lydia ran for the back door, and the cackling laughter followed her down the hall. "Watch out for the bogeyman, girlie."

"Better him than you," said Lydia, pushing open the metal fire door an infinitesimal crack—and seeing the bogeyman walking across the cracked asphalt parking lot toward her. Jo-Jo Jefferson's gold teeth glinted in the neon floodlight at the back of the motel.

She had no doubt he was coming for her, and she had no doubt who told him to come.

Pulling the fire door shut, thus making it impossible to open from the outside, and slinging her bag over her shoulder, she darted back to the lobby. The crone stretched out one skinny arm as Lydia veered around the desk. She felt her sleeve rip as the old woman's talonlike hand grasped it.

Lydia jerked free and whirled around. "You set me up! You manipulated me! You made a fool out of me! I can do that well enough on my own. I've never hit an elderly person before, but I've done a lot of things tonight I never thought I'd do. However, since I abhor violence and am by nature a pacifist, I'm going to walk out that front door without beating the living hell out of you."

"Where's Jo-Jo?" hissed the crone, her eyes full of rage and ancient evil.

"He's waiting for a dumb blonde hooker with no pimp to walk through the fire door. Tell me, how much does a person get these days for selling a woman into slavery?"

The woman opened her mouth in a tooth-filled snarl, but snapped it shut when her eyes shifted their angry focus to a point behind Lydia.

"Don't move! You're under arrest!" The voice was deep, masculine, and excited.

Lydia hunched her shoulders in the worst feeling of defeat she had ever experienced, turned around, and stared dumbfounded at a tall, barrel-chested, redheaded man dressed in Levi's, boots, and Western shirt. The stranger stood less than three feet away. Six or seven more similarly garbed men bunched up behind him, all staring at her like boys on their first visit to a strip show.

"Who the hell are you?" demanded Lydia.

"I'm Bill Elliot, and I'm making a citizen's arrest."

"Oh, my God, it's the vigilantes," said Lydia. "I don't need this." She glanced wildly around the lobby, then stumbled sideways against the wall and giggled.

Elliot curled his lip in what he imagined was a sneer and hooked his fingers in his belt loops. "Drunk," he announced to his followers. "Look at her, so drunk she can't stand up. Grab her arms and let's haul her into the van."

To keep herself from falling, Lydia grabbed a fire extinguisher hanging on the wall. "I think I'm going to throw up."

"Jesus, Bill," said one of the other men. "I don't want her puking on my upholstery. Let's just wait here for the cops."

"She ain't drunk," stated the old woman, glaring at Elliot.

"Ma'am, a respectable senior citizen like yourself can't be expected to recognize a drunken slut. . . ."

"Slut!" shouted Lydia, jerking the fire extinguisher off the wall and lifting it over her head

"Watch it, Bill," shouted one of his men. "She's gonna throw it!"

"I've been cheated, threatened, almost arrested, almost sold to a pimp, had my property stolen, but I'll be damned if I'm going to let you insult me!" shouted Lydia, quickly hooking one arm around the fire extinguisher and using her free hand to activate it. She prayed it had been checked recently by the fire department and was fully pressurized.

It was.

She coated Elliot and his fearless band with a thick layer

of foam, added a carpet of the white slippery chemical to the linoleum floor, then turned and hurled the extinguisher through the plate-glass window behind her and vaulted through after it.

CHAPTER NINE

THE BUTCHER CARESSED THE WALLET'S SMOOTH LEATHER as he listened to the phone ring. He breathed shallowly through his mouth, trying to control his excitement as he waited for the sound of the man's voice on the other end of the line.

He waited for John Lloyd Branson to pick up the receiver.

John Lloyd Branson, the only adversary who was his equal. Branson the eccentric, the successor to Templo Houston in Panhandle folklore; Branson the knight errant, the defender of the defenseless, the useless, and the hopeless; Branson the strategist, who would appreciate the game even as his queen was taken.

The phone was picked up. "John Lloyd Branson."

"Is Lydia there?" He was proud of his deep, husky voice, so unlike that of his other self.

The hesitation was brief, only long enough for a game master like Branson to respond to an unexpected move. "Who might this be?"

The Butcher fingered the business card he'd found in Lydia's billfold, the one describing her as a legal clerk for Branson. "I'm one of her admirers."

"It is customary in this society to possess a name, young man."

Branson's voice had been sharper, with less of a drawl. Time for another unexpected move. "You her father?"

"My relationship with Miss Fairchild is not the subject of this conversation. Your identity is. Calling yourself an admirer may be adequate if you are placing an ad in the personal column of *The Village Voice*, but it is insufficient to convince me that your intentions are benign. While calling me at ten o'clock in the evening to ask the whereabouts of a young woman may be evidence of overwhelming love, it is more likely to be the result of a sudden glandular secretion. I am neither a dating bureau nor a procurer, young man."

Branson's voice sliced across the distance between Amarillo and Canadian like a scalpel cutting through flesh, drawing blood from his listener while telling him what he needed to know: The attorney would guard his queen.

"You're her watchdog, aren't you, Branson? An old, icicle-cold cripple warming yourself with dreams of her musky woman's heat and snapping at anyone who comes too near her."

"You are hysterical. I suggest a cold shower might restore your hormone balance."

The Butcher twisted around in the telephone booth and looked across the street at Lydia hesitantly pausing to glance over her shoulder. He gripped the receiver harder. He had not yet heard the emotion beneath Branson's icy tones that he wanted, *needed*, to hear. "You don't know where Lydia is, do you, Branson? I do. I'm watching her right now, watching her whore's face and whore's body. She's tall, isn't she, and ripe, like a fruit just on the verge of being putrid with decay? I'm not touching her yet, just watching, but soon, perhaps sooner than I'd planned, I'll know her, know her very flesh and bones. Yes, I think it will be sooner. It wouldn't do to allow you too much time."

"Young man, you are quite mad!"

"No, not actually. I'm competent; I know exactly what I'm doing, and it's what I choose to do. Madness is the rationale others use."

"Others?"

The Butcher touched the glass walls of the telephone booth that enclosed him. "The ones outside, to explain me."

"I see." There was a moment's silence. "Are you planning to sexually assault Miss Fairchild or to take her life?"

"What's wrong, Branson? Scared somebody's going to fuck your blonde? Or scared I'm going to wring her neck like a chicken's? Do you suppose she'd jerk around, maybe run in circles like a chicken does when it loses its head? Are you scared, Branson? You want to beg me? Better yet, offer your body for hers?" The thought of John Lloyd Branson begging was giving him an erection. "Come on, Branson baby, what's your best offer?"

There was the sound of a quick breath sucked in, then slowly expelled. "If any harm should come to Miss Fairchild, I shall, without mercy, without regret, without remorse, and without regard to my legal oath, hang you and leave your body for the buzzards to consume."

There was a soft click, then only the sound of the dial tone and the Butcher's own heavy breathing.

CHAPTER
TEN

"HEY, SWEETIE, WANT A DATE?"

The prostitute cocked one hip and thrust out her chest, a wind-up merchant displaying her wares. The wind whipped clumps of bleached hair around a thin, pasty face. A pungent odor of peroxide and Evening in Paris stung Jenner's swollen sinuses. A whore on her way down was his first thought. Bleached blondes weren't that common on the street; they were generally reserved for the high-dollar trade, the so-called escort services where a well-dressed, well-groomed girl could earn two or three thousand a night. When her looks were gone, she ended up here—on the Boulevard—where the pimps were too cheap to pay for professional bleach jobs, and she resorted to peroxide for as long as her pride held out. Unfortunately pride was an early casualty on the Boulevard.

But Jenner wasn't looking for a blonde. He wanted the dark-haired whore with the ghost-white face, and after a week on the Boulevard, he wasn't any closer to finding her than he was when he started.

The blonde hooker stepped backward and folded her arms over her chest. "What you looking at, huh? Staring at me like I was a piece of meat. You deaf and dumb or what?"

Jenner stepped closer to the woman. "I'm looking for a special girl. Maybe you know her. Long dark hair, real white face, wears a leather skirt and cowboy boots."

The woman backed up again. "What do you want her for?"

"Do you know her?" asked Jenner, reaching in his back pocket for a twenty-dollar bill, payment for information received.

The hooker swung her purse in a tight semicircle and slapped Jenner across the face, followed by a hard kick to his kneecap. "He's got a knife!" she screamed. "I saw him reaching for it. It's the Butcher!"

"No! Wait a minute! You got it wrong. I don't have a knife. I was reaching for some money," huffed Jenner, leaning over to grab his wounded kneecap.

"Butcher! Butcher!" The hooker kicked him again, this time catching him in the left buttock as he limped around in a circle clasping his throbbing knee.

Propelled by a kick any pro football player would be proud of, Jenner's hopping limp turned into a staggering limp. He released his hold on his knee to grab the streetlight before he brained himself on its concrete post.

"Goddamn it, lady! I'm not the Butcher!" he yelled, hooking one arm around the post and turning back to face her. "Ah, shit," he added as he saw her running up the sidewalk and waving her arms at a baby-blue Cadillac on the other side of the street.

Letting go of the lamppost, he limped, staggered, and hopped in the opposite direction. He heard the screeching brakes and didn't need to look around to know the Cadillac had made an illegal U-turn and was coming back his way. Actually, he didn't have time to look around. He knew what that Cadillac meant as well as any vice cop. Besides at least five hundred pounds of extra chrome, that car also carried the hooker's pimp and one or more enforcers, affectionately known as *muscles* on the Boulevard. If he, Lawrence Robert Jenner, wanted to see another sunrise with all his appendages firmly attached to his body, he had better concentrate on dragging himself toward safe territory.

Panting, he rounded a corner and down an alley at a fast

limp, his abused knee sending needle-sharp pains up his thigh to meet the aching spasms on their way down from his bruised hip. He wondered if his knee was broken. He wondered if his hip was broken. Then he wondered why he was worrying. If both weren't broken already, they soon would be.

Car doors slammed and Jenner crouched beside a Dempster Dumpster. Cautiously he peered around the Dumpster toward the mouth of the alley. A figure standing silhouetted against the streetlight's fluorescent glare was joined by two others. Side by side and silently, the three figures stepped forward, disappearing into the shadows that lay just inside the entrance to the alley. Jenner hadn't seen any guns, but he knew the three figures were carrying. A man with a gun walks differently from a man without one.

He looked toward the other end of the alley. Nothing but the darkness cast by ancient brick buildings for fifty or so feet, then a vacant lot, beyond which stood a few dilapidated houses, their back gates opening onto the alley. If he ran to one of the houses, he'd be dead the minute he crossed that moonlit vacant lot. If he *did* make it across to one of the houses, he'd still be dead. No homeowner in North Amarillo with any sense of self-preservation opened his door to someone he didn't know. If he stayed where he was, he'd be dead. His granddaddy's old saying about being between a rock and a hard place suddenly made a lot of sense.

"What the hell," he muttered under his breath as he wedged himself in the corner created by the Dumpster and the blank brick wall of the tallest building. "If I'm going to be pulped, I'm gonna take somebody else's balls with me."

Slipping his belt out of its loops, he wound one end around his fist. A heavy Western buckle dangled from the other end. If he were Chuck Norris armed with such a weapon, he could break one enforcer's wrist, blind the second, and choke the pimp. Unfortunately, he was Larry Jenner, and he'd be lucky to raise a bruise.

He braced himself against the wall, wiped the sweat out of his eyes, flexed his wrists, and tightened his grip around the belt. He wished he were home watching television. Or investigating a ten-car pileup on the expressway. Or even writing the mayor a speeding ticket. Anywhere but hiding in a filthy alley.

And while he was wishing, he also wished he didn't need to take a leak. Somehow the idea of wetting himself disturbed him more than the idea of dying. Because, he realized suddenly, he really didn't believe in his own death, but he *did* believe in the very real possibility of pissing in his pants like an old wino.

"Police! Do you men know anything about this Caddy parked on the curb?"

Jenner tried to melt into the side of the Dempster Dumpster as a cop leaned out of the passenger window of a patrol car and pointed a flashlight at the pimp and his enforcers. Like cockroaches caught in light, the three swiveled their heads to look at one another. Jenner could almost see antennae waving from their skulls. There was one distinctive difference between the three and a cockroach: Cockroaches were too smart to scratch their heads with the same hand that held a gun.

"Drop the guns and freeze, you bastards!" shouted the cop as his partner threw the patrol car into reverse, then forward, to get a straight run down the alley.

"Shiiit!" yelled the pimp as he and his two associates scuttled toward the far end of the alley.

Jenner estimated he had five minutes tops, two until the pimp and his two dwarfs were stopped, and three more until the cops decided to search the alley. The instant he saw the patrol car's taillights whip by his hiding place, he limped in the opposite direction—back toward the Boulevard. Even the Boulevard was safer than being caught by the cops. Even the pimps were safer than the cops. The pimps were simply going to break off anything that stuck out and dump what was left in the trash. He might even have lived through it. He would most definitely, positively, without question, not live through Sergeant Ed Schroder. Schroder would ignore the wig and earring; Schroder would even ignore the six tattoos, including the full skeleton on his chest, carefully faked by the makeup artist at the little theatre. Schroder *would not* ignore the fact that he, Sergeant Larry Jenner, was not supposed to be on the Boulevard dead or alive, or in any stage between.

He burst out of the alley and limped down the sidewalk for a few feet until the shakes made his teeth chatter. He leaned against a building and bent over, hoping all that blood to the brain would at least keep him from fainting. That is, if he had a brain. Deciding to pose as a derelict on the Boulevard while he looked for his prostitute witness wasn't exactly proof of its existence.

"The Butcher!"

Jenner raised his head. "Ah, shit," he mumbled with a groan as he recognized the same blonde prostitute whose screams had brought the pimp. Same scream, too, he observed, as the hooker tilted her head back, closed her eyes, and started through her scales, beginning low with earsplitting and progressing through deafening to a squeal that rendered all auditors brain dead. That was what was wrong with him, Jenner thought. He was brain dead. Otherwise, he wouldn't be leaning up against a sleazy motel known for renting rooms by the hour, listening to a hooker whose adenoids had failed to atrophy at the proper age.

He pushed himself away from the wall, put one hand over his left kneecap, the one that needed help staying on, and slung his belt over his shoulder. He would never make it to his car, which was hidden in a rented garage a block south of the Bimbo Bar. He would die right here on the Boulevard with a blonde hooker singing an aria over his brain-dead body.

He hobbled down the sidewalk and wondered how long before someone reported an air-raid siren had gone off by mistake. How long before a wolf pack of Boulevard beasts circled around him, smelling a helpless cripple to feast upon? How long? He looked down the block and smiled. Not as long as perfectly good transportation stood at hand. Actually not at hand, more on the curb, but he didn't want to get too specific when God had just provided a baby-blue, late-model miracle. Actually not God, but he didn't like to impute good motives to evil men like cockroaches.

He decided to leave the pimp's Cadillac in a tow-away zone across the Boulevard from the Bimbo Bar.

CHAPTER
ELEVEN

"WHAT'S HAPPENED? IS IT THE BUTCHER? WHY IS THAT GIRL screaming? Can anyone understand what she's saying?"

Lydia impatiently tapped a scrawny boy who was nearly as tall as her five feet ten inches—not counting her three-inch heels. Of course, if she subtracted his rooster crest of green hair, he was considerably shorter. But tougher, she thought as he turned around and she saw the safety pin through his right nostril.

"Who the fuck knows?" drawled the kid, tilting his head and flaring his nostril to make his safety pin jiggle.

"You're standing here. You must have heard something. Has anyone talked to her?"

"Who the fuck knows?" he answered, now wiggling his nose up and down to add a new step to his pin dance.

Lydia swallowed. That pin sent chills down her arms. "Has someone called the paramedics?"

"Who the fuck knows?" The boy giggled as he flicked his safety pin.

"Are those the only four words you know?" demanded Lydia, gripping the strap of her shoulder bag with both hands to control the temptation to shake his pointed green head right off his shoulders, safety pin and all.

He giggled again. "Wanta fuck?" he asked, and reached for her breast.

Lydia grabbed his safety pin and twisted. "Not even if you ask nicely," she said, letting go of the pin to shove him backward into the gutter.

"You'll have to hurt him," said a hoarse voice.

Lydia turned around, then quickly shook her hair forward to cover as much of her face as possible. The girl in front of her with the improbably orange hair was the hooker from John Lloyd's office, the one called Cowgirl.

"I did hurt him. I may have even made his nose bleed. He'll leave me alone."

Cowgirl looked at her curiously. "Honey, all you did was make it smart. Where you been playing? In the Junior League?"

Lydia lit a cigarette and let it dangle from one side of her mouth. It served two purposes: she looked tough, *and* she could puff and exhale without ever inhaling. She didn't intend to end up with a smoking habit just to masquerade as a prostitute. "I've been on the game long enough to take care of myself. I've just never been to Amarillo before. Me and my man came down from Kansas City. Heard about the Boulevard and decided to check out the action. Maybe open a branch office."

Lydia wondered if she was using the right words? The right tone? God knows she hadn't earlier in the evening. She knew better now. Don't admit you're without a pimp, and don't talk as if you're collecting signatures on an ERA petition. Most important: act tough. Nice girls not only finished last on the Boulevard, they got stomped at the starting line.

Watching Cowgirl's face to gauge the hooker's reaction to her story was no help either. For one thing, the smoke from her cigarette was making her eyes water, and for another, the other woman didn't *have* a reaction. Her face was hard and blank and so were her eyes. Or were they? Was there a residue of emotion mirrored in her eyes? Something more positive than resignation?

"Here he comes, honey," said Cowgirl.

"Who?" asked Lydia, catching sight of some emotion in Cowgirl's face at long last.

"Hey, bitch. You think your ass is too good for Benny?"

Lydia gulped and whirled around. The green-haired rooster stood holding a turquoise bandanna to his bleeding nose. "If you're Benny, I don't think so. I know so." She hoped he didn't hear her voice shaking.

He did. She could tell by his smile, a wide one that revealed pointed incisors. Predator teeth, her orthodontist always called such dental development. Her orthodontist was absolutely right. She could almost feel those teeth buried in her jugular vein.

"Come on, bitch," he said, and giggled as he grabbed her wrists.

She looked back over her shoulder at Cowgirl. "Help me!" she pleaded, her cigarette wobbling in the corner of her mouth.

Cowgirl shrugged. "This is the Boulevard, honey. No man can let some bitch hit him and still be a man."

Lydia clenched her teeth and jerked backward, twisting her body sideways at the same time. The kid's eyes crossed as he lost his balance and stumbled groin first into Lydia's hipbone. He dropped her wrists and grabbed his crotch. Lydia twisted the other way and put her whole weight into the uppercut that landed squarely on the point of his chin. His eyes rolled up until the whites showed, his legs quivered, and he passed out in the gutter.

Lydia spit out her cigarette and rubbed her throbbing knuckles. "I don't like that macho shit, Benny. You remember that the next time."

She swaggered over to Cowgirl. "Why didn't you help me?"

Cowgirl lifted an eyebrow. "What if you'd lost?"

"He couldn't have beaten two of us."

"I don't know that for sure, and I don't want to be cut. That's what Benny's kind does—they cut. Among other things."

Lydia shuddered. "Do you think he's the Butcher?"

Cowgirl's eyes widened, and Lydia saw the fear in their depths. "Hey, don't talk about him, huh? It's bad luck."

"Do you know something? Did you see something?"

Cowgirl shook her head violently. "Benny's not the Butcher. No hooker with any sense at all would even get within feeling distance of Benny. He's into pain in a big way, and all the girls on the Boulevard know it.''

"Maybe he grabbed them before they had a chance to run.''

Cowgirl glanced furtively at the crowd. "Shut up! I didn't see anybody.''

"But you saw something, didn't you? You know something . . .''

Cowgirl grabbed Lydia's arm. "Shut your mouth! For God's sake, some of these people standing here watching would sell their mothers for a bottle of wine or their next fix, and you're making me out to be a witness. I don't want the Butcher looking for me.''

Lydia felt the cold spot again and glanced at the crowd. "Oh, God, do you think he's here? Do you think he's listening to us?''

Cowgirl released Lydia. "I don't know. The Butcher is sort of like a shadow that you see out of the corner of your eye. You think you saw it move, but when you look directly at it, it's just another shadow. So you tell yourself you're crazy and walk on, and all the time the shadow's following you, getting closer until it finally swallows you up.'' The prostitute rubbed her arms where Lydia saw huge goose bumps of fear. "Hey, I don't want to talk about it, so stop asking questions like you were a cop.''

Lydia laughed uneasily. "Do I look like a cop?''

"Honey, I've seen women cops who look more like hookers than hookers do. But I know most of the women undercover cops, I make it my business to know, and you're not one of them.'' She jerked her head toward the blonde who had finally wound down to a hoarse whine. "That so-called hooker you were so concerned about? She's a cop, honey. That's why nobody's offering her a hanky. That's how my pimp and his muscles got dropped on so fast. A cop car was shadowing her, and they followed Jo-Jo right up the alley.''

"Jo-Jo?'' asked Lydia, thinking about cold eyes and hard diamonds.

"Yeah, my pimp. Serves the bastard right. I tried to tell him about that girl, but he just backhanded me and told me I'd better stop messing in his business. He was out trolling for new girls''—her voice changed, deepened into bitterness—"and when he saw that blonde start to run from that john and no pimp came out of the cracks, he figured she was trophy size. He followed the john into the alley to show the blonde what a big man he was, and the cops followed him."

"And the cops are in the alley?" asked Lydia, backing away.

"Yeah, some of them. Others will be here as fast as their little squad cars can hustle—till cops are thicker than flies on a garbage can. See that old Ford parked next to the alley—the one with the smoking tailpipe and two different colored doors? I recognize that car. The chunky guy getting out is Schroder. He's the homicide dick in charge of catching the Butcher. The skinny guy next to him is Lieutenant Green, head of Vice." Cowgirl whistled softly. "Look what's coming there."

Lydia looked. And didn't like what she saw. "Oh, God," she breathed.

"That guy who looks like he had an accident with a can of shaving cream is Big Bill Elliot. He thinks he's God's gift to city hall, but he's so damn stupid he can't count his balls and come up with the same number twice."

Lydia started edging away. "Look, I've got to leave. I just remembered an appointment with a client—er—I mean john. He'll be mad if I'm late. I mean, I promised to meet him."

Cowgirl grabbed her wrist. "Wait a minute. I thought you said you and your pimp just got to town from Kansas City."

Lydia stared down at Cowgirl's large, well-shaped hand curled around her wrist and noticed the bitten nails. "That's right."

"But you already know about the Butcher, and you're already picking up johns." She made an exaggerated bow. "Excuse me, you're making *appointments* with johns, like you were a damn hairdresser or something. Your story's got more holes than a junky's veins. High-dollar whores make appointments, but they don't work the Boulevard. The ones who do, well, we're blue-collar hookers, twenty-five to fifty bucks depending on the frills, fifteen minutes to turn a trick, and we don't make change. We work out of flophouse motels that cut a deal with our pimps, and we pick up our dates off the street in front of it. Now you want to start over and tell me who you are."

Lydia looked past Cowgirl's shoulder at Elliot. All he had to do was turn his head a fraction of an inch, and he would be looking straight at her.

"Can we exchange job descriptions some other time? Elliot's looking for me and so are the cops. I've got to get out of here." She tried to pull her hand free.

Cowgirl hesitated, then tightened her grip and tugged Lydia along behind her as she elbowed her way through the small crowd gathered around watching the various acts. Between Benny trying to crawl out of the gutter, the blonde trying to catch her breath from nonstop screaming, and the cops chasing Jo-Jo Jefferson, tonight on the Boulevard was better than a three-ring circus.

Lydia staggered after the Cowgirl, still trying to jerk her hand free. "Where are we going?"

"To a safe place."

"The last person I trusted tried to sell me to a pimp."

"Old Annie is your basic scumbag."

"Who?"

Cowgirl gently pushed Lydia around a corner and down an unpaved street. A weed-choked pasture of vacant lots stretched for three blocks toward the west. "The old witch at the motel. I was with Jo-Jo when Old Annie called him about you. That's another reason I know you're not a cop. Annie can spot a cop faster than a junkyard dog can smell out rotten meat. Jo-Jo took off like wildfire when you jumped out that window. You're why he went up that alley. He thought the screaming blonde was you. What's your name anyway?"

Lydia hesitated for a moment. "Blondie," she said finally.

Cowgirl nodded. "That's as good as any, I suppose. Besides, I don't want to know your real name 'cause I don't really want to know you."

"Then why are you helping me?"

"To spite Old Annie and Jo-Jo. Or maybe my charitable instincts haven't atrophied yet. Or maybe just for the hell of it, I don't know. Why are you trusting me?"

Lydia glanced at Cowgirl's hands. "You bite your nails."

Cowgirl let go of Lydia's wrist. "So what's my manicure got to do with it?"

"You're not as tough as you want me to think you are.

You're vulnerable and scared. And . . .'' Lydia stopped abruptly as she realized she was about to say she remembered Cowgirl stepping in to protect the little Oriental prostitute from Jo-Jo during the pimp's visit to John Lloyd.

Cowgirl looked at her intently. "And?"

"Uh, nothing."

The hooker studied Lydia's face. "Who are you? And don't give me any crap. If you're a hooker, then I'm a nun."

"Why is everyone so sure I'm not a hooker?"

Cowgirl smiled, and Lydia noticed it reached as far as the hooker's eyes. "I know about shadows, remember? And you don't have any shadows in your eyes, just light, all the way inside. Besides, I think I've seen you before, but not on the Boulevard."

"Never mind," said Lydia hastily. "I'll admit I'm a ringer, but I want to help you."

Cowgirl laughed. "Blondie, you can't help yourself. You got Bill Elliot and the cops looking for you. Worse than them, you've got Jo-Jo after you now and he's steamed. Old Annie's charging him for the window you broke 'cause she said he was stupid enough to let you see him. Now the cops are going to land on him and it's going to cost him bail money, all because he thought that blonde undercover cop was you."

"That's his problem," began Lydia.

Cowgirl laughed. "That's *your* problem. Jo-Jo's going to blame you. He never thinks anything's his own fault. So just how do you think you can help me?"

Lydia opened her purse. "I'll give you a card. You call the number, and John Lloyd Branson will get you off the Boulevard. He'll protect you and help you find a job. . . ."

Cowgirl grabbed Lydia's arms and shook her. "You're the woman in his office, his partner. That son of a bitch sent you down here to hand out business cards like some Girl Scout selling cookies!"

"No!" exclaimed Lydia, twisting away. "He doesn't know I'm here. And I don't want him to know. I just wanted to find the Butcher and help you women escape your pimps. . . ."

Cowgirl's mouth twisted into a sneer. "You do-gooding little bitch! You're gonna save us, huh? Send us to church twice on Sunday, maybe? The only way off the Boulevard for most of us is the Butcher's way, don't you realize that?''

"It doesn't have to be that way," argued Lydia. "There are other options."

"Not for me and I'm not about to stand here arguing about it either." Cowgirl took a deep breath and grasped Lydia's shoulder. She pointed across the expanse of vacant lots. "See that flashing sign? The one that says Bimbo Bar? You go over there, call your lawyer friend, and get the hell off the Boulevard. You don't belong here, and we don't want you, damn you!"

"Come with me," Lydia urged, reaching out to touch Cowgirl's arm.

The hooker shied away. "Get away from me. I've done you all the favors I'm going to. If Jo-Jo ever finds out I helped you, he'll break my arm, and you're not worth it. Now run, damn it. Don't you hear the sirens?"

Lydia did, but stood frozen in the middle of the unpaved street. She, who could always make a decision even if it was the wrong one, couldn't decide what to do, and she hated herself for it. "What are you going to do?" she asked.

Cowgirl started walking up the street toward the Boulevard. "Look for my friend. We're traveling in pairs now, and I haven't seen her in a while."

Lydia started after her. "Let me help."

Cowgirl whirled around. "I'm gonna knock you on your ass if you don't get out of here. You can't help, don't you understand? You don't know how to play our games. Besides, the cops would pick you up the minute you stepped back on the Boulevard, and maybe me, too, if one of those zombies in the crowd told them I was with you. Then there'd be nobody looking for China Doll, would there? And I need to find her. She bites her nails, too, you know."

Lydia closed her eyes to hold in the tears. She had cried more tonight than she had done since—since John Lloyd fired her. "All right," she said. "I'll go."

She was halfway across the first lot when she heard Cowgirl's voice. "Blondie, thanks for the favor."

Lydia turned around, but the hooker had disappeared.

CHAPTER TWELVE

THE BUTCHER STOOD IN THE SHADOWY DOORWAY LISTENING to Lydia and Cowgirl. He smiled to himself. Such a touching conversation.

And so enlightening.

Such dedication, such selflessness, such commitment. Lydia Fairchild was as committed to the game as he, even if she didn't know she was a player. She would not abandon the poor soiled doves of the Boulevard.

Such loyalty.

Such stupidity.

Such luck.

He had taken a risk by not following her after she vaulted through the window at the motel, but the game demanded he kill between midnight and 1:00 A.M. Fortunately a victim had been close at hand, fearfully strolling from that very same motel. Easy to find, easy to kill. Actually, the hardest part had been tying the silk scarf around her neck into a bow. He hadn't thought to practice tying bows.

Lydia had been equally easy to find. She could no more avoid being the target of Boulevard bullies than a rabbit could avoid being torn apart by a pack of wolves.

He smiled again. Except a wolf with any instinct for self-preservation would circle around this particular rabbit.

He wasn't a wolf.

Originally, he had planned on Lydia's being the evening's first kill—until he had discovered her identity. Then he had thought to make her his second kill, which, according to the game, would be much more . . . extensive.

Until he had talked to John Lloyd Branson.

Then he knew Lydia would be his last victim.

He watched her trudge across the vacant lots toward the Bimbo Bar. "Patience, Lydia, your turn will come," he mouthed silently, then glanced down at the luminous dial on his watch.

It was time.

Moving silently he slipped out of the doorway and followed Cowgirl as she disappeared into an alley.

CHAPTER
THIRTEEN

THE BIMBO BAR HAD FOUR SMALL TABLES, AN L-SHAPED BAR with stools of uncertain age and unexpected comfort, and three booths reputed to be padded. The door sat squarely in the east wall, for no reason anyone had ever been able to discern, as the Boulevard was south, and the Boulevard was the magnetic pole.

The bar was not actually on the Boulevard, but squatted like a befouled hen on a little intersecting side street. The patrons ignored that technicality and continued to refer to the Bimbo as being "on the Boulevard." It was tradition, and the Bimbo supported tradition, or rather tradition supported it. It was traditionally the filthiest watering hole, traditionally patronized by the worst dregs of the prostitution, drugs, numbers, gambling, and other, less socially desirable professions. It was also home to a few harmless, eccentric derelicts.

Jenner sat in the middle booth, the one in which the red vinyl was still distinguishable from the stuffing, and the tabletop was flat enough to set a drink on without spilling it. Not that it mattered if he spilled a drink—the floor in the Bimbo was only mopped when the patrons began sticking to its surface. The middle booth was the one piece of furniture closest to what might be found in a respectable bar. The three patrons who customarily claimed it were the closest of all the Bimbo's denizens to being actual examples of Homo sapiens. The middle booth and its occupants were living proof that the Bimbo was located on planet Earth.

"Have a drink, young fellow, and forget the unkindness of this world." Theodore carefully wiped a cheap glass with a handkerchief and poured Jenner a shot of equally cheap whiskey.

"Uh, thanks, Theodore," said Jenner, eyeing the handkerchief and feeling relieved that it looked clean. Ordinarily he bought a drink, then took it back to the cesspool the Bimbo furnished as a bathroom, poured the liquor out, and washed the glass with a rubbing-alcohol–soaked cloth he carried in a plastic baggy. Then he bought a refill, assured at least his glass was clean and that the alcohol content of the whiskey would kill any remaining bacteria. Or he hoped so. For all he or the health department knew the Bimbo could be breeding some super strain of bacteria along with the cockroaches.

Theodore tucked his handkerchief back in his breast pocket and delicately lifted his glass. "To us, society's leftovers, Saturday's baked beans served up on Wednesday." He sipped at his whiskey, holding it in his mouth to savor.

"Baked beans is bad enough fresh, Theodore, and you better swallow that varnish remover the Bimbo sells as liquor before it melts your tongue." Maude, aged somewhere between fifty and death, pulled her brown crocheted cap farther over her ears and nudged Jenner. "Ain't that right, son?"

"Maude, my dear woman, don't put the poor boy in the position of having to insult his mentor," said Theodore, blinking eyes so red-rimmed they looked ready to bleed.

Maude snorted. "There you go with them fancy words again. That's what comes of being a professor. What's *mentor* mean, Theodore?"

Theodore set his empty glass on the table, adjusted his frayed cuffs, then gripped the lapels of his ragged suit. "Mentor means guide or teacher, one who instructs a novice in the path which he should follow."

A large-knuckled fist slammed the table. "Thou shalt not teach him the ways of rum and evil women. Direct his feet from the way of perdition and onto the path of righteousness.''

Theodore frowned at the tall, awkward figure seated across from him. ''I wish you would quote from a Bible we all recognize. Your verses are very suspect.''

Preacher Paul's watery blue eyes peered at Theodore. ''Only an atheist like you wouldn't recognize the Lord's voice. I tell you that our Father is watching and will smite you if you dare endanger this man's immortal soul.''

Theodore leaned across the table until he was nose to nose with the itinerant evangelist. ''I am not an atheist. I am a Unitarian.''

From the expression on Preacher Paul's face, Jenner decided that atheism was preferable to Unitarianism. ''It is not too late to denounce such godless associations and follow Jesus.''

Theodore's sallow face seemed to swell and Jenner interrupted to prevent the old man from having a stroke. ''Hey, Preacher, my soul's not in danger. I'm just having a run of bad luck is all. Got laid off when the oil patch dried up and I'm killing time until I find something else. I'm not gonna end up like everybody else on the Boulevard: trash for the garbage man to carry off.''

Theodore sat back, his complexion losing its dull red color. ''It is an old argument. Preacher Paul tries to save my soul, there being no other available except Maude's, which has long since been saved by the Methodists and I resist his narrow-minded view of paradise.'' He leaned forward again. ''I do resent being accused of leading this young gentleman astray,'' he said, looking at the evangelist. ''I only meant I would show him the ways of survival on the Boulevard. If you didn't look for sin in every utterance, you would know that.''

''Your tongue, coated with lies, fails to persuade,'' replied Preacher mildly.

Maude took a drink of her draft beer and wiped the foam from her upper lip. ''Hush up. It gets tiresome listening to the two of you. I want to hear about Larry. Me and Preacher and Theodore wondered what you're doing on the Boulevard.''

Jenner shifted in his seat and winced as his bruised hip protested. He wondered if he should have used an alias rather than his own first name. Probably not. He had enough problems without worrying about forgetting what alias he had chosen. "I, uh, told you. I'm killing time until I find another job."

Maude's sharp brown eyes examined him. "Not many oil rigs on the Boulevard, and the Bimbo ain't a fit place to kill time."

Jenner gagged down a drink of the cheap whiskey. "It seems like a good enough place. The whiskey's okay and I like the company."

"You get better company down at the city jail. In fact, that's where most of this company spends their time." She waved her arm at the other people crowding the bar. "There's folks in here who'd sooner kill you than look at you. This is the first stop after something goes down, a robbery or a break-in or murder."

Jenner felt his hands start shaking again. He'd heard Schroder say that just being in the Bimbo Bar was almost enough probable cause for arrest, but he'd never believed the sergeant until now. "You're exaggerating, Maude. It's nothing like that bad."

Maude pointed to the walls and ceiling. "See them pieces of duct tape? The cops had to start covering up the bullet holes. Got to be so many they couldn't tell which holes were the latest. Now, whatever bullet hole ain't got duct tape over it is the one they investigate."

"What keeps anyone from covering up their own bullet hole before the police get here?" asked Jenner curiously.

Theodore looked offended. "It's a matter of honor."

Maude giggled. "That would be cheating. Folks like to brag. I've seen men get liquored up and shoot at each other just to put another bullet through the wall."

Jenner started to count the patches of duct tape but lost track. "Why do you stay here?"

"It's a matter of choice, my boy," said Theodore, pouring still another drink. "Take myself for example. I am a drunkard. I use that word rather than alcoholic because I predate the more fashionable condition. An alcoholic has a certain respectability. I have none. I used to be a professor of classical studies and a drunk. Now I am a drunk, period. I chose to be one, and I chose to live on the Boulevard because I don't have to apologize to anybody. It's a fallacy to believe that a human being will always choose the good and honorable course, my boy. There's no guarantee of that at all. As my friend Preacher says, it's free will."

"But don't you think you've wasted your life?" asked Jenner.

Theodore reached over and patted his hand. "Of course, my boy, wasted every minute of it from the time I took my first drink. But that's not the point of my philosophy. It's choices. Choose your course, change it if you will, but don't whine about it."

Maude nodded her head. "He's right. Choices are what the Boulevard is all about."

"Just a minute. You're confusing me." A glint in Theodore's eye made Jenner think the old man didn't believe that was too difficult. "You have to make choices wherever you live. There's nothing special about Amarillo Boulevard."

"Good and evil abound," said the stentorian voice of Preacher. "You must follow the path of righteousness, and always choose the right fork in the road."

"Preacher is saying that the choices are clearer here. Evil isn't hiding behind a Sunday shirt," said Maude.

"The Lord has called me to this Gomorrah to seek his lost sheep."

"Preacher is a little confused in his choice of metaphor, but he is sincere in his vocation," said Theodore. "What better place to find sinners than Amarillo Boulevard? Of course, finding them and saving them isn't quite the same thing, but Preacher has made his choice."

"But what about you, Maude?" Jenner asked. "You're not a drunk or a preacher, and there are shelters for bag ladies, someone to help you find relatives and friends. Why are you staying here?"

Maude set her glass of beer down and pushed up the sleeves of her coat. "Honey, I don't need to find any relatives. I've got five kids, the oldest on the other side of town, but I'd rather live at the mission halfway house and have those folks trying to save my soul than my daughter trying to change my ways. After all, I'm used to ignoring Preacher. It's no bother to ignore the do-gooders at the mission. But my daughter is another proposition. She's like having a horsefly buzzing in your ear all the time. I choose not to listen to her, and I choose not to live with her. I have my little room and I have a part-time job at the library. That's where I met Theodore. He brought me to the Bimbo for a drink, and I chose to stay. If you want to stay, you have to make a choice."

"Are you telling me everybody in this bar, in this whole part of town, made a choice? What about the prostitutes? What kind of free will do they have?" demanded Jenner, pointing to a hooker with a sad look sitting at the bar.

"Pimps and harlots, fornicators and adulterers," said Preacher, his Adam's apple slipping up and down his scrawny neck.

"Lord Almighty, boy, you've got him started. He's a mite unbalanced about prostitutes. Theodore and I think he was injured by one once, maybe got the clap. Or maybe his son was tempted and fell from grace, if he had a son. Or maybe his daughter took to the streets, if he had a daughter." Maude made shushing noises at Preacher.

"Whores and strumpets and trollops, wenches and hussies and sluts."

Jenner leaned closer to Maude. "You don't know if he had a son or daughter. What about a wife?"

"Jades and baggage, tarts and chippies and floozies."

Theodore poured himself another drink. "We don't know. Each of us may tell whatever story he wishes. It is one of our choices, you see."

"Bitches and drabs and trulls and wantons. Streetwalkers, hustlers, and hookers."

"For God's sake, doesn't anybody tell the truth!" shouted Jenner, and turned sideways in the booth, wishing he'd never made the choice to go undercover. Then he'd never be drinking with these dingbats.

"Truth? What is truth, dear boy, but one man's lies," replied Theodore. "I only knew one honest man in the sense you're speaking of, and I found him a very irksome creature."

"Courtesan, adventuress, and vamp. Seductress, painted woman, doxy."

"Doesn't he ever shut up?" moaned Jenner.

The door opened and a tall woman wearing spike heels and a tight leather skirt and low-cut blouse came in. Blonde hair tumbled past her shoulders and deep blue eyes peered from a puffy, round face. Jenner swore she looked familiar, but maybe he just had blonde whores on the brain. At least this one wasn't screaming.

"Scarlet woman!" shouted Preacher, pointing at the blonde.

The blonde stood tottering in the doorway, her mascara smeared and a large run in her black, patterned hose. She looked at Preacher and cleared her throat. "If you call me or any other woman that name again, I'll kick you in the balls."

CHAPTER
FOURTEEN

THE SILENCE WAS ABSOLUTE, AND LYDIA FELT LIKE A RABbit caught in a circle of hunters as everyone in the bar turned to look at her. Wrapping the straps of her purse around her wrist, she backed against the wall next to the door and peered through the dim, smoke-layered atmosphere at the crowd. The Bimbo Bar was small, perhaps twenty by thirty feet, and every inch of it seethed with the vilest assortment of human beings Lydia had ever seen. They leaned against a tiny bar, slouched in rickety chairs around cheap pedestal tables, crowded into ripped and patched booths, and even crouched on the floor like starving hounds waiting to be tossed a bone.

Lydia felt like the bone.

If this was Cowgirl's idea of a safe place, she would hate to enter a dangerous one.

She gripped her purse tighter and waited for the next move from the feral beasts watching her.

"My dear young woman, please excuse my friend." A tall, old man neatly dressed in an ancient brown tweed suit rose and bowed to Lydia. "No insult was intended toward you personally. He was merely reciting a litany of sinners in preparation for his next street-corner sermon, such litanies being very popular with his congregation. They prefer their theology straight, like their drink. Hellfire and brimstone instead of love and forgiveness, the latter two virtues being in short supply on the Boulevard in any case, and considerably misunderstood.''

There was a pedantic tone to the old man's voice that seemed to calm the waiting beasts, and Lydia felt the easing of tension in the bar. Whoever the man was, he seemed to command some respect. Probably because he was the only person besides herself who didn't look as if he harbored fleas.

Lydia felt her legs began to shake as she relaxed. She wasn't sure she could walk without stumbling, but then stumbling was an accepted means of locomotion in a Boulevard bar, and she couldn't stand alone with her back to the wall all night. She had to attach herself to a group—for protective coloring, if for no other reason. And the only safe group seemed to be the one with the pedantic old man and the religious nut who had called her a scarlet woman.

She walked over to the booth, sidestepping grasping hands and ignoring invitations to indulge in sexual practices both unappealing and physically taxing.

"You're a minister?" Lydia asked the awkward-looking man who was blinking his pale blue eyes at her. He reminded her of Ichabod Crane with a bad case of pink eye. Given the company in the bar, pink eye was probably the most pleasant contagious disease going. At least it was curable.

"I have received the call," pronounced the man in a deep, hollow voice that sounded as if it issued from a cave.

"I think the Lord got a wrong number," retorted Lydia. "Didn't you learn in divinity school not to cast stones?" She winced. Great, she thought. Insult the only man in the room who might not be contemplating rape.

"Alas, my dear, no school of theology lists Preacher among its alumni," said the old man in the tweed suit, smiling at her and answering for Ichabod. "He is a self-taught man. I believe you are a stranger, or at least I have never seen you on my daily convivial stroll down the Boulevard. Let me introduce myself"—he waved his hand at the others sitting in the booth—"and my friends, and invite you to share a drink with us. I am Theodore, and this lovely lady sitting by me is Maude. Our man of God calls himself Preacher, and the young man sitting across from me is Larry.''

"My name is Blondie," said Lydia, studying the man called Larry. There was something very familiar about him. And something suspicious. Most men who wore earrings didn't wear clip-ons.

"Sit yourself down, Blondie," said Maude. "Theodore, get the lady a chair. And a beer. It's the only drink in the place that's not watered down. Not that it makes much difference. Even watered down, the Bimbo's liquor would still take the enamel off your pretty white teeth."

"No, thank you," Lydia said hastily as she sat on the splintery wood chair that Theodore conjured up from God only knew where. "I, uh, lost my money earlier this evening. I'll just take a glass of water."

Theodore patted her shoulder. "My dear, I, too, have found myself financially embarrassed on occasion. No need to apologize. Let me treat you to a beer. Besides, I don't recommend the water. No, not at all. The bartender is nearsighted and often misses certain residue from a previous drinker when washing the glasses. Alcohol sterilizes the glassware."

Lydia's stomach heaved as she wondered exactly what kind of residue, and she took several deep breaths through her mouth to control the nausea. "Thank you," she said when she could speak again.

"Are you a whore?" demanded Preacher, blinking his eyes.

"Preacher," said Maude. "Don't agitate. Blondie's Theodore's guest, and he wouldn't like it."

Lydia's shoulders slumped. Even a religious nut like Preacher was suspicious of her. As an undercover prostitute, she was an abysmal failure. She noticed Larry staring at her, a puzzled look on his face, and knew she had seen him somewhere before and not on the Boulevard. And if she had seen him, the reverse was true. She had to convince Larry *and* the Preacher she was what she claimed to be. Otherwise— well, she didn't care to contemplate the otherwise.

"Yeah, I'm a whore," she said, shoving her face close to his. A mistake, she thought a second later after getting a whiff of his breath. She leaned back in her chair to get out of range and crossed her legs. "You interested for business reasons or personal ones?" She reached over and squeezed his knee. "I might consider a quickie on the house if I weren't broke. I guess you're out of luck tonight."

Preacher jumped up as if her hand had been hot grease. His mouth worked soundlessly for a few seconds, its grimaces in perfect time with his blinking eyelids. "Get thee behind me, Satan!" he practically shouted as he cowered back in the booth.

"Preacher!"

Preacher flinched at the sound of Theodore's voice. "She tempted me with the evils of the flesh."

Theodore sat the beer in front of Lydia. "You provoked her, and she retaliated with her own weapon: her woman's flesh."

Preacher turned condemning eyes on Lydia. "The wages of sin is death," he intoned, pointing a bony finger at her. He turned and left, the bar's occupants parting before him like the Red Sea.

Lydia huddled in her chair, feeling the cold dread enveloping her. She also felt something else; she felt ashamed. "I'm sorry," she said, looking up at Theodore.

Theodore sat down and took a delicate sip of his drink before smiling at her. "My dear, don't worry. As I told you before, he doesn't bear any ill will toward you in particular. He just isn't too fond of your profession."

Maude leaned over the table. "Theodore, tell the girl the truth. Preacher's crazy as a cootie. But he's harmless."

"What if he isn't?" asked Lydia. "What if he's the"— she hesitated, took a breath—"Butcher?"

"Who's the Butcher?"

Lydia jerked around to gaze at an alien. Actually he wasn't, but anyone in clean clothes and without a dissipated expression was an alien in the Bimbo. "W-who?" she stuttered.

Theodore cleared his throat. "Blondie, this young man is Louis Bryant, the reporter who christened our, uh, murderer."

The clean but unprepossessing young man slid into the booth next to Larry—who, Lydia noticed, was combing his long, dusty hair over his face. "I heard you call someone the Butcher, and I'm very interested in him."

Theodore cleared his throat. "Blondie was just talking, Louis. Speculating, you might say."

"It didn't sound like speculation to me, Theodore," replied Bryant, examining Lydia with the biggest, brightest blue eyes she had ever seen. "How about it, Blondie? Were you speculating or do you know something?"

Lydia rubbed her hands together and noticed her palms were damp. Wet hands, scared heart, she thought. "I, uh, was just asking Theodore and Maude why they were so sure that Preacher was harmless. I mean, he seems to hate prostitutes, and those invitations point to a religious fanatic. What if he got mad when the women didn't, uh, change their ways and he decided to cleanse them in their own blood?"

"Theodore."

Lydia looked toward Larry. She was glad to know he could talk, but she wished he would brush his hair away from his mouth while he did it. It was disconcerting to hear a voice issue from behind that blanket of hair.

"Theodore," continued Larry. "Do you know where Preacher was when the first two girls were killed?"

The old man took another sip of his drink before answering. "Preacher was here or there, to or fro, back or yon. In many ways he is a very fey creature."

"In other words, you don't know?" asked Larry.

Theodore's lips tightened. "Young man, I and my friends took you to our bosom when you arrived on the Boulevard, shared our booth and our companionship. I am offended by your questions." He turned to Lydia. "You, my dear, have an excuse. A stranger may be forgiven her ignorance. Let me assure you, though, Preacher is innocent. I guarantee it."

Bryant lit a cigarette and took a deep drag, letting it trickle through his nostrils. It made Lydia's nose hurt to watch him. "Let's see the fine print on that guarantee, Theodore. In other words, how do you know?"

Theodore took a mended white handkerchief from his breast pocket and patted his forehead with it. Carefully replacing it, he folded his hands and contemplated the reporter. "In the first place, Preacher is a man of the cloth, however bedraggled his cloth may be, and consequently adheres closely to the Ten Commandments. Thou shalt not kill, said the Lord, and all of that. Preacher has never raised a hand in violence to any man as long as I have known him."

"What about women?" demanded Lydia.

"Nor women. Preacher simply is not violent. Unbalanced, perhaps, but then aren't we all?" He chuckled. "Yes, I think we are all a bit crazy."

Maude finished her beer and sat her glass on the table with the exaggerated care of one whose depth perception is addled by drink. "Blondie, Theodore is right. Preacher isn't the Butcher because he would have to touch the women, and you saw what he did when you touched him. Took off like a scalded cat."

"That's not proof," insisted Lydia.

Theodore sighed. "How did you hear about the Butcher, my dear?"

Lydia glanced around the table and saw the same expression in three pairs of eyes: curiosity verging on suspicion. She was sounding like a cop again, and she had better think of some believable explanation for her questions.

She looked down at the table and saw Louis Bryant open a small spiral notebook and had a sudden inspiration. "My pimp and I read it in the papers, and we wanted to check out the situation before we hung out our shingle."

"Who's your pimp?" asked Bryant, his pen poised over a blank page in his notebook.

Lydia wiped her hands on what there was of her skirt. "The Undertaker."

Bryant grinned in disbelief. "He sounds more like a hit man. What does this private-eye pimp look like?"

Lydia's mouth suddenly dried up. She hadn't thought of what her mythical pimp might look like. She gulped at her beer, absently noting that it tasted as if it had been brewed from old boots rather than barley.

"Look like?" she croaked, then improvised. "The Undertaker is six feet five inches, blond with black eyes, carries a cane weighted with lead, and doesn't like people asking questions about him."

Actually John Lloyd was only a little over six feet four, but if he ever found out she borrowed his physical description for what he would consider an obscene purpose, she could argue that adding an inch or so to his height masked his identity. She hoped he never found out because her argument wouldn't convince John Lloyd of anything except his wisdom in firing her.

Theodore rose and straightened his coat. "Blond hair and black eyes, an unusual combination. I shall watch for him and do my best to avoid him. He doesn't sound like a man I would like to meet in the dark. If you will excuse me, I have to find Preacher. I don't want him walking the Boulevard in his agitated condition. Good night, Maude." He leaned over and kissed her wrinkled cheek, then hurried toward the door.

Lydia turned in her chair. "Wait a minute! Where's your proof that Preacher's innocent?"

Theodore paused in the open doorway and looked over his shoulder at Lydia. "Get off the Boulevard, young woman."

As the door slammed behind him, Maude picked up his glass. "Theodore's upset about something. He didn't finish his drink."

Lydia picked up her purse. "I'm going after him."

"Theodore don't like people poking around in his business. You best just leave him and Preacher alone," said Maude, making an ineffectual grab for Lydia and closing her fists around empty air at least a foot to Lydia's right.

Double vision, maybe even triple vision, thought Lydia, as Maude took another swipe at the air six inches in front of Lydia's nose.

Maude blinked, then shook her head. In Lydia's opinion, combining head shaking and beer drinking usually had dire consequences: one either threw up or passed out.

Maude passed out.

"Will you gentlemen excuse me?" asked Lydia, pushing back her chair and slinging her purse over her shoulder.

Larry nodded glumly, and Lydia threaded her way between the tables to the door.

"Hey, Blondie!"

Lydia looked back toward the table. In the dark bar, the flashbulb had all the intensity of a miniature sun. She groped her way forward, blinking furiously to clear away the polka dots that danced in front of her eyes. "Bryant, you low-life worm, I'll break that camera over your head!" she shouted.

She bumped into a table, felt someone pinch her thigh, and struck out blindly with a left hook. She heard the grunt a split second after she felt her fist connect with someone's front teeth. The clatter of a chair falling over and the thud of a body hitting the floor followed immediately.

"Next time keep your hands to yourself, you horny bum," she said calmly to the unconscious body at her feet.

One of the horny bum's companions leaned over his chair and peered bleary-eyed at the unconscious body. "We ain't gonna be able to call him Bucky no more," he announced to the hushed room. "The whore done fixed his front teeth better than braces."

Lydia felt someone grab her left arm and jerk her around.

"I don't allow no hooker to beat up my good customers, especially no hooker who already chased out three customers and coldcocked another one." The bartender was covered in tattoos, built like a professional football player, the kind who enjoyed sacking the quarterback and blocking the kicker, preferably by breaking legs, and the strength of his grip on Lydia's arm threatened to cut off circulation.

Lydia stood very still. She had read somewhere that a bull won't charge if you don't move. She hoped it worked for bartenders, too. "I never chased away your customers."

The bartender snorted. "Like hell you didn't. Theodore left eight drinks shy of his usual load. Preacher didn't down his usual six beers, and that reporter didn't order anything at all."

"Louis Bryant's gone?" asked Lydia. "But he took my picture without permission."

"Who the hell you think you are, Princess Di? Nobody asks a whore for her permission." The bartender turned Lydia around and shoved her toward the door, which a snickering patron obligingly opened.

Lydia stumbled on the wooden steps outside the Bimbo's front door and sprawled on her hands and knees on the ground. The dirt smelled sour, like an open sewer, and she scrambled up, gagging and wiping her hands on her skirt.

Staggering the few feet back to the Bimbo's wooden steps, she sank down on the bottom step and leaned over to rest her head on her knees. She had been evicted from the foulest bar on Amarillo Boulevard, tossed out like a used cocktail napkin, except the Bimbo didn't provide cocktail napkins; its patrons used their sleeves or the backs of their hands. Being declared persona non grata at a place like the Bimbo had to rate as the nonachievement of the century.

She felt a thousand years and a million miles from the Lydia Fairchild who stepped off the plane how many hours ago? Six? Eight? God, she didn't know; she'd given her watch to Old Annie. She did know that the old Lydia would have marched back into the Bimbo Bar and flattened the bartender, or at least attempted to flatten him.

The old Lydia was an immature, impulsive fool.

The new Lydia was cautious.

The old Lydia would have had to be tossed out of the Bimbo in pieces, screaming defiance as each part of her landed in the dirt.

The new Lydia sat very quietly on the step, wondering how in the hell she was going to get her bruised and totally penniless body back to Dallas.

The old Lydia would immediately start searching for Theodore and Preacher and knock their heads together to learn the truth.

The new Lydia was very much afraid she would call the cops—if she could borrow a quarter.

Lydia decided becoming a mature, responsible adult was a demoralizing process.

She raised her head and looked around. The weed-filled, refuse-littered expanse of vacant lots stretched before her to the east. South, a block away, the Boulevard sliced through the city like an open wound, spewing its tainted blood in the form of pimps and hookers, gamblers and number boys, thieves and burglars, wife beaters and child killers, arsonists and murderers, pushers and addicts. To the west were derelict motels, scattered convenience stores, and open country. Low-income housing for the desperate huddled on cracked and buckled streets to the north. But nowhere did she see

Theodore, Preacher, or that unethical bastard, Louis Bryant. She was alone in the dark.

Alone, that is, except for the three figures she saw loping up the street toward the Bimbo, their voices becoming audible over the sounds from the Boulevard.

"What's you planning to do now, Jo-Jo?" asked one of the figures.

"Jo-Jo," whispered Lydia to the darkness.

"I'm gonna find that bastard what stole my car, and I'm gonna pull his lower lip down over his shoe tops and step on it. Then I'm gonna pull his upper lip over his eyeballs and down to his heels. And then I'm gonna pick him up by his feet and shake him outta his skin and make seat covers out of it. See, that's kinda what the army calls a de-terrent. The next motherfucker thinks he can steal Jo-Jo Jefferson's new Cadillac is gonna look at them seat covers and he's gonna be de-terred."

Jo-Jo pantomimed his verbal threats, and Lydia scrambled up and assessed her strategic situation: flee or fight? The Bimbo crouched like a malodorous animal in the middle of the block with no cover closer than a hundred yards; Jo-Jo and his men were between her and the Boulevard, so her chances of fleeing looked dim. That left fighting. If she were betting on the outcome, she'd put ten bucks on Jo-Jo. However, the Marquis of Queensbury wouldn't be present at this fight. She did have a way of evening the odds, she thought, as she took her can of Mace from her purse. Holding the can behind her back in her right hand, she gripped her purse with its concealed brick in her left and waited.

One of the pimp's muscles, a new term for the old role of enforcer, pulled on Jo-Jo's sleeve. "Hey, Jo-Jo."

Jo-Jo slapped the hand away. "Quit pulling on my silk jacket. I didn't pay no thousand dollars for this rig so some asshole with hog jowls for brains can be jerking on it. I got shit enough on the pants"—he balanced on one leg and raised the other—"runnin' up that fuckin' alley. Just look at my pants. And my shoes—Jesus, brand-new shoes scuffed up like some honkie wino's."

He lowered his leg and grabbed a handful of his muscle's shirt. "And it's your fault, you motherfucker."

"I didn't do nothing, Jo-Jo," whined the muscle, a black man at least as tall as the pimp and not much more muscular.

"Just who yelled out that the screaming bitch was the one I was lookin' for?"

"But . . ."

"And who said let's chase the Butcher and whip his ass?" Jo-Jo punctuated his questions by pounding his fist on top of the muscle's head.

The muscle slipped to his knees and tried to cover his head with his hands. "But . . ."

"And who about got me caught by the cops after I been running my ass off all week to stay away from them? Asshole!" yelled Jo-Jo, bringing his knee up under the muscle's chin. The enforcer sprawled backward, landing with a grunt in the dirt.

Jo-Jo kicked the limp body and Lydia heard ribs crack. "Stop it, you bastard!" she screamed impulsively, leaping off the steps and into the circle of light cast by the neon sign over the Bimbo's front door.

Jo-Jo jerked around in surprise and stared at her, then put his hands on his hips and examined her with cold, dead eyes. Lydia knew how a fish felt just before a shark swallowed it. "Well, look what we got here, Skipper," he said to his other muscle.

Lydia glanced at Skipper. His name reminded her of peanut butter, skateboards, and Donna Reed reruns. His appearance was straight out of *The Twilight Zone*: lank brown hair, big head, big neck, big shoulders, skin as pale and unhealthy-looking as Dracula's between transfusions. The best that could be said for him was that he was proof that Jo-Jo's hiring practices weren't biased. Skipper was the ugliest white man Lydia had ever seen.

"Yeah," said Skipper, popping his knuckles to limber up his hands.

Lydia gripped her can of Mace tighter and wiggled her toes inside her shoes. On the proper person's feet, spike heels made a deadly weapon. Hers were the proper feet.

"You're the one what stood me up back at the motel," continued Jo-Jo, sauntering toward her. "Left me standin' at the back door."

Lydia licked her lips. "I don't go on blind dates."

Jo-Jo snickered. "You hear that, Skipper? She don't want a blind date. Well, I ain't asking for one. I got a business arrangement to discuss with you, bitch. I hear you ain't got a pimp, and it just so happens I got a vacancy."

"I've got a pimp," answered Lydia, backing up a step. "The Undertaker."

Jo-Jo grinned, his diamonds flashing green and red in the neon lights. "Never heard of him. You ever heard of him, Skipper?"

The muscle grinned without drooling. "Nope," he said.

"He's tough. He'll pick the diamonds right out of your teeth and make a pinkie ring with them," warned Lydia.

Jo-Jo pretended to flinch. "Oh, I'm real scared. Ain't you scared, Skipper?"

"Huh," grunted Skipper, looking confused. "I ain't scared, Jo-Jo."

The pimp cuffed Skipper on the side of his head. "I was bein' sarcastic." He looked at Lydia. "A businessman just can't find no decent people to hire anymore. They ain't got no manners and they got shit for brains. Speakin' of manners, I don't allow no honkie bitch employee to call me names."

"Are you talking to me?" asked Lydia.

"Are you talking to me?" mimicked Jo-Jo. "I don't see nobody else, do you?"

"I'm not your employee!"

"You're on my turf. That makes you my bitch."

"Listen, are you deaf as well as stupid? I told you I already have a pimp, and I wouldn't work for you even if I didn't. I don't like your business methods, your pay scale's too low, and your fringe benefits stink."

Jo-Jo snapped his fingers. "Skipper, shut her mouth."

The muscle lumbered toward her, and Lydia backed up. She noticed Jo-Jo step away and stand with his arms folded like a coach who had just sent in his meanest player with instructions to bust head. Jo-Jo Jefferson didn't know it yet, but she intended to do a little head-busting of her own. She felt the wind blowing against her cheek and carefully circled around until she stood with her back to the wind, always a good idea before dousing someone with Mace.

"What are you waiting for, Skipper? You scared of a woman?" she taunted as she gripped the can of Mace and tensed, knowing she would have only a fraction of a second to step inside those outstretched arms, Mace him, and jump back.

"Huh?" said Skipper as he stopped to give his brain a chance to assimilate her insult.

"Some people just can't think and walk at the same time," said Lydia as she whipped her arm forward, Maced Skipper, and danced away as he staggered backward like a poleaxed steer, clawing his eyes and gagging. One down, one to go, she thought as she whirled toward Jo-Jo.

The pimp was gone.

She smelled the scent of his cologne at the same instant he reached around from behind her and viciously chopped at her wrist with the edge of his hand. "Drop it, bitch," he grunted.

The can of Mace dropped from Lydia's paralyzed fingers.

CHAPTER
FIFTEEN

As Jenner reached the Bimbo's door, he felt the tattooed bartender's eyes boring into his back. Damn it, he'd just been trying to help Maude out of the bar and home. Of course she was unconscious, but that was no excuse for the bartender to accuse him of dragging her out for an immoral purpose. Did he look so hard up for female company that he would pick on a woman old enough to be his mother and dead drunk besides? Did he *look* like a sex pervert? Did he *act* like a sex pervert? He shrugged his shoulders. Those were stupid questions to be asking himself. A pervert could look like a doctor, lawyer, plumber, or like one of the derelicts who snickered, guffawed, or snored at Jenner, depending on their state of sobriety.

Or Lydia could be right; it could be Preacher.

Lydia?.

Jenner sagged against the door in shock. The prostitute who called herself Blondie was Lydia Fairchild! He'd known there was something familiar about her when she walked into the bar, but the Bimbo was darker than a black Angus at midnight, and he hadn't gotten a good look at her until Bryant took her picture. The flashbulb had turned her face whiter than a ghost's, whiter than the prostitute's face he'd spent a week on the Boulevard looking for.

He was wrong.

He had to be wrong.

What in the hell would Lydia Fairchild be doing on the Boulevard dressed up like a two-dollar tart?

Feverishly he examined his memory of her face caught in the harsh light of the flashbulb. Blue eyes, almost turquoise, blonde hair that he would swear didn't owe its color to peroxide, full mouth, high cheekbones, face puffy, but not puffy enough to prevent anyone from recognizing her. And he'd spent enough time admiring her face during the two murder investigations she and John Lloyd Branson had been involved in.

Besides, how many nearly six-foot-tall gorgeous blondes with legs like hers were there in the Texas Panhandle?

Just one. Lydia Fairchild.

Then why hadn't he recognized her immediately when the flashbulb went off?

He had—that's why her name popped into his mind, but only subconsciously. Why should he expect to see John Lloyd Branson's beautiful legal clerk in the Bimbo Bar?

He shouldn't.

But she was. Furthermore, she was out on the Boulevard this very second hunting Preacher. If she was right, if Preacher was the Butcher, then she might be lying in some alley dead as a gutted perch.

"Holy shit!" he shouted, and jerked open the Bimbo's door.

He saw the two men first, one stretched prone on the ground, and the other on his hands and knees gagging and whimpering. Then he heard the sounds, over to his right and outside the circle of the Bimbo's flashing neon lights.

"Let go, you son of a bitch!" Jenner heard a familiar voice hiss. Jerking his head around he felt himself freeze with shock a second time as he saw Lydia stomp one spike-heeled foot into her assailant's instep at the same time she swung her purse backward to connect with his crotch. The tall black man let out an agonized shriek and released Lydia in favor of grasping his injured body parts. His arms jerked up and down as he grabbed first his foot, then his genitals, in response to his brain's scrambled message of pain. Jenner felt a sympathetic twinge between his own legs, but he didn't let it prevent him from leaping off the steps and putting all of his one hundred seventy-five pounds behind an uppercut to the man's chin. He heard the crunch of teeth grinding together as his fist snapped the man's head backward.

He watched the man sprawl backward in the dirt and thought that at least the bastard wouldn't have to decide whether his balls or his foot hurt worse.

"Look out behind you!"

Jenner heard the urgency in Lydia's voice and whirled around to see a fiercely blinking, teary-eyed, hard-breathing creature that looked as if it had just escaped from Dr. Frankenstein's lab. The ogre was coming at him with outstretched arms. Jenner ducked under the arms and butted his head into the man's belly. He heard a crack and thought at first he'd broken the other man's ribs, but that didn't account for the man's sudden, unexpected sagging to the ground to lie motionless like a puppet with its strings cut.

"Is he dead?" asked Lydia in a voice that sounded hoarse with strain.

Jenner crouched down and felt for a pulse. "He's just out cold. I didn't think hitting him in the belly could put him away like this." He rocked back on his heels and looked up at Lydia. "You don't think I ruptured something, do you, like his heart?"

"You didn't knock him out. I did. I hit him with my purse."

Jenner got up, rubbing his right hand. The way it was throbbing, he figured he'd broken his knuckles. "What the hell do you have in that purse?"

"A brick," she answered impatiently. "Listen, thanks for your help. Wish I could stay and visit, but we just wiped out Jo-Jo Jefferson and his muscle, and I don't want to be around when he wakes up."

"Jo-Jo Jefferson! God Almighty, Lydia, did you have to coldcock the Boulevard's number-one pimp?"

"I suppose I should have let him drag me off to his"—she

stopped, her mouth falling open and her blue eyes widening in surprise—"what did you call me?"

"Lydia. You're Lydia Fairchild, and what the hell are you doing on the Boulevard dressed like that?" He gestured at her short skirt that in his opinion left too much leg bare to the elements. "In fact, what are you doing on the Boulevard, period?"

There was the sound of a groan, and Jenner glanced over his shoulder to see Jo-Jo flop over on his side and curl into a fetal ball. "Never mind. You can tell me while I drive. I've got my car stashed a block away." He grabbed Lydia's arm and started pulling her toward the Boulevard.

"I don't think so," she replied, and swung her purse.

"Goddamn!" Jenner hissed as he clenched his teeth against the pain radiating down his arm from his elbow. "You broke my arm."

"No, just tapped the ulnar nerve, funny bone to you. I really don't like violence."

"Tell that to Jo-Jo Jefferson and Frankenstein back there. Why the hell did you hit me anyway? I saved your butt."

She ignored him, standing braced against the wind, swinging her purse. "Who are you?" she demanded.

He pulled his wig off and heard her gasp. "Sergeant Larry Jenner. Now, can we get the hell out of here?"

Her shoulders sagged, then straightened. "Are you going to arrest me?"

"No, but you're going to wish I had if we're still standing in this parking lot when Jo-Jo stops hurting and starts hunting. Nothing pisses off a man more than getting hit in the, er, between the legs."

Lydia and Jenner glanced back at Jo-Jo, who had progressed to the grunting stage, but wasn't quite up to worrying about more than whether or not he was emasculated or merely temporarily incapacitated. Jenner didn't plan to wait around for the pimp to decide. Evidently Lydia didn't either because she took off across the vacant lots, long legs pumping as if she were trying to break the three-minute mile.

"Hey, my car's in the other direction!"

Lydia didn't answer and Jenner cursed. By the time he got to his car, she'd be in the next county and he might never find her. But he couldn't leave her alone on the Boulevard. She would be helpless against the Butcher. Well, maybe not helpless, he thought, hearing Jo-Jo groaning behind him, but not evenly matched either. The Butcher was a hell of a lot meaner than Lydia ever thought about being, and having virtue on your side didn't mean a damn thing in a face-off with a murderer.

Jamming his wig back on and cradling his throbbing elbow, Jenner followed her.

He was panting by the time he caught up with her at the mouth of an alley several blocks from the Bimbo. He didn't understand how anyone could run so fast in three-inch heels. "Why did you run away?"

She stopped, breathing hard and holding her side as if she had a stitch in it. "I'm not getting in a car with you. I'm not explaining anything to Sergeant Schroder."

"Do you see Sergeant Schroder anywhere?"

"You work with him."

"I'm not working for him at this particular minute, so you explain to me. What are you doing on the Boulevard?"

She straightened up, and Jenner sensed she was preparing to run away. He grabbed her arm. "You're not going anywhere, Lydia, until you give me an explanation."

"I'm trying to help these women, show them that there are other options, other choices. And I'm—I'm looking for the Butcher."

Jenner swung her around to face him. With her heels she was an inch or so taller than he, but be damned if he intended to be intimidated by her height, her looks, or that brick in her purse. "Are you certifiably nuts? What will you do if you find him, hit him over the head with your purse? Kick him in the balls like you did Jo-Jo? Do you have any idea what the Butcher does to women? Do you want your throat cut? Do you want to be sliced open by some do-it-yourself coroner?"

She gulped and shook her head. "No," she whispered.

Jenner heard the wet sound of tears in her voice and was perversely glad. He hoped she was crying because she was scared. In fact, he hoped she was scared witless; that is, if she had any wits to begin with, which he doubted, or she wouldn't be pulling this kind of a stunt in the first place.

But if she was witless, someone close to her wasn't.

John Lloyd Branson.

Jenner grabbed Lydia's shoulders, wincing as pain spiraled up his arm from his swollen hand. "Where's your boss? What's that stuffed shirt doing while you're flashing the winos, druggies, perverts, and other slime?"

She twisted away. "I don't think we'd better stand here any longer. Jo-Jo's probably put a price on our heads, or called in the bloodhounds, or whatever it is people like him do." She disappeared into the alley's black mouth.

Jenner followed her, cursing under his breath. The alley was darker than the belly of a whale, and she didn't have any better sense than to run into it. Anything could be waiting along its black length—anything or anyone.

He finally caught up with her, more by the sounds of her panting breath and crunching footsteps than by her visibility, which was zero. "Jo-Jo Jefferson's not people. He's something to step over so you don't ruin your shoes. And quit changing the subject. How come Lawyer Branson let you out to play on the Boulevard?"

She stopped and he sensed her turning to glare at him; in fact, he could see her face as a faint white blur as his eyes adjusted to the darkness. "John Lloyd fired me last week! This doesn't have anything to do with him."

"I don't believe it! John Lloyd Branson would cut off his right nut before he'd fire you."

She turned away without answering, and he heard her feet skid on the rough surface of the pavement. "Watch it, now. This alley hasn't been blacktopped since the Truman administration, and"—he felt her hand hit his arm as she fought for balance—"it's got potholes deeper than the Marianas trench." He grabbed for her hand, closing his fingers on empty air. Six feet plus of woman and he'd missed every inch of her, he thought as he knelt and groped in the darkness for some piece in the neutral zone, like an arm or a wrist. It paid to be cautious around the woman who put down Jo-Jo Jefferson.

"Oh, my God!" Lydia screamed.

Jenner felt the hair on his arms stiffen. "What the hell's wrong?"

He heard Lydia swallow. Funny, that he could hear her swallow. "Jenner," she said, her voice vibrating like fragile crystal. "Jenner, I didn't step in a pothole. I"—he heard her swallow again—"think I slipped in a pool of blood, a pool, a pond, an ocean of blood. I've got it all over my hands, and it's wet and sticky, and I think I touched someone's leg, and I don't think it's your leg. Is it your leg, Jenner?"

"Shit," said Jenner, fumbling in his pocket for a flashlight. "Don't move, Lydia. Don't touch anything else"—he found the pocket light—"until I can see what the hell's happening." He flicked the flashlight on and off almost simultaneously.

"Oh, God, God, God," he repeated, dropping the light and pulling Lydia up and away from the body, pulling her to the opposite side of the alley where he leaned against the rear wall of a dilapidated brick building. He held her while she sobbed.

CHAPTER SIXTEEN

"ARE YOU THE ONES WHO REPORTED FINDING A BODY?"

The cop was young, clean-shaven, crisp, pressed, buffed to a high shine—and suspicious.

Holding a cup of coffee in both hands and intermittently shivering, Lydia leaned against the brick wall outside the front door of POP'S LITTLE GROCERY—SERVING AMARILLO SINCE 1934—and waited for Jenner to answer the young cop. Jenner was more in control than she was. Jenner was accustomed to dealing with horror.

She started shivering again and not from the wind whipping around the edges of the building and lashing her bare legs. Even her blouse, wet from repeated rinsing in Pop's bathroom sink, couldn't account for the intense cold she felt. It was exposure. She felt exposed, as if some shell she hadn't even suspected she inhabited had suddenly split and fallen away, leaving her naked. Her defenses were gone or at least seriously weakened. Another assault on her sensibilities and she would surrender to an attack of hysteria worse than the one she'd had when she stumbled over the corpse.

She shifted her weight from one foot to another, suddenly restless. If she hadn't been hysterical from discovering the body, if she and Jenner hadn't clutched each other, if she hadn't felt the tears on his cheek, she would never have confessed the whole terrible evening to him.

Those tears had fooled her. She had forgotten he was a cop.

It was the blood.

If she had not fallen in the puddle of blood, touched the corpse's warm bare leg, wiped her bloody hands on her blouse, on Jenner's shirt, marked them both with the stains of violence, she would not have lost her objectivity. She had seen dead bodies before; she had even seen a murder victim before. But seeing is not the same as touching. It is the difference between being an observer and being a participant.

Dear God, how did cops stand it?

"I'm Sergeant Larry Jenner, and I'm the one who reported the body. This is Ms. Lydia Fairchild."

Lydia heard Jenner's introduction and held her breath. When he didn't enumerate her various offenses against the persons, peace, and dignity of the state of Texas, she relaxed and nodded to the officer. "How do you do," she said, hearing herself speak in a monotone. Hadn't she read somewhere that speaking in a monotone was one indication that the speaker was denying emotions?

The young officer watched her warily. "You got something wrong with your neck?"

"No, no, I'm fine." She consciously commanded herself to stop nodding and wondered if her brain had switched from automatic to manual.

"May I see some identification, please?"

Jenner frowned. "I told you who I am, and I gave the dispatcher my badge number when I called in. Look, Officer"—Jenner glanced at the other cop's name tag—"Masters, cut the crap and call for a backup and Special Crimes. The Butcher left another body in the alley about three blocks from here."

Masters touched his holster as if to assure himself he was armed. "Yeah, buddy, about that badge number. The officer it belongs to is listed as being temporarily suspended from duty. The dispatcher checked with the officer's wife, and Mrs. Jenner hasn't seen her husband in a week."

Lydia jerked around to stare at Jenner. If he were suspended, then he didn't have any legitimate business on the Boulevard either. In fact, he was as much of an impostor as she.

Jenner glanced at Lydia, then back at Masters and cleared his throat. "It's like this, Masters. . . ."

"*Officer* Masters," interrupted the cop. Lydia decided that if the young man looked any more suspicious, she and Jenner might find themselves handcuffed and in leg irons.

Jenner frowned. "Then my name is *Sergeant* Jenner. As I was saying, I didn't exactly tell my wife what I was doing or where I was going. I didn't want her to worry. You know how wives are about undercover work. . . ."

"I'm not married," Masters said. "And you're not undercover either. The dispatcher checked. So you better come up with some ID."

"For God's sake, Jenner, don't you cops carry ID cards of some kind?" said Lydia, pleased to note her voice held some expression, even if it was panic.

"I don't have it with me," answered Jenner with exasperation. "Can you imagine what some of these slime buckets on the Boulevard would do to me if they caught me with an ID?"

"No, but I imagine it's something similar to what I'd like to do to you right now," said Lydia, leaning over to set her Styrofoam coffee cup on the sidewalk. She straightened up and noticed she wasn't cold anymore; she was sweating and her chest hurt. Anxiety reaction, she thought. If Jenner didn't manage to convince Masters of his identity, then the young cop might start looking more closely at both of them, and she couldn't stand the scrutiny. No one could who had downed two police officers, even if it was an accident.

"Officer Masters," she said, pointing to Jenner. "He's who he says he is. I've met him before on another investigation. I'll vouch for him."

"Uh, Lydia," Jenner said uneasily.

Masters examined Lydia from her mussed blonde hair to her spike heels, paying particular attention to her wet blouse, still stained pink with blood, her short skirt, and her tattered black mesh hose. "You got any identification, lady?"

Lydia opened her purse before she remembered. "Uh, no.

My billfold was stolen earlier this evening. But I'm a law student at SMU. The dean will vouch for me."

Masters nodded his head. "A law student, huh. In Dallas, huh. What are you doing on Amarillo Boulevard, taking extension courses?"

"Well," began Lydia, feeling herself blush under her heavy makeup.

"That's enough!" exclaimed Jenner. "We've got a body getting cold and an unsecured crime scene, Masters. Move your ass and call for backup. Sergeant Schroder of Special Crimes will identify me when he gets here. And he's going to land on your butt with both feet when I tell him how long you held things up."

Masters nodded. "Right," he said as he pulled out his handcuffs. He snapped one cuff on Lydia's right wrist and motioned to Jenner. "Stick your hand out, buddy."

"What the hell are you doing, Masters?"

"I'm moving my ass just like you told me to," said the younger officer, snapping the other cuff around Jenner's unresisting wrist. "The two of you just get in the backseat of the squad car and be real nice while Officer Masters calls for backup."

"What detail do you work?" asked Jenner, grinding his teeth together in what Lydia thought was a credible effort not to lose control.

"Traffic."

"Goddamn it, I'm a sergeant in the traffic division!"

"I've never seen you before"—he prodded Lydia and Jenner toward the patrol car—"and I've been working traffic for two weeks—ever since I graduated from the academy. I was top of my class."

"Congratulations," said Lydia.

"Thanks," he replied, squaring his shoulders like a West Point cadet on parade.

Jenner's face seemed to swell. "A rookie! A goddamn rookie! Of all the cops in the Amarillo PD, we catch a rookie!"

"Watch your language, buddy," warned Masters.

"And don't call me buddy!" roared Jenner, standing nose to nose with the younger cop.

"Oh, shut up and get in the car, Jenner. I think the officer is entitled to use reasonable force if you don't cooperate, and I've seen enough force tonight. I don't want to see any more," Lydia said, sliding into the backseat followed by Jenner and immediately wrinkling her nose. Judging by the smell, she decided none of the squad car's previous felonious occupants had been either clean or sober. She felt at home because she didn't think she would ever feel clean again.

"A goddamn rookie," repeated Jenner again, pounding his fist on his knee and jerking Lydia's arm up and down with each blow.

"Would you stop that, or at least use your other fist before you dislocate my wrist or elbow?"

"Sorry. Did I hurt you?"

He sounded so concerned that Lydia pressed her lips together to keep the lower one from trembling. "No, but could you do me a favor and talk about something else? You've called Masters a rookie at least three times. Unless he's deaf, he knows what you think of him. Besides, he's just doing his job."

Masters twisted around and looked at them. "Here comes your good buddy, Sergeant Schroder. You did say he was your good buddy, didn't you, fellow?"

"Not exactly," muttered Jenner, slumping down in the seat. "How come you know Schroder, rookie?"

"He taught a class at the academy. All business, but seemed to be a hell of a nice guy."

"So is a grizzly as long as it's caged," said Jenner, blotting his forehead with his sleeve. Lydia wondered why he looked sweaty and nervous.

"Where's the body, Officer?" asked Schroder, not glancing in the backseat.

"Schroder, it's me," said Jenner, leaning over the front seat.

Masters pointed his thumb toward Jenner. "He says it's three blocks down and up the alley on the right."

"Follow me," said Schroder, and walked back to his car without a backward glance.

"Schroder didn't act like he knew your ass from a hole in

the ground, buddy," said Masters, swinging in behind the detective's old Ford.

"Watch your language, asswipe," said Jenner. "There's a lady in the car."

Lydia ignored their bickering, leaned her head back against the seat, and closed her eyes. Masters stopped the car, and she heard the door slam as he got out.

Jenner twisted around to look out the rear window, jerking Lydia halfway across his lap in the process. "Schroder's checking out the body. When he finishes, he'll come over and identify me. Don't worry about a thing. Hey, see, that goddamn rookie's talking to him now."

Lydia kept her eyes closed. If she looked, she might see the body—what was left of it—and she'd seen enough when Jenner had flicked on his flashlight to know she didn't want to see any more.

She felt Jenner nudge her. "Here comes Schroder," he said, and she wondered why he sounded so uneasy.

Lydia pulled herself upright, opened her eyes, and looked straight ahead as Schroder opened the car's front door and leaned in. She flinched and blinked when the burly sergeant shone a mega-watt flashlight in her face.

"Is your name Lydia Fairchild?"

Schroder's voice sounded totally impersonal. Foreboding tightened Lydia's throat like a ligature until she wondered if she would be able to speak.

Jenner had no such problem. "For Christ's sake, Schroder, you know who she is, and you know who I am. Tell that rookie to unlock these cuffs."

Schroder shifted the flashlight's beam to Jenner. "You the one claiming to be Sergeant Jenner?"

Jenner's mouth worked soundlessly for several seconds. "What kind of game are you playing, Schroder?"

"That ain't the question, son," replied Schroder in a voice so cold it could freeze the blossoms off a plum tree. "What kind of game are *you* playing?"

Lydia heard Jenner swallow. "I can explain. . . ."

"And I want to hear it, too—at the station." He snapped off the flashlight, then addressed Masters: "Take them downtown and lock the would-be sergeant in the interrogation room in the detective division. We'll hold him for investigation."

"What about her?" asked Masters.

Schroder hesitated, touching his ID card clipped to his breast pocket. Lydia had the oddest feeling that he had just made a decision he was already regretting. "Book her . . ."

Lydia sank back against the seat and covered her eyes. Schroder must have matched her face with the description of the blonde hooker who had sent two cops to the hospital. Otherwise he would have arranged to have her statement taken then released her.

". . . for capital murder," the detective finished.

CHAPTER
SEVENTEEN

JENNER TWISTED IN THE METAL FOLDING CHAIR AND LOOKED around the interrogation room—the official name for an eight-by-eight cubbyhole with acoustical tiles on walls and ceiling, indoor-outdoor carpet in a shade somewhere between gray and mud, and furnished with one institutional steel desk, one chair with a vinyl seat, his own metal chair, and a reasonably comfortable padded office chair with arms, now occupied by Lieutenant Roger "the Bean" Green.

"Your ass is grass, Jenner," said Green. "And I'm the lawn mower. What the hell did you think you were doing running around the Boulevard dressed up like some candy-assed faggot?"

"Where's Lydia?"

"Your little sweetie's upstairs getting a new wardrobe and having her picture made."

Jenner felt his stomach lurch upward into his throat. He gritted his teeth to keep from vomiting. The only thing *up-stairs* in the Amarillo police station was the jail. Until that moment, he hadn't really believed Schroder was serious when he told the rookie to book Lydia for capital murder.

"Listen, Green, she's no murderer. She's a law student,

for God's sake! She was trying to help the prostitutes. She's into causes, I guess, but all she's guilty of is acting stupid.''

Green propped his feet on the desk. "If anybody can recognize stupid, it's you, Jenner. You got a fucking monopoly on it.''

"You got to get her out of there! Jesus, that jail bait will eat her alive.''

"She's got a cell all to herself, the one up by the desk. Got a shower and everything. She's even got a choice of beds—the upper bunk or the lower bunk. 'Course there's no satin sheets and feather pillows, but it beats a gurney all to hell.''

Jenner came out of his chair like a coiled spring and stood poised on the balls of his feet, his cuffed hands curled into fists. "You're full of shit, Green. She's not going to end up on a gurney in Huntsville waiting for a lethal injection.''

"Sit down, Jenner," warned the lieutenant. "Whoever's convicted of being the Butcher is gonna get the death penalty, no doubt about it. Being a woman won't save her life.''

"She's not the Butcher, damn it!" He dropped back in his chair and wiped his forehead. "Where's Schroder? I want to talk to him.''

"You ought to worry about talking to a lawyer, Jenner. At the very least you're off the force. At most, well—" Green wiggled his eyebrows "—there's always accessory to murder.''

"What!"

Green made a languid gesture toward Jenner's white shirt. "You got blood all over you. Want to bet a DNA check will prove that blood comes from our latest corpse?''

Jenner wiped his face again. "I told you how I got blood on me. Come on, Green, you don't really believe this bullshit!''

"How about it, Lieutenant? You believe Jenner gutted that hooker or helped Lydia Fairchild do it?''

Schroder stepped inside the interrogation room and closed the door. His collar was frayed, his tie dotted with tiny cigarette burns, one button was missing from a two-button coat, the back of his shirt had crawled out of his trousers and was peeking beneath his coat like a lady's slip, his shoes were scuffed, cracked, run over at the heels, and had last been polished during the Watergate crisis. To Jenner, he was beautiful.

"God, Schroder, I'm glad to see you!" exclaimed Jenner.

Schroder shot him a look that Jenner translated as *say one more word, and I'll chop off your nuts*. He shut up.

"Do you believe he's guilty, Green?" asked Schroder.

Green scratched his paunch. "Jesus, Schroder, don't you think it's suspicious? Jenner finds the first body, shows up at the scene of the second one in spite of being told to keep his ass off the Boulevard, and now tells us he stumbled over the third body. Anybody else, and he'd be up in the cell with the blonde."

"Holy shit, Green!" exclaimed Jenner, forgetting to keep quiet.

Schroder gave him another look, this one, if anything, worse than the last. This one told Jenner what would happen to his balls *after* Schroder cut them off.

"You think Jenner's gone bad?" the detective asked Green.

Green wiggled in his chair. He studied the ceiling, the toe of one shoe, the acoustical tile on the back wall, the one with large chunks gouged out. He scratched his paunch with both hands. He looked up at Schroder, opened his mouth, then closed it again. Finally, he nodded his head. "I smell something that stinks worse than rotten beef and I think maybe it's him or at least he's got something to do with what I'm smelling."

Jenner smelled something rotten, too, and its odor didn't come from him. If anybody was walking around with dog shit on his shoes, it was Sergeant Ed Schroder.

"Congratulations, Jenner," said Schroder, teeth showing in a smile, or what the detective considered a smile. Jenner had seen friendlier expressions on a shark, and sharks didn't have nicotine-stained teeth.

"What do you mean?" asked Jenner.

"What do you mean?" echoed Green.

Schroder pulled a cigarette from a crumpled pack in his coat pocket and lit it with a battered Zippo. Smoke trickled from his nose and curled around his face. "Of course, we set it up well, but I still figured Jenner had less chance of pulling it off than a three-legged mule in a horse race.''

"Huh?" said Jenner.

"Huh?" said Green.

"I'm proud of you, son, real proud of you." He lumbered across the room, put his hand on Jenner's shoulder, and looked at Green. "Never thought there'd ever be anybody so good at undercover work that he could fool Lieutenant Green."

"Underc—" Schroder's grip on his shoulder cut Jenner off in midword.

"Undercover? That fuckup?" said Green.

Schroder smiled again, or his approximation of a smile. "Jenner's been working undercover for Special Crimes this week."

"I have? I mean, yeah, I have."

"His suspension was cover," continued Schroder, squeezing Jenner's shoulder again.

"That's right, it was cover. Sergeant Schroder figured if no one knew I was on the Boulevard, then no one, meaning you, Lieutenant, would be looking for me, and I'd be free to move around, meet people, ask questions—"

"Quit while you're ahead, son," said Schroder under his breath, tightening his grip until Jenner thought his arm would be permanently paralyzed. "So you see, Green, Jenner here was under orders."

"I don't like people being on the Boulevard without checking in with me," said Green.

"The Butcher is Special Crimes's case."

"*Is* did you say? Don't you mean *was*?" demanded Green, lifting his feet off the desk and standing up. "We just charged the blonde bombshell with capital murder. The case is done, finished, closed."

"No!" interrupted Jenner. "That's not right. Lydia didn't murder Cowgirl. . . ." He stopped abruptly when he saw the expressions on the other men's faces.

"Cowgirl?" asked Schroder in a voice that sounded like silk drawn through a gravel bed. "How did you know the deceased's name was Cowgirl?"

Jenner swallowed. "Uh, Lydia told me."

Green punched Schroder's arm. "She even knew the broad's name. How the hell does an *innocent* young law student make the acquaintance of a cheap hooker?"

"Because Jo-Jo Jefferson brought all his girls with him when he talked to John Lloyd Branson. Except Purple Rain, and she was already dead. Branson threw Jo-Jo out of his office, and Lydia decided to play hooker to help the girls and maybe find the real Butcher." Jenner stopped to take a breath. "Something else, Schroder. Cowgirl was the witness I saw, the one I've been looking for. I guess you didn't pull her in for a lineup because of the orange hair, but I recognized her anyway."

"The orange hair was a wig," said Schroder absently, stubbing out his cigarette while it was still two inches long. Jenner felt a premonition of disaster. Schroder always smoked his cigarettes down to a minuscule butt; for him to do otherwise meant the detective was suffering a major emotional upset.

"I know it was a wig," snapped Jenner. "He ripped it half off her head."

"So Ms. Fairchild knew the victims, is that right?" asked Schroder.

"Well, yeah," agreed Jenner, his premonition growing stronger.

"So the victims wouldn't be suspicious if Ms. Fairchild approached them, is that right?"

"Well, I guess not. But she's disguised. They wouldn't necessarily recognize her."

"But she recognized Cowgirl?" asked Schroder, rubbing his hands together while he watched the younger sergeant.

"Yeah, but—"

"—and Cowgirl is the witness that got away, the one you think might have seen something?"

"Yeah, but like I was trying to tell the Bean here, I was with Lydia tonight for maybe an hour before we stumbled over the body. And before that she was running from Jo-Jo Jefferson. In fact, she had a little altercation with him outside the Bimbo Bar, and before that she had to teach some creep some manners, and before that she was at a motel . . ."

"Ah," said Green with a leer.

"It was nothing like that," said Jenner, wanting to wipe the carpet with the lieutenant's face. "She was hiding out because two cops tried to arrest her, but she had to leave the motel because Bill Elliot tried to make a citizen's arrest. So see, she didn't have time to kill anybody, and that corpse was pretty fresh, Schroder."

"How do you know all this, Jenner?" asked Green, a suspicious expression replacing the leer.

"She was hysterical after she fell in that pool of blood and she sort of dumped on me. It was no act, either. She was telling me the truth."

Schroder dropped into the padded office chair, and Jenner held his breath while the chair creaked and shuddered, but held together. Somebody built like a Sherman tank should not drop into a chair.

The detective rubbed one massive hand over his face as if trying to erase something he didn't want to see. "I know all about it, Jenner. I've been picking up after Ms. Fairchild all night, including that creep with the green hair she knocked unconscious and left in the gutter. She ought to have a team of paramedics following after her. The Boulevard looks like a war zone."

"Schroder, listen to me. She didn't kill Cowgirl. I know Lydia Fairchild. Not very well maybe, but enough to know she's not the type!"

"You got good instincts for homicide, son. I always said that."

"Then release her!"

Schroder rubbed his face again. "I can't, son. We found evidence that ties Lydia Fairchild to the murder."

"What evidence?" demanded Jenner.

Schroder looked up at Green. "Bring Ms. Fairchild down here as soon as she's been processed."

"What evidence?" asked Jenner again.

"It'll be a pleasure," said Green, and left the room all but salivating at the thought of grilling Lydia.

"What evidence, goddamn it, Schroder?" yelled Jenner.

Schroder looked at him and Jenner swallowed and shut up. The detective cleared his throat. "Green's out of hearing range, so we can quit playacting and get down to the nut-cutting. I saved your ass, son, by covering for you, and do you know why?''

Jenner shook his head.

''Because you're a good cop, but that ain't the main reason. It's because you're the luckiest son of a bitch I've ever met. You know why?''

Jenner tried to think of something lucky that had happened to him lately—and failed. ''No,'' he answered.

''You went nosing around on the Boulevard with no identification and no backup. Nobody goes undercover clean unless he's got backup watching his behind. Anybody else pulling a stunt like you did would have ended up dead or with his kneecaps busted by some cretin swinging a baseball bat. But not you. You not only don't get blown *or* blown away, you find Lydia Fairchild. You're a fucking miracle worker.''

''Don't jerk me around, Schroder. What evidence?''

''I'm not telling you. You ain't being objective. Haven't I always told you that you got to be objective?''

''Yeah,'' admitted Jenner. ''But that's not all you've told me. You said motive was important, maybe the most important investigative tool a detective has, even if the D.A. doesn't have to prove motive when the case comes to court. Evidence don't mean shit if you can't match it up to a suspect, and you don't have a suspect until you know the motive. Unless you catch somebody in the act, of course, but you didn't catch Lydia Fairchild in the act of doing a damn thing except being a fool. She's got no motive, and I don't care what kind of evidence you've got. I don't care if you show me a Polaroid of her ripping that woman open. I wouldn't believe it.''

Schroder's face was expressionless, more so than usual, thought Jenner, and it usually looked like a blank wall. For some reason that scared him, gave him *free-floating anxiety* that his wife was always talking about since she'd taken that psychology course last spring.

''More homicide cops have been ruined by working too hard to prove somebody either guilty or innocent according to what the cop feels, instead of gathering evidence and letting the evidence point the way. I've arrested people I didn't want to arrest because the evidence said I had to.''

''Bullshit, Schroder! You've never arrested anybody you

didn't want to arrest because you've never arrested anybody who wasn't guilty—until now. You hate murder worse than any cop I know except maybe me. If you believed somebody was a murderer, really believed it, you wouldn't whine about not wanting to arrest him. You'd strap the bastard to the gurney and administer the lethal injection yourself."

"So you think I'm wrong?"

"Yes!"

"Without even knowing what evidence I've got?"

"Yes!"

"Because your gut instinct tells you so?"

Jenner hesitated, sensing a trap in Schroder's words. "Yes!"

"Seeing as how your gut instinct is working overtime, I'm sending you undercover again since you were so good at it. Your job is to gather evidence, but since you don't know what I've already got on Ms. Fairchild, you don't dare take the chance of ignoring a piece of information because it might just be the piece she needs to clear herself. I'm keeping you objective, son."

"Objective, shit! You're sitting there like a Buddha telling me I'm a bad cop, that I'd cover up evidence for Lydia. I wouldn't cover up for my own mother!"

Schroder studied his stubby fingers before looking up at Jenner. "I know that, son. I also know how bad it guts a man when he has to arrest somebody he likes. You lose an illusion, and a cop don't have many illusions to start with. We like to keep what we have. Keeping the worst about Ms. Fairchild to myself lets you hold on to an illusion a little longer."

"What are you doing, Schroder, keeping me objective or covering your ass?" asked Jenner, swallowing hard and feeling his eyes prickle. He saw Schroder's trap, knew he had to step in it, knew he didn't have a choice. But damned if he'd let the bastard think he didn't smell the rotten bait.

"If you have enough evidence for an arrest, then you have enough for a conviction. But you're still investigating, which means you're not too sure of yourself. You're not protecting my illusion, Schroder, you're protecting your own illusion that you're some kind of super cop. You're the Dirty Harry of Amarillo. Well, Harry, you fucked up. You arrested Lydia Fairchild without any evidence, or not enough anyway, and now your ass is in a crack. Worse than that you might get canned. John Lloyd Branson'll sue you for false imprisonment if he doesn't shoot you first with that antique revolver he carries in his briefcase.''

Schroder lit another cigarette and peered at Jenner through the smoke. ''Maybe. Maybe not.''

''Why, Schroder? Why are you doing this? Why don't you just file a supplemental incident report that you've got insufficient evidence to present the case to the district attorney for prosecution? Don't screw around with Branson and don't do this to Lydia Fairchild.''

''You ain't running this investigation. I am—and I know what I'm doing. You just nose around and see what you can find out. Do a good job, a *professional* job, and I'll forget you went against my orders and I had to lie to protect you.''

''Don't worry about that, Schroder. I won't fail you.'' Jenner blinked his eyes to keep the tears back. ''But not because I want to save your ass like you saved mine. The only reason you lied to Green was to manipulate me into helping you. I'm doing it for Lydia Fairchild because, goddamn it, she tried to help those women. Maybe she was stupid and not very capable of playing a hooker, but she at least did something for the right reason. Tonight an old drunk told me about choices, Schroder. That's what Lydia did. She made a choice, and I'm making one, too. I'm going to save her from you.''

''I knew I could count on you, son.'' Schroder grinned. ''Because nobody on the Boulevard knows you're a cop, you're going upstairs to share a cell with one of its slugs. I picked him up tonight as a material witness because he knows all the victims.''

''Who?'' asked Jenner.

''Jo-Jo Jefferson.''

CHAPTER EIGHTEEN

CAPITAL MURDER.

The words brushed against Lydia's consciousness as she watched Masters lock up his gun inside one of the carpet-lined wooden boxes. She mentally flinched away from the words and concentrated on examining her surroundings instead. She would worry about the words tomorrow. Any number of things might occur before tomorrow: World War III, a twenty-four-hour virus that wiped out mankind, the Second Coming. Or Ned the cop might not be dead after all.

Don't think about Ned the cop!

She closed off part of her mind and looked at the little numbered wooden boxes set into the wall beside the heavy metal door with the sign above it reading JAIL. By counting the number of locked boxes, one knew how many cops were on the other side of the door since no cop was allowed to enter the jail area with a gun. One locked box equaled one gun equaled one cop.

She wondered when Ned the cop had died. In the hospital? Who ever heard of anybody dying of a glass jaw? Maybe it was a brain concussion from hitting the pavement. But he was alive when she left him. Wasn't he?

Don't think about Ned the cop!

Lydia wished Jenner were still with her.

"What happens next?" she asked, not because she didn't know, in theory at least, what procedure was involved in booking a prisoner, but because she couldn't stand the silence anymore. Not that the hall was precisely silent—cops were walking in and out, and she could hear other voices down the hall, and around the corner demanding to see such and such a prisoner—but no one was talking to her, least of all Masters. She was a nonperson.

She was a cop killer.

Masters punched several buttons on a panel beside the jail door—evidently a code, thought Lydia—and took her arm to lead her inside. "This is the booking room."

"This?" said Lydia in disbelief, looking at a narrow room. To her right was the elevator, to her left a chest-high shelf ran down the wall, a shelf now lined with several officers filling out forms while prisoners leaned against the opposite wall. Past the elevator was a metal desk, and on the other side of that was a cement staircase. Beyond that, the room, or hall, which is what it looked like, was empty.

She shook her head. "You people have to be kidding. Don't you ever watch TV or go to the movies? You have to meet people's expectations. The public judges by outward appearances. This doesn't look like a booking room. It looks like a wide hall in a low-rent apartment building. You need to hang very inexpensive prints. Perhaps a poster or two, something in primary colors—preferably humorous."

Masters couldn't believe his ears. "Are you setting up an insanity defense?"

"No, I'm just trying to make conversation. This is my nightmare and I'll handle it the best way I know. Of course I could hyperventilate and faint, but I've never been able to identify with heroines who faint and fall into the nearest man's arms. That sort of behavior has been responsible for some very bad press for women in the past. I could have another fit of hysterics, but more than one a year is self-indulgent, don't you think?"

"I think I'm gonna tell the jailer you're a candidate for the funny farm."

"No, I'm just trying to remain in control. This place could really depress me if I let it."

Masters looked around the booking room. "If you think this is depressing, wait till I take you upstairs."

The Butcher stood across the street from the jail. He jammed his fist into his mouth to prevent a scream from erupting.

Damn that bitch!

She had escaped him!

He bit down on his fist, the pain piercing the red haze that blinded his reason. Lowering his hand, he sucked in several deep breaths. In his frenzy to have her, he had forgotten the game. He could afford to wait and to watch the other players. Her protectors, his challengers. In the end, Lydia would be his, her long, slender throat bared to his hands, her white body his to feed upon in his own way. He only had to play out the game.

He leaned against the brown stucco building as exhaustion weakened him, made his legs and hands tremble. At the same time, he felt restless, unsatisfied, his appetite unappeased.

He hungered.

He needed her.

He wanted her.

Depressing was the proper word for the actual jail, thought Lydia, as she got off the elevator and was led through the barred door—if by depressing one meant low in spirits. Her spirits were so low they were dragging along the tiled floor behind her.

"What you in for, lady?" asked a man dressed in a jail-issue white cotton jumpsuit and sitting in a tiny cage to the right of the barred door.

"Why are you in that cage?" demanded Lydia. "You don't even have room to lie down. My God, that's cruel and unusual punishment." She looked toward the jailer who stood behind a half moon–shaped desk. "Sir, unlock that cage and get that man out. Give him a decent cell. You people simply have to do something about the facilities. First that so-called booking room and now this. Someone should turn you in to the Texas Jail Standards Board.''

"Hey, lady," said the prisoner uneasily. "It ain't what you think."

The jailer looked at her as if she were a new species of animal, one that should be exterminated before it could breed. "He's a runner. That's why he's in the cage."

"What does he run? Drugs? Guns? Whatever it is, you still aren't allowed to treat him like an animal." Actually, Lydia thought drug runners *were* animals, but it was the principal involved.

"Lady, would you shut the fuck up before somebody thinks I know you?" complained the prisoner. "Hey, you don't think I put this broad up to this, do you?" he asked the jailer.

"You want to be in that cage?" asked Lydia, both in disbelief and uncertainty.

The jailer heaved a sigh. "Lady, a runner is a trustee. We call them runner 'cause they run up and down the stairs carrying papers and messages. He just stays in the cage between trips. Being a trustee is an earned privilege."

"Oh, I'm sorry. I didn't know."

"That's what a lot of my prisoners say," said the jailer.

Before Lydia could formulate a reply, Masters slammed the jail door shut, and she jerked around to look through bars from the inside for the first time in her life.

Capital murder. For the rest of her life, every door she saw would be locked.

"It's really happening, isn't it?" she asked no one in particular.

"Sure is," agreed the prisoner in the cage, leaning back in his metal folding chair. "That is, unless you're on one of them tours of the jail, and I ain't never seen one of them touring folks in handcuffs."

Lydia flexed her hands, felt the handcuffs rub against her wrists. She, Lydia Ann Fairchild, Sunday-school pupil, Girl Scout, honor student, was in jail!

It was an accident!

She leaned on the half-circle desk and tapped her foot against its front panel to get the jailer's attention again. "Sir," she said to the uniformed man shuffling paper in a determined effort to ignore her. "I want to report an accident. If you would please call Sergeant Schroder, I'll explain to him what happened. I should have done it before, but I was so shocked at being charged with capital murder—"

"Capital murder! You're a real champion badass, lady," said the prisoner in the cage, awe in his voice. "Hey, listen, I didn't mean nothing when I told you to shut up. Don't take it personal."

"—I wasn't thinking very clearly. But I am now, and I'm ready to discuss the situation with Sergeant Schroder." Lydia smiled. Schroder was a rational man. Once she explained, the worst charge she might expect was involuntary manslaughter. She felt the pain in her chest ease a little.

The jailer finally looked over his glasses at her. "You want to confess?"

"No!"

He began sorting papers again. "Then sit down," he said, nodding toward a wooden bench against the wall opposite the desk.

"It's my constitutional right to confront my accuser."

The jailer removed his glasses and gazed toward the ceiling, either looking for divine guidance or contemplating his next sentence. Lydia couldn't tell which. Finally, he rubbed his eyes and replaced his glasses, fussing with their position until they perched precariously on the end of his nose. Then he peered over his lenses at her. "Fairchild—"

"No."

"No?" he repeated, thumbing through the papers Masters had handed him.

"No," said Lydia firmly. "It's Ms. Fairchild. Even in these circumstances I'm entitled to be addressed correctly."

The officer consulted the ceiling again, then sighed as he shifted his gaze from the acoustical tiles to her face. He looked as if he preferred the tiles. "*Ms*. Fairchild, it's after three A.M., my bunions hurt, my ankles are swelling, I'm behind in my paperwork, and I'm *not* in the mood to listen to a lecture from a jailhouse lawyer."

"I need to call one."

"What?"

"I need to call a lawyer. May I use your phone, please?"

"No."

"It's my constitutional right to consult with a lawyer," Lydia reminded him.

He responded by communing with the tiles for a few more moments. As much time as he spent with his head bent back, he ought to have a pinched nerve in his neck, thought Lydia. "*Ms*. Fairchild, I notice from the paperwork that you understood your rights when Officer Masters read the Miranda warning—"

"Actually Sergeant Schroder read them to me," Lydia interrupted, realizing she was babbling again.

Ned the cop is dead.

It was an accident.

But it was an accident caused by you.

"—and you chose to remain silent?"

"Yes. It is very unwise to answer questions without an attorney present. I'm a lawyer—well, almost a lawyer—actually I'm a law student, and I know that one can incriminate oneself without meaning to, so—"

"Then why don't you do it?"

"Do what?"

"Remain silent!"

"That is excellent advice, Miss Fairchild. I suggest you follow it."

The voice was sharp, commanding, angry—and very familiar.

Lydia turned to look through the bars at the man standing on the other side. "Hello, John Lloyd."

CHAPTER
NINETEEN

A BUNK BED, A CEMENT FLOOR PAINTED MAROON, A SINK, a shower with no door or shower curtain, a toilet with no lid, a metal bunk bed with inflammable mattresses. A solid metal door with bars over its peephole, a barred window painted over with the same institutional bilious green paint that covered the cell walls. This was the model cell, the one shown to visiting schoolchildren and civic clubs; the others weren't as fancy. Jenner thought it was a hell of a place to live, and a hell of a place to die, and die he would as soon as Jo-Jo walked in and recognized him.

The cell door opened, and the Boulevard's premier pimp limped in like a crippled crab. That was the only way Jenner could think to describe the bent-over, spaddle-legged, sideways, limping gait Jo-Jo exhibited as he sidled across the four feet between the cell door and the bottom bunk.

The pimp sat down gingerly and leaned back against the wall. His upper lip was split and poked out like a sausage. He eased his foot out of his shoe, and Jenner saw that it was bandaged. Lydia had done a hell of job with her size-ten spike heels.

"Son of a bitch," Jo-Jo groaned. His swollen lip gave his voice an almost imperceptible whistle.

"Bad night?" asked Jenner, combing his hair over his face and buttoning his jail coverall all the way to the top to hide his fake tattoo. There were lots of bums he resembled, but none of them had a skeleton on his chest. If Jo-Jo had seen that tattoo just before Jenner hit him, then—well, he didn't want to think about the ifs. On the other hand, there was always a chance the pimp wouldn't recognize him since Jo-Jo's eyes had been rolling around in his head at that particular time. A brick in the balls does that to a man.

Jo-Jo closed his eyes and shook his head. "Bad night?" Opening his eyes, he turned his head to stare at Jenner with no recognition. "Bad night?" he repeated. "Shit, man, but that don't cover it. This been the worse fucking night of my life. I ain't never had one this shitty. I tell you, there ain't a man on the Boulevard been done so wrong as me. I got my brand-new baby-blue Cadillac with the velour seat covers and silver-plated steering wheel stole before I even had a chance to put the TV antenna on it. When I catch the motherfucker what did it, he'll be singing soprano and crawling on his belly 'cause I'm gonna bust his balls and both knees."

"Stole your car, huh?" said Jenner, crossing his legs and pitching his voice low. Damn it, but he thought Jo-Jo Jefferson drove a white Lincoln.

"That ain't all," said Jo-Jo, responding to Jenner's sympathetic tone. "I was chasing him up the alley when the cops come along and I had to dump my gun, and it was brand-new, too. Just bought it from a pawn broker what got it in an estate sale."

"Why did you dump it?" asked Jenner.

"Your hair roots growing through your brain, boy? The police got no sympathy for a businessman's problems. Won't approve no permit for me to carry a gun 'cause I've had me a little trouble now and again. They catch me carryin', they goin' to send me down to Huntsville. That ain't no real hardship, you understand, since I can get paroled about as soon as I get my prison uniform, but I'll lose money. Man's gotta stay on top his business."

Jenner winced at Jo-Jo's choice of words, but he knew the pimp didn't intend a double entendre. To a pimp, sex is serious business.

"Take this Butcher business," continued Jo-Jo. "Lost three of my stable to that motherfucker. That's three fourths of my inventory. I can't make no money like that."

"Stable?" asked Jenner even though he knew what Jefferson was talking about. It galled him to hear women discussed as if they were horses. Of course, a pimp would probably treat horses better.

"My bitches! Shit, don't nobody speak English no more?" He poked at a loose front tooth with his tongue, wiggling it back and forth until its diamond stud flashed like a strobe light. "Like I was saying, my profit-and-loss statement gonna look bad this quarter. My accountant's gonna crap."

"Profit-and-loss statement," repeated Jenner slowly, unable to believe he was in jail with a pimp who talked like a Harvard Business School graduate.

"It's a business document," said Jo-Jo, looking Jenner over. "But I guess you don't know nothing about that."

Jenner shook his head. "Never had any use for them." A cop never drew enough salary to have a profit left at the end of a pay period.

Jo-Jo's voice took on a lecturing tone. "See, a good whore, and my whores is good 'cause I train them right, anyway, a good whore can turn a trick every fifteen minutes and that includes the time it takes to flag down a car and make the date. Generally, the asking price is twenty-five to fifty bucks, depending, of course, on what the customer asks for. Something special runs a little more. Anyway, let's figure each unit earns an average of $175 an hour and I got four units so that's $700 an hour times fourteen hours on a good day equals $9,800."

"Jesus Christ!" exclaimed Jenner, not at the amounts Jo-Jo was quoting—any sleaze lord could tell you sex paid—but at the calculated way the pimp reduced human beings to units. That was worse than referring to them as his stable. Color aside, Jo-Jo Jefferson and a slave trader had a lot in common.

"That's gross," continued Jo-Jo. "Net ain't nearly so high. Man in my position's got a lot of expenses. There's the motel rooms, and my car—gotta have a good-looking car to keep my image up, people expect it. Then there's the girls' clothes, but I buy them at Goodwill or Lighthouse for the Blind. No sense spending good money on clothes for a whore. Customer ain't interested in what a whore's wearin' so long as it's short and tight. He don't pay no attention to no labels."

Jo-Jo stopped and pulled his jail suit away from his genitals.

"Got a problem?" asked Jenner, suppressing a snicker with some difficulty.

"Had me a run-in with a bitch tonight. I was recruiting, to replace my stock, you know, and she caught me when I wasn't looking, and then this bitch's pimp and four or five of his muscles worked me over. My balls feel like they're swelled up like basketballs."

"A pimp and four or five guys?" repeated Jenner, wishing Lydia had cracked Jo-Jo's nuts until they rattled when he walked. "Did you recognize any of them?"

"Hey, man, it was dark as an armpit, but one of them muscles was a big bastard, maybe seven feet tall. But the cops caught the bitch and I filed charges. Can't say Jo-Jo Jefferson ain't a good citizen when he has to be. Anyhow, I been hearing about how this bitch's badass pimp who calls hisself the Undertaker is moving into town. It's gonna be war 'cause I can't have that. Got everything on the Boulevard divided up, so many blocks to this pimp and so many to that one. Keeps everything peaceful, keeps expenses down. You get a coupla pimps fighting over the same turf, then you got people maybe getting dead, and that means the cops is coming around hassling everybody, and *that* means spending more money on bail bondsmen and lawyers. Lawyers—it's getting so you can't buy a good one. Fuckin' country's goin' to hell, that's what's wrong. Anyhow, cops is bad for business. The johns stay away 'cause they don't want to get picked up in no raid, and faster than a whore can quote a price, income is falling. I ain't in business for the fun of it—ain't no fun no how between problems with the cops and complaining from the whores. If things weren't bad enough what with the Texas economy kinda shaky, now we got this goddamn Butcher. What the fuck are we paying the cops for? If I paid taxes, I'd be madder than hell. The Chamber of Commerce ought to get a delegation together and go down to talk to the chief. The Butcher's bad for business."

Jenner clenched his fist. He wondered if knocking Jo-Jo's loose tooth out of the pimp's mouth without benefit of anesthesia would be police brutality. "It's pretty bad for the women, too," he said.

"What women?"

Jenner considered extending his practice of dentistry. He'd like to pull Jo-Jo's molars out with a pair of pliers—a centimeter at a time. "The women in your stable, the ones the Butcher killed. It's pretty bad for them, too."

Jo-Jo pulled at his coveralls again. "Sure as shit is—they're dead. I can't think of nothing badder. Now I got to train a whole new bunch, and I'm laying out for room and board while I'm doing it."

"No, I mean, don't you feel sorry for them?" asked Jenner. Surely Jo-Jo Jefferson had a redeeming character trait somewhere.

"I done what I could. I told them bitches to pair off and watch each other, but some johns just don't like an audience." He spread his hands in a helpless gesture. "What you in here for anyhow?" he asked, as if it suddenly occurred to him that he had talked to a stranger about things even his accountant didn't know.

"Aggravated assault," Jenner improvised. "Listen, didn't you think maybe you should've kept your girls off the streets, especially since they got one of those invitations?"

Jo-Jo waved the suggestion away. "Shit, man, them invitations didn't mean nothing."

"How can you say that when the paper said the Butcher always sent his victim an invitation?"

Jo-Jo drew back from Jenner. "I knew about them invitations. I seen the ones Purple Rain and Honey Bran got. My bitches can't hide nothing from me 'cause I turn their rooms over every day, make sure they're not skimming off the top, or taking tips in jewelry, or maybe trying to set themselves up to sell a little coke on the side. Everybody's a fucking pusher these days. Between the narcs trying to sting you and the amateurs trying to cheat you, a man don't hardly know who to buy from anymore. Anyhow, I found them invitations, but I let the girls keep them. Why not? There weren't no money in a piece of paper with a bunch of words glued on it. See, I'm a good pimp. I let the girls keep what they get—so long as there's no money in it."

"God, but you're generous," said Jenner.

Jo-Jo folded his hands over his chest. "Yeah, I am," he agreed. "Sometimes I give my bitches ten dollars apiece and take them out to the mall, you know, let them shop. Just in the mornings though. Business ain't too good much before noon."

"You got a big heart."

"I always treat my girls right," said Jo-Jo. "Don't knock them around any more than I have to. It ain't right it's my girls the Butcher's killing."

"Why is he?"

"I don't know, man. All I know is the police landed on me like flies on a turd, so they's wondering the same thing. I'm in a shitload of trouble if I don't figure it out."

Jenner saw his opening and took it. "I can feel sorry for a man who's just trying to make a living, so I'll help you. I used to be pretty handy at puzzles, so let's you and me figure together."

Jo-Jo looked at him suspiciously. "What you figuring to get out of it?"

Jenner shrugged his shoulders. "You're a generous man. I'll trust you to do right by me."

Jo-Jo nodded, satisfied with the answer as Jenner knew he would be. The Boulevard dealt in favors. Favors were sometimes a stronger currency than money and more likely to be honored than a cash debt. Unless you owed a loan shark and that was a whole other story.

"So what we gonna do?" asked the pimp.

"Did the girls get the invitations through the mail?"

"I told you them invitations don't mean nothin'."

"Just answer the question," commanded Jenner, crossing his fingers. At present he was top dog, but Jo-Jo could bite him any minute. Jo-Jo liked being in control.

The pimp thought a moment, a process that wrinkled his brow. Jo-Jo's mind resembled that of an idiot savant's: bril-

liant at solving complex formulas dealing with dollars and
cents, but slow at any other type of reasoning.

"The girls don't get no mail. No permanent address, you
know."

Jenner released his breath; the pimp had decided to cooperate instead of biting. "Okay, then where did they get
them?"

Jo-Jo thought some more. "They got them on Wednesdays
'cause I found them on Thursday mornings when I tossed
their room."

Jenner felt a particular shiver along his spine, the kind he
always felt when he sensed that just beyond the next question
was the truth. "Who did the girls see on Wednesdays?"

The pimp shrugged. "Anybody with twenty-five bucks."

"Didn't they have regular customers?" asked Jenner desperately, feeling his shiver die away.

"They ain't call girls. They's street whores. And they don't
remember faces—they remember cars."

"What are you talking about?"

"Cowgirl told me. She was always talking philosophy"—
Jo-Jo pronounced the word carefully, as if he were proud he
knew it—"and she said whores never remember men's faces.
They don't want to, you know. Cowgirl called it a *defense
mechanism*." The careful pronunciation again. Jo-Jo was definitely speaking a foreign language. "That's why the bitches
got arrested four or five times by the same undercover cop.
Cost me a lot of money in fines, so I slapped them up beside
the head pretty regular until Cowgirl told me about it. They
never notice no faces. But you can't fool them about cars.
They caught most all of their dates driving down the Boulevard. They knew repeaters by their cars, but once them johns
got out of their cars and got their britches down, them bitches
couldn't no more've told you what they looked like than the
man in the moon. To a whore, johns ain't got no faces. Don't
understand it myself. It's just business, but you can't tell shit
to a woman."

Jenner swallowed hard and took his time asking the next
question so he wouldn't have to explain why he sounded as
if he wanted to cry. "Then maybe the Butcher is one of the
girls' repeaters."

Jo-Jo shook his head emphatically. "I don't allow my whores to bird dog each other's repeaters. Too many bitch fights. Besides, I told you the girls recognize cars. If the same john in the same car what made Purple Rain's last date tried to pick up Cowgirl, she'd know it. I always told my bitches to watch out for each other even before this Butcher thing. Anyway, like I told you, we're talking street whores here, and they ain't got what you'd call a regular clientele."

"Maybe he drove a different car each time," suggested Jenner.

Jo-Jo sneered. "You think he's going to Avis before he drives down the Boulevard to kill one of my bitches? He's on foot, man, just like the whores."

Jenner scratched his head through his wig. "If they don't all see the same johns, then what about places? Do they ever go to the same place? Besides the motel, that is."

Jo-Jo grinned like a student who suddenly realized he knew the right answer. "The Bimbo Bar! I always took the girls to the Bimbo Bar for a drink on Wednesdays."

"Then somebody at the Bimbo slipped the girls those invitations," said Jenner, the shiver along his spine returning as he thought of Preacher.

Jo-Jo's eyes opened wide, and he began breathing hard through his nose like an angry bull. "Nobody at the Bimbo better be fucking around with me. That's my bar! I own the fucker!"

"Then the Butcher is somebody at the Bimbo. That's why your girls are the ones being killed."

Jo-Jo licked the spittle off his lips. "I told you the Butcher don't send them invitations."

"How can you say that?" demanded Jenner.

Jo-Jo looked at him, and Jenner saw the glimmer of a tear in the pimp's eyes. "Cowgirl never got no invitation."

CHAPTER
TWENTY

LYDIA SQUIRMED ON THE METAL FOLDING CHAIR IN THE IN-
terrogation room while she watched John Lloyd. Since the
moment upstairs in the jail when he had told her to follow
the jailer's advice and remain silent, he had not spoken to
her. While the police made her feel as if she were a nonperson, they at least admitted she was alive.

He sat at the small desk reading her file without comment
or facial expression except for the tiny white lines radiating
in a semicircle from each corner of his mouth. On anyone
else those lines would signify strong disapproval. With John
Lloyd, they were open to interpretation—disgust, distaste,
dislike, disbelief. The possibilities were endless and none of
them good. The only positive factor in the whole equation of
John Lloyd Branson was that he was here at all.

Which brought up an intriguing question: why *was* he
here?

"John Lloyd?"

He closed her file and swung around in the chair to face
her. Lydia wished he hadn't. Those obsidian eyes held an
expression that resembled anger in the same sense that a
tornado resembled a spring rain. He was unmistakably furi-
ous.

"Yes, Miss Fairchild," he said, biting off each word.

She closed her eyes for a moment, exactly as she always believed she would—if she were jumping into an ocean full of sharks. "Why are you here?" she blurted.

He cocked one blond eyebrow. "In your situation I should be more concerned with asking my opinion of your chances to avoid a most unpleasant, if not fatal, future."

Lydia twisted her hands together, absently noticing the fingerprint ink embedded in her cuticles. "Please, tell me why you came, how you *knew* to come. I'd rather know that than your legal opinion."

"That is an emotional judgment, not an intellectual one. Whatever you learned during your sojourn on the Boulevard, it was not wisdom."

Lydia smiled. "I think we both agree that I'm not wise. Maybe wisdom isn't part of my basic personality profile. I'll never be a Solomon, John Lloyd. I could never order a baby cut in half because I was confident the real mother would renounce her claim to save her child's life. I've seen things tonight that make me doubt any kind of human selflessness."

Amusement momentarily replaced the anger in John Lloyd's eyes. "I suspect, Miss Fairchild, that were you that biblical mother, you would first embrace your infant, then assault King Solomon for frightening you. And speaking of assaults—"

"We aren't," interrupted Lydia. "Speaking of assaults, that is. We are speaking of motives. What is your motive for coming to my rescue, and how did you know I was—uh—in distress?"

John Lloyd folded his hands and stared at her. No, thought Lydia, not *at* her, but *through* her—as though the wily lawyer were watching a film projected on the wall behind her. And whatever he saw frightened him.

"John Lloyd," she said, rising and taking a step toward him. "What's wrong?"

He waved her back. "Sit down, Miss Fairchild. Stop hovering over me like a mother hen with her chicks."

"I'm not hovering, but if you don't mind my saying so, you look like hell. You look tired, you missed a button on your vest, and the bow on your string tie is crooked."

He sighed and began rebuttoning his vest. "My minding a comment of yours has yet to prevent you from uttering it, and as for my appearance, your own is so disreputable as to render any opinion of yours completely invalid. What is the matter with your face? It looks swollen."

"Soybean."

For the first time since she had known him, John Lloyd looked disconcerted. "I beg your pardon."

"Soybean. I'm allergic to soybean. It makes my face swell. When I needed a disguise and I didn't want to pad my cheeks or whatever, I ate some soy burgers. They tasted awful, by the way."

"I am certain they did," he agreed dryly. "So, to summarize: aided by a skirt so short as to be almost indecent, a blouse that exposes you to lung fever, makeup more appropriate to a circus clown, ungroomed hair, and soybean-stimulated alteration of your features, you masqueraded as a lady of easy virtue on an infamous street whose alleys and shadows conceal enough evil and human misery to frighten and sicken us all. Is that correct?"

"Why are you here?" countered Lydia, distrusting his drawl, and not anxious to discuss her own motives.

"Is—that—correct?" John Lloyd repeated the question, a heartbeat between each word.

"Yes!" she shouted.

He rose with his customary, though almost imperceptible, stiffness and crossed the tiny room to rest his hands on her shoulders. "Miss Fairchild, I am here because God watches over fools and children. As God was otherwise occupied with such trifling concerns as war and famine, I am here in his stead."

Lydia stared up at his angry face through a shimmery curtain of tears. "Since I'm not a child, I must be a fool, is that what you're saying?" she asked, her throat burning from holding back what she knew would be a succession of humiliating sobs.

John Lloyd uttered a short expletive and let go of her shoulder to whip a handkerchief from his pocket. Gently he dabbed her eyes. "Lydia, my dear, I apologize for my remarks. This is not the time nor the place to point out your errors in judgment.''

She took his handkerchief and wiped her eyes, leaving large smears of bright blue eye shadow on the pristine white linen. "I deserve to be called much worse. After all, I killed a man—"

"Miss Fairchild—"

"Don't say anything! Please! But I'm not crying because you called me a fool—"

"Miss Fairchild—"

"Shut up, John Lloyd! Please! Let me finish while I'm able. When I saw you upstairs looking like some kind of avenging angel, I thought, like the fool I am, that you came because it was me, Lydia Fairchild, a particular fool, in trouble, and not because you'd come to the rescue of any child or fool in general. I wanted you to be here because you respected me, because you *liked* me. Under the circumstances I ought to be grateful you came whatever the reason, but then we've already agreed I'm a fool.''

She blew her nose and looked up at him in time to see an undisguised expression of concern and disbelief in those black eyes. He probably thought she was suffering from schizophrenia. "So what's your opinion of your client's chances, Lawyer Branson?''

He cleared his throat, and Lydia considered crying again. In her experience, throat-clearing was a delaying tactic to put off saying something unpleasant. She blotted up new tears and old eye shadow and calculated her chances at getting a job in the prison library.

"Miss Fairchild," began John Lloyd, his voice a peculiar soft drawl unlike any she had ever heard him use. "If you believe that I would expend not only my energy, but a considerable sum of money to charter a plane to Dallas"—she gasped—"break into your apartment, bully the Dallas police, not to mention Dean Johnson, spend half an hour conversing with a young woman of questionable integrity and less common sense named Cindy Spencer, return to Amarillo, and use up whatever goodwill has accrued to me from the Amarillo Police Department over a period of years in order to ascertain the whereabouts and condition of just *any* client, you are mistaken!''

His drawl gradually changed into a shout. John Lloyd never shouted. ''What?'' she asked numbly.

He paced around the room, favoring his stiff knee and running his fingers through his graying blond hair. Finally he turned and pinned her to the chair with both hands, this time digging his fingers into her flesh as if he were afraid she would escape. He didn't have to be concerned, she thought; she was too shocked to move.

''Shortly before eleven o'clock I received a phone call from a man I presume to be the Butcher threatening your life. He spoke as if he were physically watching you. Naturally assuming you to be in Dallas, an assumption based on logic and a very human need to deny that logical thinking is *not* your forte, I flew to your side only to discover you had flown the coop, to use one of Mrs. Dinwittie's deadly homilies. After indulging in unspeakable behavior which has undoubtedly left the impression in the minds of the authorities, not to mention the dean, that I am suffering from a virulent form of insanity, I thought to listen to your telephone message machine, on which were recorded a series of increasingly acrimonious calls from Miss Spencer. After visiting with that young lady, an experience I do not wish to repeat in this lifetime or the next, she repeated your very cryptic remark about taking *a walk on the Boulevard*. By the way, Miss Fairchild, I do not believe that Miss Spencer is very fond of you. She blames you for the cancellation due to lack of popular support of a scheduled protest meeting, something to do with a brewery. She took great pleasure in describing you as a political reactionary whose social goals were inherently suspect. I accepted the compliment on your behalf.''

Lydia swallowed. ''John Lloyd, you are distraught.''

He abruptly released her and straightened up. ''Miss Fairchild, as usual, your use of understatement is mindboggling.''

''You did all that for me?'' she asked, stunned by his behavior.

''It seems so, Miss Fairchild, and I might add that I am as distressed over my own behavior on this occasion as I am by yours. Your irresponsible impulsiveness must be contagious.''

"Thank you," she continued, rising and stepping close to him. "Thank you very much." She clasped her hands behind his head—and kissed him.

A few seconds, or minutes, or hours later—who worries about trivia when one's body is dissolving into a trembling, quivering, toe-curling mass of basic female chemical reactions?—John Lloyd gently but impersonally pushed her away and returned to his chair with no sign of weak knees, heavy breathing, or sweaty palms. Other than a glitter in his black eyes that could very well be a reflection from the fluorescent light, he revealed no reaction at all. If Lydia's lips weren't practically singed from the hottest, most potentially lethal kiss she'd ever received, she wouldn't believe it actually happened, not if her only evidence was an acknowledgment by the other participant. Obviously John Lloyd would acknowledge that kiss when hell froze over.

Lydia hoped he owned a pair of ice skates.

She handed his handkerchief back. "Passionate Red is not your color," she said primly, then whirled and sauntered back to her own chair. "No need to apologize for kissing me, John Lloyd. You *were* distraught." She felt better when she heard him sputter.

He wiped his mouth while glaring balefully at her. "If we may dispense with any further remarks concerning your feminine advances and my imagined response—"

"Imagined!" retorted Lydia.

"—there is the matter of a capital murder charge."

"John Lloyd, that's a mistake. I didn't intend to kill that cop—that Ned. It was an accident!"

"Miss Fairchild, I noticed earlier your remark about killing a man, but your insistence at knowing my motives for representing you, and then the other matter"—Lydia had no doubt what *other matter* he was referring to—"distracted me. However, allow me to reassure you that according to the IR, or incident report, the police officer named Ned, while not in good health—a broken jaw, I believe—is alive."

"Then who am I supposed to have murdered?"

"Margaret Jeanne Jefferson, better known to you as Cowgirl—'' He stopped abruptly and half rose from his chair. "Miss Fairchild, what is wrong? Your face is flushed."

"Those damn bastards! Throwing me in that zoo upstairs! Letting me worry that I killed somebody when all the time the charge is pure crap!"

"Miss Fairchild, your language—"

"Don't tell me your opinion about my language. I've had all I can tolerate for one night of men foisting their opinions on me, and ordering me around, and manhandling me, and treating me as if I didn't have sense enough to tell time with a digital watch. And to top it off, the culmination of what has been one hellish night, is that moron Schroder charging me with murdering Cowgirl." Lydia ran out of breath.

"Miss Fairchild, if you would kindly let me finish, I was about to say that I find your language surprisingly inoffensive compared to the linguistic excesses of which you are capable, and which in this case may even be justified."

She waved away his comment. "Did you say Cowgirl's name was Jefferson?"

John Lloyd nodded. "She was Jo-Jo's wife."

Lydia wrapped her arms around her waist. "I may vomit. He prostituted his own wife."

"Miss Fairchild, such arrangements are not uncommon. You cannot understand it because you and Jo-Jo do not have a common frame of reference."

"I suppose you do!"

"Yes," he replied. "Now, to return to the subject of your defense, please begin your statement with your first ill-conceived step upon the Boulevard and continue your narrative up to the point at which I interrupted your garrulous exchange with the jailer. Leave nothing out. I want a full description of everyone you met, a verbatim account of every conversation, and please do not neglect to mention all impressions, however vague, you had of your environment."

"Including the cold spot in the middle of my back?"

John Lloyd stared intently at her until his black eyes appeared to smolder red. "Most particularly I wish to hear of that phenomenon."

Lydia leaned forward and began talking while John Lloyd listened, his eyes never moving from her face, his tall, lean body motionless. She finished and leaned back, feeling empty, a husk that would rustle dryly if hung out in the wind.

"I'm in a hell of a mess, aren't I, John Lloyd?" she asked.

John Lloyd tapped her file. "Not from a legal standpoint, Miss Fairchild. The charges against you are trivial and easily dealt with."

"A capital murder charge is trivial?" Lydia blurted. "Since when?"

A flicker of irritation crossed his face. "Since I am representing you," he snapped. "I am more concerned with the Butcher's interest in your well-being, or perhaps I should say your lack of well being, than in any ill-advised charges the police may have filed. You realize, of course, that he has your wallet. I suggest you report your credit cards stolen."

"Is that all you have to say?"

"For the present," he replied. "If you are composed, I shall call Sergeant Schroder who has by now contacted the chief, and we shall dispose of your criminal record. That is, with the possible exception of the broken window. Couldn't you have left in a more conventional manner, Miss Fairchild? Vandalism is an indication of an uncontrollable rage."

"I *was* uncontrollably angry!"

He waved his hand nonchalantly as he rose and tugged his vest down. "Never mind, I shall arrange something." He opened the door. "Ah, Sergeant Schroder and Lieutenant Green."

He ushered in the two officers, neither of whom looked pleased. However, they appeared ecstatic compared to the third man who followed. From the pajama leg showing beneath his trousers, and a patch of unshaven whiskers in the shape of a sunflower on one cheek, Lydia concluded he was a man roused from his bed and distinctly unhappy about it.

"Miss Fairchild, have you met Chief Mostrovich?" asked John Lloyd, motioning the man forward like a host intent on introducing guests at a cocktail party.

Lydia debated whether or not to smile. Should she smile, and risk his thinking she was a happy Butcher? Or be sober and frown to let him know she understood the seriousness of the charges against her. Damn it, ever since she'd met John Lloyd Branson, she'd found herself in situations not covered by Emily Post. She finally decided on a smile that didn't show any teeth, polite but noncommittal.

"Chief Mostrovich."

Amarillo's chief of police was a slim, middle-aged man of medium height whose bland, even features disguised what Lydia knew had to be tough personality and an intelligent mind. The days of mentally deficient, redneck police chiefs had passed, along with nickel beer. No civil government would trust responsibility for several millions dollars' worth of vehicles and equipment and two hundred and forty-three men, not to mention some very formidable firepower, to an idiot.

Mostrovich nodded curtly at Lydia and removed a pipe from his coat pocket. Under the guise of filling, tamping, and lighting it, the chief studied her. Finally he tucked his pipe in the left corner of his mouth and wiggled it until the customary teeth found their customary dents in the stem. "So this is the young lady who's responsible for my being dragged out of bed at four in the morning. Did you know, Miss Fairchild, that police chiefs rouse themselves from sleep only for a nuclear disaster, a riot involving hostages, a shortage in the coffee fund—and John Lloyd Branson."

Lydia wondered how John Lloyd managed it—blackmail probably. But what puzzled her even more was the purpose of this meeting. It wasn't to question her officially because there was no stenographer present. There was an air of menacing sub rosa intimacy about this group, and contrary to what the ordinary person might think, the menace did not originate with the police. The source of the menace she felt emanated from the silent, watchful figure of John Lloyd Branson.

Chief Mostrovich turned his head to look directly at John Lloyd. "You owe me for this one."

John Lloyd displayed the composure of a gambler holding a straight flush. "I believe you have forgotten the incident of the black motorcycle, the yellow paint chips, and your brother-in-law."

Lydia knew it; it *was* blackmail.

The chief flushed, and Schroder and Green looked interested. Mostrovich inverted a lighter over the bowl of his pipe and inhaled several times while watching the attorney like an honest gambler scrutinized a card sharp. Lydia thought his alertness commendable, but it wouldn't prevent John Lloyd from dealing from the bottom of the deck.

"John Lloyd," Mostrovich asked between puffs, "has anybody ever told you what a son of a bitch you are? Excuse my language, young lady."

Lydia shrugged. "I've heard him called worse."

"As your attorney, Miss Fairchild, I advise you against any gratuitous comments to the police," said John Lloyd, sitting down in the padded secretarial chair and picking up his silver-headed cane off the desk.

"I only said—" began Lydia.

"I know what you said," interrupted John Lloyd with a note of disapproval in his voice. Actually, thought Lydia, it was more than a note; it was a whole choir.

Mostrovich sat in the only other unoccupied chair while Green and Schroder leaned against the wall like scruffy Praetorian Guards. At least Schroder looked scruffy. He also looked dangerous.

The chief puffed contently on his pipe while he perused Lydia's file. Finally he closed the file and glanced from Green to Schroder as if seeking an explanation before glowering at John Lloyd. "Suppose you tell me why my presence was required here. It's sure as hell not to—how did you put it to Schroder?—avoid a serious miscarriage of justice. Good God Almighty, John Lloyd, your clerk's got damn near every kind of assault charge on the statute book filed against her. She's a one-woman crime wave!" The chief waved a paper in the air. "Two counts of aggravated assault on a peace officer—"

John Lloyd waved his hand as if swatting a meddlesome insect. "Miss Fairchild had an unfortunate accident—"

"Unfortunate accident!" squawked Green. "Poor Ned's gonna be eating through a straw for six weeks! And Tony's hand is swelled up bigger than a baseball mitt!"

"—but avoided injury, no thanks to the negligence of the city of Amarillo. Had Miss Fairchild not stepped in that crack in the sidewalk and fallen, neither Ned nor Tony would have sustained any injuries at all. I shall advise my clients to sue the city for reckless endangerment due to poor street repair.

We can reasonably expect to recover very generous medical expenses. A broken jaw often leads to extensive orthodontia. One's bite is ruined. And, of course, Tony may need lengthy physical therapy for his hand. Nerve damage and infection of the carpal tunnel is common with injuries of that sort.''

"Wait a damn minute!" yelled the chief. "Are you representing Miss Fairchild or my cops?"

John Lloyd assumed an expression of surprise so exaggerated that in Lydia's opinion he deserved a felony charge for overacting. "Why, both, Chief Mostrovich. I *did* speak of *clients*, in the plural. I had an opportunity to speak to both gentlemen while I was waiting for Miss Fairchild to be fingerprinted. While Miss Fairchild may be impulsive and somewhat foolish, she is far too intelligent to assault two police officers. I knew it was an accident of some kind, and after noticing her unaccustomed footwear, I had assumed that she tripped over her own feet. I apologize, Miss Fairchild, for assuming you were clumsy.''

He inclined his head in her direction in that imperial way of his that never failed to irk her. "Ordinarily I would sue for illegal arrest''—he emphasized the words—"but I feel a certain responsibility for the officers' injuries as Miss Fairchild is in my employ although not acting under my orders in the present instance. However, just being in her vicinity can be hazardous to the unwary. In a legal sense she might be considered as an attractive nuisance.''

Lydia drew in a deep breath to respond but thought better of it. If John Lloyd succeeded in getting the charges dismissed, he could tattoo a surgeon general's warning on her forehead if he wanted.

The chief, whose face was an interesting color of puce, finally admitted that John Lloyd had won that hand. He chewed his pipe stem and picked up another piece of paper. "Seven counts of simple assault with a''—he peered at the fine print on the P-3 form—"fire extinguisher?" He looked at Lydia. "You assaulted Big Bill Elliot with a fire extinguisher?''

"No, I squirted him with it.''

"Seven times?''

"I squirted the other six men with him.''

"Miss Fairchild, please do not answer any questions without consulting with me first," snapped John Lloyd. "My client was defending herself against an attempted kidnapping."

"She squirted that foam on Elliot and he broke out in a rash," said Green. "Allergic to the chemicals I guess. When he came in to file charges, he was scratching like a dog with fleas."

"Attempted kidnapping?" asked the chief.

"He was attempting to make a citizen's arrest," said John Lloyd.

"I wish civilians would stop watching those lousy cop shows on TV," said Mostrovich. "There's no such thing as a citizen's arrest. The most the civilian can do is interfere with a felony in progress."

"Which is what Miss Fairchild did," said John Lloyd. "In a manner of speaking."

"Kidnapping being a felony," said the chief.

"Exactly," said John Lloyd.

The chief grinned. "I'll have Schroder explain it to him." He picked up another P-3. "What else do we have here? Criminal mischief—throwing a fire extinguisher through a window. Same fire extinguisher?"

"A small motel lobby usually only has one," said John Lloyd. "Surrounded by danger in the form of kidnappers at the front door, a pimp at the back door, and a white slaver—i.e., Old Annie—at the desk, Miss Fairchild took the only expedient route from the motel."

"Now we got the perils of Pauline," muttered Green.

"The proprietor of the motel, this same Old Annie, also defrauded my client of a gold watch," added John Lloyd.

"Discuss the gold watch with Old Annie, Schroder," said the chief, relaxing enough to cross his legs and expose several inches of pajama leg. He picked up another P-3. "Two charges of aggravated assault with a brick—with a brick?—on the person of Jules Jefferson—"

"Jo-Jo," said Schroder.

"Self-defense," said John Lloyd.

"He's not a person," said Green. "She should've used a whole load of bricks."

"—and one charge of simple assault: complainant is Benjamin Hunter."

"Bennie with the knife and green hair," said Lydia.

"Self-defense," repeated John Lloyd. "He made unwelcome advances toward Miss Fairchild. I am considering filing a sexual harassment suit."

"Explain it to him, Schroder. Tell him it's not nice to grab at ladies," said Mostrovich, picking up the last P-3 form and reading it.

Lydia swallowed and waited, watching the chief's face. All humor had disappeared and his features looked stiff. As stiff as Cowgirl's body must be by now, she thought.

The chief carefully laid the form back in the file, then looked at John Lloyd. "Capital murder. Do you have a snappy answer for that one?"

Lydia watched John Lloyd's long, slender fingers fondle the silver head of his cane like a surgeon seeking the proper spot to make an incision. Or a gambler seeking the right card to palm.

"If Miss Fairchild were an ordinary client, I would demand an examining trial and have the charge dismissed by the judge. However, she is not ordinary. She is a law student, and any felony charges at all, even if later dismissed, would call her integrity and ethics into question. It is not inconceivable that she would be refused admission to the bar. I cannot risk having a future member of my firm in that position." He shot Lydia a look that promised retribution if she opened her mouth.

Lydia kept very quiet. After all, John Lloyd hadn't lied—exactly; just used the present rather than the past tense when speaking of her employment status.

John Lloyd looked at each of the officers in turn. "Also, I respect this department and Sergeant Schroder in particular, and I do not wish to harm the reputation of either—"

"Here it comes, Schroder, the iron fist," said Mostrovich.

"—by filing two lawsuits for violation of Miss Fairchild's civil rights, one for false arrest, another for false imprisonment."

"Holy shit!" said Green. "You sure you haven't left out anything?"

John Lloyd arched one eyebrow. "It is possible a more complete study of Miss Fairchild's file will turn up other violations of her rights," he admitted.

"You had to ask, didn't you, Green," said Mostrovich. "How about you just stand there against the wall and keep your mouth shut while I listen to John Lloyd's devious reasons *for threatening this department*!"

John Lloyd's hands tightened on his cane's silver head, and Lydia felt her stomach tighten at the same time. Please don't let him be bluffing, she thought. Please let him say the magic words, whatever they are, that wake me up from this nightmare. Otherwise, she had no recourse except to take that elevator back upstairs. And wait behind closed, barred doors.

John Lloyd's fingers gripped his cane until they turned white. "You should be aware that I do not bluff where Miss Fairchild is concerned. I have read the incident report on this matter and this victim is one of a series. Miss Fairchild was in Canadian with me at the time of the first murder and in Dallas at the time of the second. Thus your evidence in either of those murders in nonexistent. As for the most recent atrocity, the presence of my client's business card in the victim's handbag does not ipso facto prove she is the murderer. As evidence it is pitifully inadequate, grounds for an investigation to be sure, but *not* for an arrest. Therefore I must conclude that I am not the only devious individual in the room." He looked directly at Schroder

"You filed that charge, Schroder," said the chief.

Schroder lit a cigarette. "So let's give Branson a chance to prove I treed the wrong coon."

Lydia saw John Lloyd loosen his grip on his cane. "An excellent suggestion, Sergeant. However, I thought I already had. I wonder what your motive is—beyond the most obvious one that Miss Fairchild is innocent."

Schroder's blue eyes were bland. "Justice."

John Lloyd's black eyes were equally bland. "Which is blind and totally merciless."

"Can be," agreed Schroder.

"I prefer cutting the cards before the deal, Sergeant. Much less chance of a stacked deck," John Lloyd said.

"What are you two talking about?" demanded the chief. "This isn't a damn oriental gambling den."

"The game has changed, Branson," answered Schroder, pulling a small plastic bag out of his pocket and handing it to the attorney. "We found that by Cowgirl's body."

Lydia froze as she watched John Lloyd's face lose all color. "John Lloyd," she whispered. "What is it?"

Slowly he turned his head to look at her with eyes as black and lifeless as two pieces of coal. "Your driver's license, Miss Fairchild."

CHAPTER
TWENTY-ONE

JENNER SLAMMED OPEN THE INTERROGATION-ROOM DOOR. "Schroder, you bastard, I've got your evidence. He screwed up when he handed out those damn invitations. We've got a suspect with motive and opportunity. You can sic the lab on him now, let the tech people match up fibers and hair and whatever the hell else you've got that will prove up the case and strap that sick bastard to the gurney. File that supplemental IR, Schroder, and let Miss Fairchild go."

He closed the door and leaned against it, light-headed with exhaustion, but feeling good in spite of it. No, he felt more than good; he felt wonderful, fantastic. He felt as if he had just scored the winning touchdown at the championship game, won an Olympic gold metal, slain the dragon. He felt like a goddamn hero.

But nobody was looking at him as if he were a hero; in fact, everybody except Lydia acted as if he had just told a joke at a wake. He saw Branson and Schroder exchange glances. "What's wrong? Is everybody deaf? I said I got—"

"We heard you," said Schroder.

"Don't everybody hug my neck at once," said Jenner.

Lydia glanced at Branson and Schroder in puzzlement. "I

165

will, Jenner," she said, rising and stumbling toward him to wrap her arms around him for the second time that night.

"Miss Fairchild, if you will refrain from choking Sergeant Jenner until he can give us a coherent explanation of his miraculous, or should I say impossible, feat, Sergeant Schroder and I would appreciate it."

Jenner thought Branson sounded pissed off. The best way to get a reaction from the lawyer was to put your hands on Lydia Fairchild. He'd never seen anybody with such a bad case of the hots, nor anybody so determined to deny it. He gave Lydia an extra squeeze and watched Branson's eyes start to burn.

Lydia's eyebrows flew together and she whirled around to lean over John Lloyd, her hands clutching the arms of his chair. Jenner leaned back against the door again to enjoy the fight.

"Damn you, John Lloyd," she said. "Jenner says he's found evidence to free me, and you and Sergeant Schroder act as if he stole your toys. Do you want me in jail?" She closed her eyes for a second and shuddered. "Have you ever been in jail? No, of course you haven't."

"On the contrary, Miss Fairchild, I frequently interview my clients in jail."

"That's different! When you finish your interview, you can walk out. Not me! The doors were locked!"

"Miss Fairchild, you are becoming hysterical."

"Not yet, but I'm working on it." She stopped, and Jenner waited for her to catch her breath. "Do you know what it feels like to be processed like a piece of Swiss cheese, to be told to stand here, stand there, when you haven't done any-thing wrong? It's awful. There's a sign hanging on the wall in the little room where prisoners are photographed and fin-gerprinted that sums up jail. It says this ain't Burger King; you can't have it your way."

There was silence until the lawyer broke it with an oath Jenner would have bet he wasn't even aware of saying. "Damn it, Lydia, I wanted you safe!" he roared, grasping her around the waist.

Her face turned white under the caked makeup and she started trembling. "You *knew* I was in jail. It was a deal between you and Schroder, wasn't it? That's why you weren't worried about the charges. You thought Schroder would drop them after you played your famous lawyer game. You put me through hell, you son of a bitch!''

Jenner winced at the sound of her slapping John Lloyd.

John Lloyd rubbed the side of his face where a hand-shaped welt was rising. ''As usual you are jumping to conclusions, Miss Fairchild,'' he said in a muffled voice as he spat blood into a lipstick- and eyeshadow-stained handkerchief. Jenner concluded that the blow had been hard enough to lacerate the inside of Branson's mouth.

John Lloyd folded his handkerchief and wiped his mouth. ''I was in Dallas while a madman was stalking you. I had no choice but to call Sergeant Schroder, tell him the circumstances surrounding the Butcher's call to me, and ask him to find you. I knew you would not go peaceably, so I instructed the sergeant to charge you with theft under fifty dollars, a class C misdemeanor which would of course be easily dealt with.''

''What theft?''

''When you left Canadian after our misunderstanding, you took the telephone from your apartment.''

''It was my telephone!''

John Lloyd raised one eyebrow. ''I told you the misdemeanor charge would be easily dealt with.''

''And what misunderstanding? You fired me!''

He shrugged. ''It seemed the best way to prevent you from doing exactly what you did, in fact, do: interfere in a situation about which you knew nothing. I understand you, Miss Fairchild, perhaps better than you understand yourself. You feel deeply about injustice, and you do not hesitate to—how shall I put it?—redress wrongs. I knew if I allowed you to stay in Canadian, you would have attempted to contact those prostitutes again. I foolishly believed that if I fired you and forced you to return to law school, distance and the distraction of studies would protect you. I was also arrogant enough to believe that you might be preoccupied with our personal relationship. I was wrong, it seems, in all of my assumptions.''

Branson glanced toward Schroder. ''I also had an ulterior motive in contacting Sergeant Schroder. If the Butcher were planning to harm you, I had to protect you, and that required being privy to the police investigation. As the attorney for a potential victim of the Butcher, I had a legal, although unorthodox, share in the investigation. I did not expect to find you charged with enough felony counts for ten people. I believed I had been betrayed, or rather that Sergeant Schroder was holding you hostage to insure that I would keep my word.''

Jenner had heard enough. ''You aren't the only one that's been jerked around and lied to, Lydia. Schroder handed me more bullshit tonight than you'd find in the average barnyard. No wonder you wouldn't close the case, Schroder. It was just like I figured. You knew you had the wrong person, but you didn't tell me because you didn't want anybody to know about your deal with Branson. And there was a deal, wasn't there? That's why you weren't scared Branson would scalp you. You want the Butcher caught, but the investigation is going nowhere, and then you get a phone call from John Lloyd Branson who has to be the smartest defense attorney in the state, maybe the country, and we all know a smart defense attorney is also a damn good investigator. You see your chance to get maybe the best investigator next to yourself on your team, so you and Branson cut a deal. According to Branson, charging Lydia with capital murder wasn't part of the deal, so why did you do it?''

The chief cleared his throat. ''You're skating on the edge of suspension, Sergeant, so your answer had better be good. We don't arrest innocent citizens, and we don't cut deals with civilians. So help me God, Schroder, I'll testify for the plaintiff in Miss Fairchild's civil-rights suit if you've screwed this department.''

''What is going on here?'' demanded Green. ''Why the hell doesn't anybody ever tell me anything. I'm the damn lieutenant. Schroder's just a sergeant.''

''Schroder's passed every exam up to and including the one for colonel, Green,'' said the chief. ''He's always refused promotion because he wants to stay on the street. Maybe he's been on the street too long. Maybe he's forgotten he's a cop and adopted some of the ways of the people he hunts.''

Lydia pushed herself away from Branson's chair to sit on the desk, a position that Jenner noticed gave her a height advantage over John Lloyd, who was still seated. "You know what I think, Chief Mostrovich? I think two arrogant bastards were playing games while women died. Furthermore, I'm a pawn in that game. I went to jail and I'm the lucky one. The other pawns are dead!"

Schroder stood away from the wall. If he was frightened by the chief's threat or Lydia's charge, he didn't show it. To Jenner, he looked like a mad bull stung by picadors but determined to kill the matador. "I hate murder, and I hate this kind of murder more than any other kind. I can understand killing for love or money or jealousy or because you hate somebody so damn much you snap. That's murder for reasons that any of us can have. Those are human reasons. When a murderer sits in the courtroom because he killed for one of those reasons, we can understand him. We don't approve, and we might think he ought to be hanged, but we recognize he's human. He's one of us. But the Butcher kills because he—or she—likes to see women die, then he gets a sexual kick out of mutilating their bodies. I won't go into details, but we can prove the sexual angle to the mutilation from autopsy findings. The Butcher isn't human. He's got a head and two arms and legs, but he's not human."

The detective wiped his forehead, the first time Jenner had ever seen him sweat. "When John Lloyd called me, I didn't think twice about maybe stretching department regulations or policy. Besides, I never read anywhere that we couldn't work with civilian consultants or defense attorneys or whoever the hell we wanted so long as they could further the investigations. So I said I'd pick up Miss Fairchild on a misdemeanor charge, just to get her off the Boulevard until he got here, and he'd agree to help with the investigation, no strings attached."

"Why didn't you just ask him for help?" asked Lydia. "Why did you both use me for a bargaining chip?"

"I did," answered Schroder. "I left a message on his answering machine tonight. He'll find it when he gets home. You ought to be fair to him, Miss Fairchild. I think he'd have sold his next ten clients down the river to get me to cooperate if that's what it cost him. He didn't know I'd let those same clients loose if that's what it cost me, and I didn't tell him. I don't get many chances to take advantage of John Lloyd Branson, so I took this one. But I didn't intend to make you part of the bargain. I'd have picked you up anyway. I just didn't see any reason to tell John Lloyd that. I figure you're one of the only human weaknesses he's got, and it would do him good to worry about you a little."

"I go to jail so you can humble John Lloyd?" asked Lydia bitterly.

Schroder shook his head. "No, John Lloyd didn't have anything to do with that. I didn't like seeing you in jail, Miss Fairchild, and I didn't like my bust. It looks good on paper, but it smells like an open sewer. You were on the Boulevard, you were the last person seen with Cowgirl, your driver's license was found by the body like you dropped it accidentally, you had blood all over you. I had to take you in just like I would've dropped on anybody else. Then things really started unraveling. You knew all the victims. They knew you and wouldn't be afraid of you. Cowgirl was the witness Jenner had been looking for, the one he believes saw something. Everything pointed to you."

"What about the phone call to John Lloyd?" asked Lydia. "Didn't you consider that at all?"

Schroder looked uncomfortable, another first in Jenner's opinion. Not even creeping underwear could make Schroder uncomfortable. "John Lloyd could've been lying about that. Maybe he knew you were the Butcher, maybe he was trying to protect you. I had to go with the evidence, Miss Fairchild, even if the evidence turned out wrong. I can always file that supplemental IR Jenner was talking about, but I can't bring a dead woman back to life."

"So you ignored your gut instinct, Schroder," said Jenner.

"No, my gut told me that I'd better arrest Lydia Fairchild. It's like I told Branson, I want justice for those women, and I'm the only one that can see they get it. And justice is a blind lady. She doesn't care if I like the suspect or not, doesn't care if that suspect's boss is a man I respect. That doesn't mean I like you, Branson. I've spent too many years on the other side of the fence from you. But I do respect you, and if anybody can prove I got the wrong coon up the tree, it's you."

Jenner looked at Branson. The attorney wore a brooding expression.

"Sergeant Schroder, I must apologize for my remarks about your using Lydia as a hostage. That is not true. We were both guilty of arrogance and of underestimating the Butcher. We both forgot that we are not the only ones involved in this investigation. Someone used Miss Fairchild as a pawn, but it was neither of us."

"And I believe in the Easter bunny," interrupted Lydia.

John Lloyd gestured impatiently. "If you please, Miss Fairchild, wait until I finish before deciding I am an unmitigated liar. To continue, the Butcher stepped in and moved the playing pieces around. He knows you, Sergeant, as well as I know Miss Fairchild. He knows what you will do in any given situation, and he set you up."

"You want to explain that?" asked Schroder, his face as expressive as the acoustical tile and about as attractive.

"Gladly, Sergeant. He knows what kinds of evidence you cannot ignore, such as a driver's license. However, when you do a background check on Miss Fairchild, you must exonerate her for the first two murders and by extension, the third, since all three are obviously committed by the same culprit."

John Lloyd tapped his cane on the floor. "So why did he bother salting the crime scene with evidence which is, in the last analysis, valueless? To manipulate me as well as you, Sergeant. In case the telephone call failed to arouse me, he framed Lydia, an action he knew would bring me into the middle of the case. He wanted another opponent."

"I guess that means the Butcher doesn't think I was a good enough opponent," said Schroder, lighting a cigarette with hands Jenner would swear shook a little. He looked at John Lloyd. "He's got us lined up on opposite sides of the board, Counselor."

Jenner flinched. "You make me sick, Schroder. All your talk about lining up worthy opponents and evidence and gut instinct. All it amounts to is Branson's right; you did exactly what the Butcher wanted by arresting Lydia. He's running this investigation, not you, and you're letting him get away with it. If you hadn't thrown me in that cell with Jo-Jo Jefferson, you and Branson would be playing mind games about does the Butcher mean this or does he mean that, and Lydia would be in jail till hell freezes over. Oh, you'd figure out she wasn't guilty when the Butcher chopped up another hooker, but by then it would be too late both for the hooker and Lydia. What really scares me is that if he's smart enough to jerk you and Branson by your chains, just maybe he might have been smart enough to get away with framing Lydia.''

John Lloyd stirred, gingerly touching the side of his face where Lydia slapped him. His cheek was still an angry red and Jenner suspected he'd have a hell of a bruise. "I assume there is a connection between Jo-Jo Jefferson and the evidence you said you found," said the lawyer. "Something about the invitations, I believe. Please elucidate, Sergeant Jenner, and forgive the earlier interruptions.''

"Somebody slipped the invitations to the hookers while they were drinking in the Bimbo Bar on Wednesday nights. Lydia Fairchild has never been in the Bimbo Bar until tonight. We can prove that because none of the regulars know her, and she's not exactly the type you'd miss seeing. But there is one man who's always in the Bimbo, one man who's down on whores as the Butcher's letter says.''

He saw John Lloyd jerk but hurried on before the long-winded lawyer could interrupt. "That one man left the Bimbo Bar tonight before Lydia did. In fact, she was looking for him when she ran into Jo-Jo. That man killed Cowgirl and dropped Miss Fairchild's driver's license by the body to implicate her because he was all worked up at Lydia. What I'm saying is that Cowgirl's death was sort of an impromptu thing. He didn't plan it like he did the others because Cowgirl didn't get an invitation on Wednesday night. It was coincidence that the victim was Cowgirl, and it was coincidence that Lydia was the last person to see her alive.''

"The Butcher sent you a letter?" John Lloyd asked Schroder.

"Yeah," answered the detective, still looking at Jenner.

"You want to compare handwriting, Schroder?" asked Jenner impatiently. "Let's go next door to the other interrogation room, and you can ask the Butcher to write you a note. I ordered him picked up before I came in here.''

"Who is it, Jenner?" asked Lydia, the only one who seemed to be excited about his catching the Butcher. Of course, he guessed she had the most at stake. It was her ass at risk.

"It's the Preacher, of course. Who else in the Bimbo is a half-bubble off level when it comes to hookers?"

"Shall we go talk to the gentleman?" asked John Lloyd, picking up his cane and offering to assist Lydia off the desk. Jenner noticed she jerked away to avoid touching him. "I will suspend agreement with your explanation of the Butcher's motives until later, but I will certainly take advantage of any evidence you have found if it will convince Sergeant Schroder to release Miss Fairchild. Once she is safe in Canadian, then I will be free to concentrate my attentions on the Butcher."

Just like Branson to disagree with anybody's theory but his own, thought Jenner. He had to be the most arrogant bastard on two legs.

"Just a minute," said Chief Mostrovich, grabbing John Lloyd Branson's sleeve. "Your standing in this investigation is quasi-legal, and with the Butcher caught, you can retire as a rent-a-cop."

John Lloyd darted a glance toward Schroder then back to the chief. Jenner thought he saw fear surface in the lawyer's eyes and felt uncertain of his own interpretation.

The lawyer folded his hands over the head of his cane. "Although I would certainly win any lawsuit against Sergeant Schroder and this police department, I do not wish to jeopardize Miss Fairchild's future by actually filing that suit. I will do so, however, if I am forced off this investigation. I will allow myself to be humiliated, to be shamed, to be mocked, if that's what is required to save Miss Fairchild, but I will not be defeated."

Lydia stepped in front of him and placed her fingers over his mouth. "Please no, John Lloyd. Don't beg."

For a moment Jenner thought the attorney planned to kiss Lydia's fingers, but he lifted her hand away from his mouth and held it between his own. Jenner didn't think he remembered ever seeing two people display so much caring in such a simple gesture. He felt his eyes burn and blinked. He didn't think heroes cried at tender scenes.

"I am a formidable opponent, Chief Mostrovich," continued John Lloyd. "Sergeant Schroder knows it, the Butcher knows it. Have you forgotten it?"

Jenner didn't know what Branson was referring to with his question, but evidently the chief did, because he visibly relaxed when Schroder interrupted. "Preacher ain't the Butcher," stated Schroder, exhaling a cloud of smoke. "And Jenner's full of crap. Cowgirl's murder was planned. We found the Butcher's invitation clutched in her hand, all crumpled up like she closed her fist on it right at the moment of death. I figure the only coincidence was the fact the victim was Cowgirl."

Jenner stared at Schroder as he tried to assimilate what he'd just heard and redesign his theory to fit the facts and still exonerate Lydia. "Then Preacher had the invitation in his pocket and when he decided to murder, he had it handy."

Schroder frowned. "You're not thinking, Jenner. Another reconstruction would be that Miss Fairchild had it in her purse and gave it to Cowgirl. She was with Cowgirl at the time of the murder according to our witnesses: Benny the green hair and the screaming prostitute who's really a cop. While Cowgirl was reading the invitation, Miss Fairchild strangled her."

"Strangled?" gasped Lydia.

"He always strangles the women before he mutilates them. Strangulation is always found in sex crimes, that and stabbing. With the Butcher, we got both," explained Schroder. "Of course, one thing in your favor is you're a woman. Most serial killers aren't women, don't have the stomach for it, I guess. It's sort of a male-dominated occupation."

"That's a sexist remark," said Lydia.

John Lloyd closed his eyes for a second. "Miss Fairchild, this is not the subject over which to debate equal rights."

"I should have said women don't lack whatever it is men lack that turns them into serial killers. Or at least, most women don't. There have been a few exceptions. But to get back to what I was saying, Miss Fairchild didn't know the invitations were always passed out in the Bimbo Bar on

Wednesday nights, because we didn't know that ourselves until tonight."

"Wait a minute, Schroder, that sounds like two Butchers," said Green.

Schroder's face had a stunned expression as if someone had just hit him between the eyes. Jenner decided Green wasn't so bad after all. Anybody who could catch Schroder with his deductions down might even be worth liking. Maybe.

"Or one Butcher who is unaware his victims had received invitations and the exact wording of those invitations until a facsimile was published in the paper," said John Lloyd. "A Butcher who is unaware of how and from whom each victim received her invitation and so is tripped up by his own improvisation and a loose-mouthed pimp. To decide between the two possibilities, we shall have to question our minister of the gospel who frequents the habitats of sinners."

He turned to the chief. "Do I continue with your blessing or without it?"

The chief shrugged in defeat. "I've got a police department to run. I can't be peering over my sergeant's shoulders. I'll have to trust him to know how to run an investigation." He clapped John Lloyd's shoulder. "Besides, I'm not about to make John Lloyd Branson beg. You'd never forget it, and that damn brother-in-law of mine might need help again."

The chief had hardly closed the door behind him when John Lloyd turned to Schroder. "I shall want to see that letter as well as the autopsy protocols as soon as we dispose of this matter of the invitations."

Jenner felt slighted. More than that, he felt tired of these two huge egos. "Maybe you two think those invitations are just so much garbage because they don't fit your fancy theories, but I happen to think they are important. They sure as hell better be since I had to spend an hour breathing the same air as that bastard, Jo-Jo Jefferson."

John Lloyd looked surprised. "Sergeant, it is possible that your information about those invitations is the single most vital piece of evidence we have. It is the first of two errors the Butcher has made and provides us with a glimpse of his thought processes."

"What is his other error?" asked Jenner curiously.

John Lloyd glanced down at Lydia and hesitated. "He challenged me," he said finally.

Jenner had a feeling the lawyer started to say something else.

The first person Jenner saw when he entered the interrogation room where Preacher waited was Theodore. "What the hell are you doing here?" he blurted.

The old man crossed his legs and folded his hands over his knee. "It's Larry. Am I right in assuming you are a policeman?"

"Yeah, Sergeant Larry Jenner, and I'm a police officer. We stopped saying policeman when women joined the force. Now, answer my question: What are you doing here?"

"You arrested Preacher. I chose to accompany him. You see, my friend becomes easily agitated, and I thought I would be a calming influence. Otherwise, you simply will not get any information out of him other than that of a theological nature."

"Bullshit," said Schroder, crowding in behind Jenner. "If you're not a lawyer, get the hell out."

"I'm not a lawyer, but Preacher does little or nothing without my knowledge. In many ways he cannot cope with our technological society, and I help him. In return, he watches over me when I'm drunk, which is most of the time. You might say we are mutually dependent."

"Did you help him kill those hookers?" asked Green, pushing around Schroder to stand over the old man.

"Whores, sluts, wanton women—"

"Now, now, Preacher," said Theodore. "This is not the time to play word games." He looked up at Jenner and Schroder. "I don't believe you've introduced your friends, Larry. I know such formalities aren't common anymore, but I'm old-fashioned."

"Oh, shit," said Green.

Theodore's hands were bloodless from being clasped together so tightly, but there remained a trace of pathetic pride in the old man's request. He was a drunk, but he had a self-acceptance about it that most drunks lacked. He would be dignified lying in the gutter.

Jenner capitulated. "Theodore, may I introduce Sergeant Ed Schroder, Lieutenant Roger Green, and the tall guy behind me is John Lloyd Branson and his legal clerk, Lydia Fairchild. You might know her better as Blondie. Everybody, this is Theodore, and I'm sorry, but I don't know your last name."

Theodore didn't answer, and Jenner took a step forward. The old man looked as if he were suffering a stroke. There was a slackness about his features as if something inside had suddenly deflated, a tremor to the clasped hands, and his color had gone gray.

"Theodore," said Jenner. "You feeling okay?"

The old man finally moved, taking a worn handkerchief from his pocket and patting his forehead, which had suddenly broken out in a greasy sheen of sweat. "I'm fine, Larry. Just a trifle tired. You asked me my name, I believe. It is unimportant, and best left unsaid."

"You are Preacher's spokesperson, Professor?" asked John Lloyd.

Jenner turned to stare at the lawyer. He looked as if he had sustained a shock of his own. "Why did you call him professor? Do you know Theodore?"

"He does," answered the old man. "He was once my student—in a manner of speaking. I believe I mentioned tonight that I was once a professor of classical literature, although he had a greater fondness for the novels of Charles Dickens than in the authors offered in my course. John Lloyd, are you well?"

Jenner saw John Lloyd's mouth twist in what on any other man would be an expression of hatred. "Our former relationship does not give you leave to ask personal questions."

Theodore's eyes dropped to focus on his folded hands but not before Jenner saw an expression of what might have been shame and resentment. Whatever conflict Theodore and Branson shared, it was still active and still virulent.

"John Lloyd," said Lydia, blushing in what Jenner decided was embarrassment.

Theodore's head came up at the sound of Lydia's voice. "My dear, although I don't have the prejudice against prostitutes that Preacher has, I am glad that you aren't one. The young ladies' souls die so young and so quickly in that profession.'' Jenner saw the old man's glance rest momentarily on Lydia's hand, still safely enfolded by John Lloyd's larger one. ''You work for John Lloyd, I believe Larry said?'' he asked.

Lydia nodded. ''I'm his clerk. I'll be his partner when I graduate from law school.''

''Why did you let her on the Boulevard?'' Theodore spat the words at John Lloyd with calculated vehemence.

''It was her choice,'' answered John Lloyd. ''She is not mine to control.''

''He had me arrested when he discovered where I was,'' blurted out Lydia. ''He thought it was the only way to protect me.''

''Do not defend me to him!'' snarled John Lloyd.

''To protect or to free?'' The old man sank back in the chair. ''Choices,'' he murmured. ''Not so easy as the young might think, are they, John Lloyd? Are you angry because he chose arrest as a means to protect you, Lydia?''

Lydia looked uncertainly at John Lloyd. ''I think he did the only thing he could do under the circumstances. If things didn't turn out the way he planned, he still made his choice for the right reasons.''

''I see.'' He straightened his shoulders, shrugging aside whatever conflict he and John Lloyd had, and looked at Jenner. ''I presume that this young lady is involved in your search for the Butcher. Might I ask how?''

John Lloyd glowered at the old man, and Jenner quickly answered before the two men could square off for another altercation. ''She's been arrested on a charge of capital murder, Theodore. Do you know what that means?''

''I'm not senile, Larry,'' answered the old man.

''Sorry, I didn't think you were. Anyway, her driver's license was found by the latest victim, and she doesn't have much of an alibi. Theodore, we know the invitations were passed to the other victims on Wednesday nights in the Bimbo. We have to know about those invitations. Did Preacher make them and give them to the girls? Did he murder them, Theodore?''

''Thou shalt not kill,'' said Preacher.

''Will information about the invitations help Lydia?''

"Yes!" interjected John Lloyd impatiently.

Theodore sighed. "We really must confess our little transgressions, Preacher. If you remember, I told you at the time that the notion was foolish, but you would go on with it. Now this young lady is in trouble, and I must help her because it's my expiation. You understand expiation, don't you, Preacher?"

"She's not a whore?" asked Preacher suspiciously, looking at Lydia's short skirt.

"No, Preacher," answered Jenner. "She was trying to help the girls."

"I was, too," said Preacher. "I thought those invitations would frighten them into changing their ways. I slipped them into their purses when they weren't looking."

"Why didn't you just give the invitations to the women?" asked Lydia. "Why do it secretly?"

"Because they wouldn't have paid no never mind of them if they knew they came from me. They laughed at me. I figured if those whores didn't know who was sending these invitations, they'd think more of them."

Jenner felt a stab of pity for both Preacher and the women. He was probably the only man they felt safe baiting because he was the only man who was afraid of them.

"Preacher only handed out two," said Theodore. "Always on Wednesday night because that's prayer meeting night in most fundamental churches. But after Louis Bryant's column appeared and we discovered that both girls had been murdered, I refused to make any more invitations for Preacher."

"I guess he started making his own," said Green sarcastically. "Because one of them damn sure turned up on Cowgirl's body."

Theodore wiped his forehead again. "Lieutenant Green, Preacher is not only illiterate, but dyslexic. Words are a jumble to him. He could no more make up one of those invitations than I could give up drink."

CHAPTER
TWENTY-TWO

LYDIA TUCKED JOHN LLOYD'S SHIRT INTO THE WAISTBAND of her new Levi's and felt clean and respectable for the first time in twenty-four hours. John Lloyd had dispatched Mrs. Dinwittie to the local ladies' dress shop for new clothes, but both evidently had underestimated her bust size because the sweater Mrs. Dinwittie bought had startled an unheard of "Good God" from John Lloyd. But then John Lloyd had done and said a good many startling things since he first appeared outside that barred door in the Amarillo jail.

She wandered into John Lloyd's study, a large room with a rolltop desk only slightly smaller than the one in his office, a couch upholstered in soft brown leather, a chair similarly upholstered with a matching hassock, and three walls of bookcases. The fourth wall had a door on one end and a sideboard on the other. Two decanters, both filled with seven-year-old Kentucky Bourbon, stood on the sideboard beside glasses that Lydia suspected were Waterford crystal.

She splashed two fingers of Bourbon into a glass and sat down on the hassock, noticing as she did so that John Lloyd was in his stocking feet. She had supposed John Lloyd had feet, most people did, but she never expected to see them, even in socks. He had a long, narrow, aristocratic foot, very attractive for a foot. And warm. She knew that because her hip was touching his feet.

"Am I missing any toes, Miss Fairchild?" His voice was a soft drawl, a sign he was relaxed. He looked relaxed, sprawled back in the leather chair with his feet resting on the hassock and reading a book. She didn't know he knew how to sprawl.

She smiled at him. "No, but you seem to be missing your coat, vest, and tie. And dare I mention that your shirt collar is unbuttoned? Very improper when a lady is present."

"I think you are a bad influence on me, Miss Fairchild." He returned her smile and she suddenly felt tears burning her eyes. "What is wrong, Lydia?" he asked, dropping his book on the floor.

She shook her head. "Nothing, except I just realized how long it's been since you smiled at me."

He looked disconcerted for a moment, then she watched his face lose all expression as though he wiped it clean. "I am not by nature a jovial person, Miss Fairchild. Does that disturb you?"

"Stop it, John Lloyd! Can't you act like a normal man for just a few hours, or however long we have before Schroder gets here with whatever files and so forth you wanted? Can't you show a little kindness instead of that damnable politeness you always wear?"

He raised one eyebrow as if in surprise, but she noticed his eyes were guarded. "Miss Fairchild, I brought you to my home, fed you, clothed you, partially from my own wardrobe, smothered you with what I believed was kindness. What else do you want?"

"I want you!"

He jerked his feet off the hassock and leaned over, resting his elbows on his thighs and clasping his hands together as if he didn't know what else to do with them. "Lydia," he began.

Lydia took a large swallow of her drink and coughed to give herself time to recover her equilibrium since she couldn't recover her words. She cleared her throat. "Don't misunderstand me, John Lloyd. I'm not inviting you to throw me on your Persian carpet and make love to me. Just please touch me. I've already had hysterics in the shower, so I won't embarrass you with any kind of emotional outburst; but I feel as though I'm shattered and I need you to hold the pieces together until I can find some kind of—of glue.''

He reached over and grasped her around the waist, dragging her into his lap so quickly she spilled two fingers of expensive seven-year-old Kentucky Bourbon on his Persian rug. ''That never happens in my romance novels,'' she said, looking at her empty glass, then at the damp spot on the rug.

He plucked the glass out of her hand and placed it on the floor beside the chair. ''Innocent young ladies in your romance novels don't fall over dead bodies, Lydia.''

She tilted her head to look up at him. His eyes were sympathetic, warm, and very wary. ''I've really upset you, haven't I, John Lloyd? You just used a contraction, and you've called me Lydia three times in the past five minutes.''

He pressed her head against his shoulder and stroked her hair. ''In the four months since you first knocked on my office door, I have sustained a number of shocks and upsets and have managed to recover, bruised but unbowed. I doubt your behavior on this occasion will have any permanent effect on my composure.''

It was the complacent tone of his voice that did it, she decided afterward. That and his proximity. He was warm and alive and smelled of bay rum and some underlying man-scent uniquely his. She was very partial to bay rum. It always evoked images of sand and sea and disreputable buccaneers. She was very partial to buccaneers, too. The word evoked images of romantic abductions on the high seas. She wondered if John Lloyd's conniving at having her thrown in jail counted as an abduction. Probably not; that would be pushing suspension of disbelief too far. But it did indicate a breach in his precious composure. She planned to destroy it altogether as a lesson in humility.

Actually, she thought as she looped her arms around his neck and laced her fingers together behind his head, she was lying to herself. What she was about to do had nothing to do with humility. ''John Lloyd, I'm going to kiss you,'' she said in a voice that sounded too thin, too high, too quivery, to be her own.

He lifted a strand of her hair and rubbed it between his fingers before letting it float back to her shoulders. "I rather thought that was your intention. The death grip on the back of my head is a technique I recognized from our previous engagement."

"I want to."

He stroked his hand down her hair, over her shoulder, and down to rest on her waist. "I assumed you did. You seldom do anything you don't wish to do."

"I need to."

He stroked her waist. "I suppose there is an element of need involved."

"I need to prove I'm alive."

His hand stroked around to the small of her back, flattened, and lifted, shifting her slightly so she lay partially on her side. "You are a most unsatisfactory client, Lydia. You never know when to remain silent."

"What?"

"It is very difficult to kiss you when you are talking. I feel as if I am aiming for a moving target."

"What?"

"It is your intention to kiss me, is it not? Since that activity is most rewarding when both parties participate, I intend to kiss you, also. Our decision is unwise, unprofessional, dangerously reckless, and one we shall undoubtedly both regret, but it is necessary."

"Why?" she asked. If this were a dream, it beat the hell out of sea and sand and buccaneers.

"Thanksgiving," he whispered. "That you are alive."

Even his whisper had a drawl was Lydia's last coherent thought for several minutes.

When he ended the kiss, he pressed her head back against his shoulder. She noticed with satisfaction that his breathing was at least affected this time. Laying her hand against his chest, she heard a definite acceleration in his heartbeat. That was only fair; her own vital signs were off the chart.

"Is your composure intact, John Lloyd?"

"You underestimate your effect," he said wryly. "However, my composure is not the issue. Yours is, Miss Fairchild."

"Lydia," she said, her voice muffled against his shoulder.

She felt his chest rise and fall as he took a deep breath and exhaled slowly. "Lydia," he repeated after her in the tone an adult uses when humoring a child.

"That's better," she said in exactly the same tone.

Other than a slight tremor in the hand pressing against her cheek, he didn't acknowledge her mockery. "It is time," he said softly.

She lifted her head to stare at him. "For what?"

"Cowgirl."

She felt the tremors start in her legs first, then her hands, then the rest of her body until she was shaking uncontrollably. "Oh, God, no!"

"Yes," he said, stroking her shoulders and back. "You have buried your feelings about her murder. Did you think I would not notice? Did you think I would believe a young woman with no experience, or very little anyway, with violent death could so casually accept it as you apparently have done? You have scarcely mentioned her name, a most normal reaction to a traumatic experience, but a very dangerous one. Tell me about it, Lydia. Sharing it is the glue you spoke of."

"If I tell you about it, can I forget it?" she asked, curling her body closer to his.

"No, but you will be able to grieve, both for her and yourself."

"Why for myself? I hate people who indulge in self-pity."

He sighed. "I warned you that the Boulevard leaves no one unchanged. A part of you died last night, an innocence, a belief in the essential goodness of humanity. You proved that by your outburst at Sergeant Schroder and myself. You assumed we would play games with your life, that I would barter you in exchange for an opportunity to match wits with a monster."

"Maybe I overreacted, but not because I lost my belief in man's goodness. Be honest, John Lloyd. Sometimes you aren't very straightforward. In fact, you can be downright devious. And arrogant."

"I am not perfect," he admitted, and placed his hand over her mouth when she tried to speak. "I can do without your flippant agreement for the moment, Lydia. I, too, have a painful experience to share. I am fond of you."

She pulled his hand away. "I don't know why that should be so painful to admit. I'm not exactly a hag, you know. I'm intelligent, well educated, reasonably attractive, if you like tall women, I don't slurp my soup or use poor grammar."

"Too fond," he continued, ignoring her outburst. "To use you for any such egotistical purpose as you accused me of, and too fond to serve as your defense against your own guilt feelings."

"W-what?" she stammered.

His eyes seemed to pierce her, to see more than she wanted to reveal. "Part of your refusal to face Cowgirl's death is because you feel responsible."

She covered her eyes as if that could prevent her from seeing what she'd been hiding from herself since the moment she touched Cowgirl's still warm leg. "Oh, God, John Lloyd, he wanted me. He wanted to kill me. That's why I felt that cold spot in the middle of my back. He was stalking me all night, but he never caught me alone in the dark so he killed Cowgirl instead. If I had listened to you, Cowgirl would still be alive. She was killed because she was with me."

He pulled her hands away from her eyes. "Look at me, Lydia. Don't hide. You were not his intended victim. Not last night anyway, if my theory is correct."

"What theory?"

"Later, my dear, when Sergeant Schroder arrives with the files and that letter from the Butcher. For now, just believe that he didn't choose Cowgirl in your place. He had already decided to kill. If the times recorded in the incident reports are remotely accurate, you were with Cowgirl at approximately one in the morning. He had to kill his second victim between one and a quarter to two."

"Second victim! What are you talking about? Cowgirl was his only victim."

"If she was, then my theory is incorrect, and my chances of trapping the Butcher are infinitesimal. To continue, your other self-accusation, that Cowgirl would not have died if she had not been with you, might be true. I am not certain because I am postulating from insufficient facts."

"Oh, God, I wish I had gone with Cindy Spencer. I couldn't have hurt anybody picketing the brewery."

"Does Miss Spencer also advocate saving the whales?"

"What's wrong with that?" demanded Lydia.

"Nothing, it is an admirable and necessary undertaking, but picketing breweries and saving whales are one step removed from the kind of personal involvement required to face another human being in need. You will always choose human contact over the impersonal cause, Lydia. You thrive on touching and giving. But you must learn to bear the consequences of your choices."

"Even if someone dies?"

"Even then. Remember, Cowgirl made her own choices."

"I suppose she walked up to the Butcher and told him she'd decided to die and would he like to sharpen his knife and do the job for her."

"No, but sometime in her past Cowgirl made that first choice to embrace prostitution or, more likely, to take that first drug trip. That is almost always how such women begin. Cowgirl was on the Boulevard at risk as a result of her own actions. Forgive yourself, my dear; her death was not your fault. She may even have died at peace knowing that at least one person cared."

"She was so white, John Lloyd, everywhere there wasn't blood. And her wig—did you know she wore a wig?—her wig was pulled halfway off her head, and I thought how embarrassed she would be to be found with her wig all askew. Isn't that stupid? Some monster disemboweled her, and all I could think of was how much a woman hates to be caught with her hair in a mess. Cowgirl had dignity, John Lloyd, when she was alive, and he left her with no dignity at all."

"I doubt he gives much thought to his victim's dignity," said John Lloyd gently. "Is the wig all you noticed about Cowgirl that was different from your memory of her alive?"

"This scarf was tied around her neck, but she wasn't wearing a scarf when I saw her and her torso was open and red, and she lay in pools of blood."

"What color was the scarf, Lydia?"

"What?" asked Lydia, her mind trying to assimilate the question.

John Lloyd repeated the question.

Lydia closed her eyes, and Cowgirl's pathetic image immediately appeared. She gagged and opened her eyes. "Red, I think, but I don't remember. I only saw her for a second when Jenner shone his flashlight on her. Why do you want to know?"

"Never mind," he said, covering her hand, which rested on his chest. "I will know when I see the crime-scene photos. Go on, please."

She rested her head against his shoulder. "That's all, just that same scene playing over and over again in my head as if someone had spliced all the death scenes in a horror movie together to make one long film."

She closed her eyes and cried herself to sleep in his arms.

She awoke abruptly to find herself lying tucked under a comforter on a massive antique fourposter bed. Must be John Lloyd's bedroom, she thought as she sat up and yawned. If it's antique, it's John Lloyd.

She slipped on her penny loafers, courtesy of Mrs. Dinwittie, who managed to get the size right. Perhaps she thought feet were more important than chests. The other alternative was that the secretary knew exactly what she was doing when she bought Lydia that too-small sweater and knew exactly what John Lloyd's reaction would be. There were all kinds of psychological overtones and undertones and halftones to a woman wearing a man's shirt. Brought out all the macho caveman tendencies—such as dragging the female into his lap and kissing her. Lydia decided that under the right circumstances, and with a little direction, Mrs. Dinwittie had real possibilities as an aide de camp—if Lydia ever planned a seduction campaign against John Lloyd.

Standing up and brushing the wrinkles out of her shirt, she glanced out the window and shuddered. The sun had set and shadows cast by a huge cottonwood slanted across the front lawn and undulated with each movement of the tree's branches in the gusty wind, and she thought how like crouching running figures the shadows were. Quickly she closed the drapes and leaned against the window frame, her fists clenched and resting against the velvet-flocked wallpapered wall. She wiped her tears on her shirtsleeve—actually John Lloyd's shirtsleeve—and gritted her teeth. She was not, *was not*, going to be afraid of the dark.

The hell she wasn't, she thought as she whirled around and rushed out of the room, down the hall, flicking on light switches as she ran, and into John Lloyd's study.

Five pairs of eyes looked up at her as she skidded through the door. "Is there a fire, Miss Fairchild?" asked John Lloyd, seated on the edge of his leather chair, a stack of files on the hassock in front of him.

Lydia glanced around the room. Crouched on one end of the sofa like a moth-eaten bear, Schroder twitched his lips in her direction, then switched his attention back to John Lloyd, while Lieutenant Green, seated next to the detective, looked at her as if he couldn't believe this well-scrubbed woman in Levi's and a man's shirt was the same slatternly waif he'd seen a few hours earlier. Jenner, slouched at the sofa's far end, his eyes sunken and blue-rimmed with exhaustion and dressed in his undercover clothes with wig and earrings, smiled and lifted a hand in a halfhearted salute. Lydia thought he looked like a wino on the downside of a hangover.

The room's other occupant sat at John Lloyd's desk, his legs stretched out and crossed at the ankles. Lydia blinked in shock. "You're that damn reporter who took my picture!"

Louis Bryant pushed up the brim of a gimme hat and smiled, his luminous blue eyes crinkling. "I'm sorry about that, Miss Fairchild, but how was I to know John Lloyd Branson's clerk would show up at the Bimbo Bar. It's not the sort of place you expect to meet a respectable woman."

"I don't like that word," said Lydia, irritated with the reporter for some reason she couldn't quite pinpoint. Maybe because she couldn't sense what he was really thinking.

"What word?"

"Respectable. Its connotation is that not all women, as women, are worthy of respect. Use reputable instead. God knows, not everybody is reputable."

"If we may discuss your feminist opinions another time, Miss Fairchild," said John Lloyd, gazing at her from beneath half-closed lids. "These gentlemen and I have a more urgent matter demanding our attention."

"What's more urgent than equal rights?" asked Lydia, seeking and not finding any trace of the tender man who'd held her earlier. This John Lloyd had his formal mask back in place and looked as if the most romantic thing he'd ever done was stroke the binding of a law book.

"Keeping women alive long enough to claim their rights," he said bluntly. "Sit down, Miss Fairchild. I find your looming over me like an omen of outraged womanhood distracting."

He sounded both irritated and exasperated; in other words, perfectly normal. She mentally canceled her plans for a seduction campaign. She'd rather seduce Schroder.

"I certainly don't want to distract you," she said, sauntering across the room to squeeze in beside him on the roomy leather chair. "Or upset your composure." She peered at him from under her lashes—in her best romantic-novel style.

He thrust a file at her. "Read this—if you can open your eyes sufficiently to see the print."

She grabbed it, feeling her own composure crack a little. "What is it?"

"The Butcher's letter."

"Do we have to sit here while she reads everything, too?" demanded Green. Lydia wanted to giggle. One didn't sit on that sofa; one sank into it, so Green's knees were almost parallel to his nose and his paunch rested on his thighs. "We've been picking our noses for an hour while you sit there stiff as a pair of starched jockey shorts reading every word of every damn IR, every autopsy protocol, every evidence log, and, for all I know, the manufacturer's label on the file folders."

John Lloyd leaned back and folded his hands over his flat belly. "I want a woman's opinion of the letter. Miss Fairchild, your analysis, please."

"Ego," said Lydia slowly, closing the file and laying it back on the hassock. "An ego that perverts every desire, every emotion, for its own amusement and self gratification. I don't think it—or he—is *down on whores* as he claims he is because they are, well, whores. Any woman would do, but prostitutes are better because they are more vulnerable, and because they are symbols of sexual desire of a sort."

"These are sex crimes," said Schroder, flicking ashes in one of John Lloyd's Waterford crystal glasses. "We agree on that much. But he gets his kicks from killing them."

"Of course he received sexual satisfaction from them, but it was a twisted form of masturbation. These women, any women, mean no more to him than a pornographic photo means to a normal male. They are merely a means to ejaculation. His detachment doesn't allow him to feel anything else."

She hesitated, feeling very uncomfortable. Equal rights simply didn't cover every eventuality such as discussing masturbation with a room full of males. She felt as if she'd been caught peeking in a men's locker room. She swallowed and continued, "He probably hates his mother, too, or at least all the literature in the field suggests that men who commit sexual crimes do, but then hating one's mother is perversion of a normal desire to love one's mother. Everything about him is reversed. He's like a photographic negative of a normal male. Even this letter proves a reversal or perversion of the norm. When a normal person does something wrong, he tries to hide it. But the Butcher is challenging you to catch him. He's perverting a police investigation into a game."

"Miss Fairchild, your intellectual prowess occasionally awes me," said John Lloyd, sitting up straight and squeezing her shoulder.

"I'm glad something about me does," she said dryly.

"So what's Miss Fairchild's analysis got to do with catching the Butcher?" asked Green. "All this talk of symbols and perversions and reversions doesn't get us any closer to laying our hands on the son of a bitch."

"It is difficult to catch a killer one does not understand, Lieutenant. And it would be impossible to understand this killer without Miss Fairchild's very astute analysis. To take this one point at a time, we will begin with games. Now that I have read the IR's and, more importantly, the autopsy protocols, I know which game the Butcher is playing. I, however, do not play games. You are withholding information, Sergeant Schroder. I want it."

Schroder looked startled, then resigned. "I don't know

how you guessed that, but Miss Fairchild will have to leave before I show you anything else.''

"Bullshit, Schroder!" exclaimed Jenner. "You dismissed charges against Lydia last night."

Schroder spread his hands apart in a gesture of helplessness, a gesture Lydia suspected he didn't make any more often than John Lloyd—which meant never. "Look at it from my point of view, Branson. You're her alibi for the first murder, and you ain't exactly unbiased. I got people checking on her alibi for the second murder, but we haven't been able to rule her out. She could have caught a plane from Dallas and been here in an hour, and she was damn sure on the Boulevard last night. She's the only person we can tie to any of the crimes with any kind of evidence at all. I don't think she's the Butcher, but Jesus Christ, what if I'm wrong. And she sure didn't help herself any by talking about reversals. We think the Butcher's a man, but what if he's a woman? What if Miss Fairchild was analyzing herself?''

He lit a cigarette from the butt of another. "Can I take a chance? Can you take a chance, Branson?''

"But I'm normal!" protested Lydia. "I'm heterosexual, and I'm certainly not detached when I'm, uh, engaged in sexual activities. What is it going to take to convince you, a videotape?''

"I believe Miss Fairchild means she prefers mutual participation," drawled John Lloyd.

"I'll speak for myself, thank you," snapped Lydia, catching the scent of his bay rum and thinking of another activity she'd like to participate in with John Lloyd: a fistfight.

"Speaking for yourself has already landed you in jail, Miss Fairchild, as well as in other interesting predicaments.''

"Are you referring to any particular predicament as being more interesting than another, Mr. Branson?'' she asked sweetly.

John Lloyd abruptly changed the subject. "If you are so uncertain of Miss Fairchild's innocence, Sergeant, why did you release her?''

Schroder rubbed his hand over his thinning hair. "Because we didn't discover the other body until after I signed the jail release.''

Lydia shrank back against John Lloyd.

"That woman died about the time you jumped out of that motel window and disappeared, Miss Fairchild," continued Schroder reluctantly.

"You said there would be another body, John Lloyd!" cried Lydia, feeling herself back in her nightmare again. "You said so this afternoon."

"How the hell did you know, Branson?" asked Green. "You been helping the little Butcheress?"

"Quiet!" commanded John Lloyd, circling Lydia's waist with his arm and pulling her tightly against his side. "I have heard enough aspersions against Miss Fairchild. You will speak civilly to her and about her."

"Or I'll deck you," said Jenner, staggering to his feet.

"Thank you, Sergeant Jenner," said John Lloyd. "But violence will not be necessary. I knew there was another victim, killed between midnight and twelve forty-five A.M. because I know who the Butcher is, or to be more accurate, whom he is masquerading as."

"Who?" asked four voices in unison.

"I also know that Mr. Bryant has received, or will receive, a postcard from the man who calls himself the Butcher predicting the two murders. I believe it refers to the crimes as a double event. Am I correct, Mr. Bryant?"

Lydia twisted around to see Bryant. Strange, but she had forgotten he was in the room.

"Right on the money," said Bryant with a relaxed smile.

Lydia knew why she had forgotten the reporter. She didn't like him.

"To be historically accurate, the postcard should have been postmarked today. However, I am assuming our Butcher could not resist mailing it before eleven last night so it would bear yesterday's postmark, technically the day before the murders. Our murderer cannot help bragging. The ego Miss Fairchild mentioned. Am I correct in my assumption, Mr. Bryant?"

"Absolutely," said Bryant.

"How do you know all this, Branson?" asked Schroder.

"Because the mood I'm in, I'm ready to throw everybody in jail except myself, and I ain't too sure about me."

"I haven't heard His Highness give us an alibi, either," said Green.

"I was in Dallas in the presence of several police officers at the time of both murders, but that is unimportant," said John Lloyd. "What is important is that the Butcher plans one more murder, this one so foul that even a hardened investigator such as yourself, Sergeant Schroder, will be sickened. He will kill in a frenzy like nothing you can imagine, like nothing we have seen in a hundred years, excepting perhaps that Nazi madman's extermination camps."

"Goddamn it, Branson, who's the Butcher?" yelled Schroder.

"Jack the Ripper."

CHAPTER
TWENTY-THREE

JENNER DECIDED THAT IF HAIR COULD STAND STRAIGHT UP, his would.

Jack the Ripper!

The fiend who appeared suddenly in the Whitechapel section of London in 1888, murdered and mutilated five women, and just as suddenly disappeared. Jenner knew that as serial killers went, the Ripper's death toll was insignificant when compared to that of Ted Bundy or Dean Corll or a dozen others he could name, but none were as terrifying as he in the public's mind. Maybe because he was never caught and so never had his psyche exposed. He remained unknown, and nothing is so frightening as the unknown.

Certainly he scared the hell out of Jenner.

As John Lloyd's deep voice had pronounced the name, Jenner could almost see it taking form in the air, blood dripping from the letters. If he had been Catholic, he would have crossed himself. He did anyway. If he had been superstitious, he would have made a sign to ward off the evil eye. He did that, too, and didn't even feel foolish.

He shivered even though he knew the temperature in the cozy room hadn't really dropped. But he felt as if it had, felt, in fact, as if something unmentionable had drained the heat from the air. He noticed Lydia shivering, and wished he had another human body he could snuggle up to like she was snuggling up to Branson. Sneaky bastard probably dropped the Ripper's name just so he'd have an excuse to fondle Lydia Fairchild without anybody thinking he had any prurient interest in her. In a minute he would admit he was making a joke. Except Jenner had never heard the attorney crack a joke.

"You're crazy!" said Green, bouncing up and down on the sofa. Jenner figured the vice cop had better cool it before he popped a button off.

"Branson's a lot of things, but he's not crazy," stated Schroder. "He doesn't believe in ghosts, either, so he's not talking about the real Ripper. He's talking about a copycat."

John Lloyd nodded. "Or a masquerade, Sergeant. We must visualize a very ordinary man masquerading as the Butcher who is himself masquerading as Jack the Ripper."

"Did you dream all this, or have you been reading tea leaves?" asked Green, but Jenner noticed his sarcasm sounded forced. The vice cop sounded more like he was pleading.

"When the first murder occurred and Mr. Bryant informed the reading public that the body was mutilated but not how, I was mildly interested because Purple Rain had written me. I thought of the Ripper as I am sure Sergeant Schroder did, but only because his name has become a generic term for sex crimes involving mutilation. It was not until the second murder, that of Honey Bran, that I discerned a faint pattern. Purple Rain was murdered on Friday, August 31. The Ripper's first victim, Mary Ann Nichols, was murdered on Friday, August 31. Honey Bran was murdered on Saturday, September 8, as was the Ripper's second victim. One murder similar to one committed by the Ripper and on the same date would be coincidence. Two is a pattern. Even the fact that the women knew each other fit. We are reasonably certain that the Ripper's victims knew one another as they all frequented the same tavern as our modern victims frequent the Bimbo Bar."

"Why didn't you call Schroder?" asked Jenner. "Jesus

Christ, were you going to wait until there wasn't a hooker left alive?''

John Lloyd closed his eyes momentarily, and Jenner had the feeling the attorney had asked himself the same questions many times since last night. "I could not be certain. The invitations obscured the pattern, and there was always the possibility that the Butcher picked those dates because they were on the weekend and he had the leisure to murder. Or the dates could have been random chance. At any rate, I did not call Sergeant Schroder to discuss my speculations. Until early this morning when Sergeant Jenner mentioned a letter and quoted the phrase *down on whores*, nebulous speculations were all I had. One of the letters signed by someone calling himself Jack the Ripper and sent to the Central News Agency in 1888 contained the same phrase. No, after having read the autopsy protocols and the letter received by Mr. Bryant, I can say absolutely that our Butcher is Jack the Ripper.''

The lawyer picked up a book from beside his chair then leaned forward to select a paper from one of the files. Jenner marveled that he managed both maneuvers without dislodging Lydia who still nestled against his side and gave no indication of wanting to change nesting places.

"Sergeant Schroder," said John Lloyd, holding out the book and paper. "If you would compare the autopsy protocol on Cowgirl with that of the Ripper's fourth victim, Catherine Eddowes, you will discover that allowing for our more advanced forensic procedures, the results are identical. There is a mortuary photograph of Eddowes which could be a print of that of Cowgirl. The mutilations are exactly the same. The left kidney was removed from both bodies. The Ripper later sent half of Eddowes's kidney to Mr. George Lusk, the head of the Whitechapel Vigilance Committee—''

"Branson!" Schroder's voice was quiet, but it held a note of disbelieving horror that Jenner had never heard before in any voice. To hear it in Schroder's was enough to give Jenner his own case of the horrors.

John Lloyd looked at the detective and whatever he read in Schroder's eyes made the lawyer's face turn pale. "Yes,

Sergeant?'' he queried, his voice steady, but Jenner could see the effort it took to maintain that steadiness.

Schroder swallowed. ''Bryant, give John Lloyd the package.''

''Gladly,'' said the reporter, handing the attorney a clear plastic bag containing a small square package wrapped in brown paper and tied with brownish string. ''This was sitting by the paper's back door this morning. Nobody saw who left it. The outside has been fingerprinted, but nothing inside, so I guess Sergeant Schroder wants you to be careful. He's ticked off at me for not turning it over to Special Crimes, but it's addressed to you in care of me, and you were the one who was going to open it, and to hell with the police.''

''Part of the deal was the pencil pusher got to ride along,'' said Green.

Bryant shrugged. ''I've been cooperating. I didn't print the letter when you asked me not to, and the deal was I got the inside shit for the paper. You don't have to like me, Lieutenant, but I keep my word.''

John Lloyd sat looking at the box without attempting to open it. ''Lydia, please leave the room.''

She shook her head, her face nearly as pale as John Lloyd's. Jenner would bet his own face looked a little ghostly and the Bean looked on the verge of upchucking. They all knew what was in that innocent little package, or they thought they knew, and nobody really wanted to make certain.

The unwrapping seemed to take forever. John Lloyd cut the string so the knots would remain intact, then, still using his pocket knife, slit the tape on the wrapping paper. A piece of white paper fell on the floor, and Lydia read the words aloud.

—From Hell

Mr Branson

Sir I send you half the Kidne I took from one woman prasarved it for you tother piece I fried and ate it was very nise I may send you the bloody knif that took it out if you only wate a whil longer

signed   Catch me when you can Mishter Branson

Jenner never saw anyone move to the whiskey decanter as fast as Lydia Fairchild. Jenner had a feeling she was only the first. When John Lloyd finally opened the box, everybody in the room would be helping themselves to his liquor.

Jenner decided to avoid the rush and joined Lydia at the sideboard. "You okay?"

Lydia took a gulp of her drink. "I think I'll take up grave robbing. Seems like a cleaner profession than being an attorney. You know, law schools should update their curriculum to include visits to morgues and asylums for the criminally insane. God, Jenner, I feel like I'm starring in a snuff film."

Jenner nodded and poured himself a drink. He heard bits and pieces of conversation from the four men behind him.

"—renal artery is one inch long which matches with that taken from Eddowes."

"—DNA check will tell us if it's Cowgirl's."

"—fucking monster."

"Miss Fairchild, would you please pour everyone a drink? I don't ordinarily advocate the use of alcohol as an emotional crutch, but frankly, I need it." Jenner decided John Lloyd was shook as hell since he used a contraction. Gift-wrapped kidneys did that to a person.

"I'm not turning around if that box is open."

"Sergeant Schroder has custody of the box, and it is closed. Its contents are hardly such that I care to have it on display." John Lloyd was sounding calmer, but not by much.

Schroder cleared his throat. "Branson, are the other autopsy protocols duplicates of the ones done on the Ripper's victims?"

John Lloyd sipped at the drink Lydia handed him. "Yes."

"So everything fits?"

The lawyer hesitated, then reached for Lydia's hand and pulled her down beside him. "Not exactly."

"What do you mean, not exactly?" asked Schroder, setting his untasted drink on the floor.

Jenner watched John Lloyd idly playing with Lydia's hand, and knew the lawyer didn't want to answer, that he wished, in fact, that they would all take themselves out of his study so he wouldn't have to say whatever it was he was compelled to say.

"His timetable is accelerated. The letter you received, Sergeant Schroder, should have been postmarked September 28. The wording differs only slightly from the Ripper's original. Our Butcher omitted a reference to a suspect mentioned in the Ripper's letter because it didn't fit with his circumstances. The original of the postcard received by Mr. Bryant was actually postmarked October 1. Last night's two murders occurred too early. The times of death match, but the date is wrong. The Ripper staged his double event on September 30, and Mr. Lusk received his unpleasant gift on October 16."

"So why did the Butcher kill his women last night?" asked Schroder.

John Lloyd frowned, then glanced at Lydia, and Jenner sensed this was the question the lawyer had been dreading. "Because Lydia was on the Boulevard last night."

Jenner watched helplessly as Lydia blanched and began shaking. He could hear her teeth clicking against the rim of her glass when she tried to sip her drink. She gave up finally and stared into the amber-colored liquor as if the answer were there. "Why me, John Lloyd? Why single out me?"

"Yes, why did he do that?" echoed Bryant, sipping his drink and jotting notes in his spiral.

John Lloyd put his arm around Lydia. "Because even dressed as you were, Miss Fairchild, he knew you were not a prostitute. Like an animal he smelled your vulnerability and stole your wallet to learn who and what you were."

"I guess I'm just a lousy actress. I didn't fool anybody except Jo-Jo Jefferson, and that says more for his lack of intellect than my thespian abilities."

Jenner didn't like the absence of expression on her face. It reminded him too much of the slack, vacant face of a mental patient.

"When he discovered your identity and your relationship to me, his ego could not resist the temptation to expand his game to include me. Imagine his elation. The Panhandle's most relentless criminal investigator and its most brilliant criminal defense attorney as opponents."

"Forget what I said about the Butcher's ego," said Lydia. "His can't compare to yours and Schroder's." She laughed, a thin, shaky sound that held no humor and made Jenner wince.

It affected John Lloyd, too, Jenner noticed, because he pulled Lydia closer to him as if that would anchor whatever part of her was tearing loose. "I was quoting from the press which seems to find Sergeant Schroder and myself fascinating. At any rate, we each have gained the reputation of being the best in our respective fields, Miss Fairchild. The Butcher's ego would not allow him to play against inferior opponents."

John Lloyd took another sip from his drink, and Jenner sensed his reluctance to continue. "He called me before eleven to issue his invitation, then mailed the postcard because he was obsessed with the Ripper's pattern and must adhere to it as closely as possible. He stalked Lydia until it was time to play out his charade as the Ripper."

"Then he dropped the license to frame Miss Fairchild just in case you didn't understand his phone call," said Green.

"I was wrong in that assumption," stated John Lloyd. "I do not believe he framed her. I do not believe it was ever his intention that she be arrested. In defending Miss Fairchild against a capital murder charge, I would be invincible. I am an attorney. Courtrooms, laws, juries, are all my milieu. He could not play my game. I believe he intended her to be his fifth victim. In a murder hunt, he would have the advantage. As I told Miss Fairchild, I am not a detective. But random events kept intervening. Jenner was in the Bimbo Bar and followed Miss Fairchild when she was ejected by the bartender."

"She must have come on like Carry Nation," said Green. "Nobody gets thrown out of the Bimbo for any reason short of murder, and not even then if they clean up the mess."

"Why did he drop Miss Fairchild's driver's license by Cowgirl's body if he didn't intend to frame her?" asked Schroder.

"It was an accident, another random event."

"You are one lucky lady," said Bryant, peering at her from under the brim of his gimme hat.

"So was Typhoid Mary," remarked Lydia. "But the people around her kept dying." She gave a hiccuping sob, and

John Lloyd uttered an imaginative curse, then pulled her completely into his embrace.

Jenner took another sip of his drink. There didn't seem to be much else to do. The Butcher was revealed as a copycat of Jack the Ripper; Bryant would print the story; there would be panic on the Boulevard, and then—what? Another unknown to terrorize the public for the next hundred years? He thought of Cowgirl's pitiful body. In a pig's eye the Butcher was going to escape.

He set his glass on the sideboard. "So how do we catch him?"

Schroder wiped his hand over his face. "A decoy."

"Decoy!" Green laughed, and Jenner thought he sounded like a bilious goat. "We got decoys all over the Boulevard. We got decoys on the decoys. I bet every third prostitute is a cop. We've transferred meter maids to Vice. We've borrowed women officers from every county within shouting distance. And what have we got? Two more women killed! It's like the damn bastard knows every move we make."

Lydia's hiccuping sobs stopped and there were no other sounds in the room but those of Schroder tapping a cigarette against his lighter and Green cracking his knuckles.

"Maybe he's a cop," suggested Jenner.

"Maybe so," agreed Schroder.

"If he's a cop, we're up shit creek without a paddle, 'cause he knows all the decoys," said Green.

"So let's give him a decoy he wants," said Schroder. "Let's give him Miss Fairchild."

John Lloyd released Lydia and lurched to his feet. "That is the most callous proposal I've ever heard! The answer is no."

Jenner decided that John Lloyd's voice held the same note of warning as the dry whir of a rattlesnake just before it sinks its fangs into your ankle. Except John Lloyd Branson would go for the throat.

"We need bait he'll swallow, Branson," said Schroder. "As I see it, Miss Fairchild is the best bait we got. Matter of fact, she's the only bait we got."

"Then I suggest you have your vision checked, Sergeant. Miss Fairchild is not a goat to be tethered."

"I'll do it," Lydia said.

"I'll not allow it!"

Lydia drained her glass and carefully set it on the floor. Jenner noticed that her face didn't look quite so bloodless. "How do you plan to stop me?" she asked quietly. "Have Schroder lock me up again? I don't think he'll cooperate this time. Or will you send me back to Dallas? That didn't work before, did it, and it won't work this time."

She kicked the hassock away and rose to face him. "You can't intimidate me because I won't let you. Besides, I learned a lot about intimidation on the Boulevard. Jo-Jo Jefferson and his two muscles make wonderful teachers."

Schroder interrupted. "If we don't catch him, Branson, he'll keep on killing."

"If Miss Fairchild is not served up to him, not before November 8, when he reproduces Mary Kelly's murder."

"That's the horrible one?" asked Jenner, and nearly laughed at his own question. All the murders had been horrible. How do you judge one horror over another? Count the bits and pieces of the body?

"That ain't the half of it, son," replied Schroder. "There's a picture of the body in that book Branson showed me. I've never seen anything like it in all my years as a homicide detective."

"Can you be sure of that, John Lloyd, that he won't kill again until November 8?" asked Lydia.

His jaw clenched until Jenner heard it pop. "It's the pattern—" he began.

"But he's already changed the pattern once. Can you guarantee he won't change it again? Can you guarantee Schroder will catch him tonight or next week or the week after that, or anytime before November 8?"

"I cannot speak for Sergeant Schroder, but I believe—"

"I already know what you believe. Sergeant Schroder, can you guarantee you'll catch him without my help?"

Schroder's jaw was clenched, too. He shook his head. "No, ma'am, I can't."

Lydia turned back to John Lloyd. "If I'm not on the Boulevard, available, then another woman will die in my place. That's what both of you are saying?"

Jenner watched the muscles ripple along John Lloyd's jaw. "Possibly," he admitted through clenched teeth.

"I'm terrified to go back to the Boulevard, but if I turn down this chance to stop the Butcher, I'll never be able to face myself again. Do you know what Cowgirl's last words to me were? 'Thanks for the favor,' she said. She was thanking me for trying to help her. I wasn't very successful, was I? She died in an alley a few blocks away. I still owe her that favor, John Lloyd."

"We'll set it up at the Bimbo," Schroder said, "since that seems to be the club all his victims frequented. We'll protect her, Branson. We'll have our people staked out all around the building. She can't take a drink without a cop swallowing for her. Green and I will be in a van in front of the Bimbo with a video camera. The minute she steps out the door, we've got her and whoever she's with on tape. We'll have men follow her, and the second anybody touches her, we've got him!" Schroder's voice sounded hoarse and tired, as if he didn't really believe his own words, but couldn't think of any that would be better.

John Lloyd wasn't listening to Schroder; Jenner knew that as surely as he knew the lawyer wasn't going to concede the fight so easily.

John Lloyd grabbed Lydia's arm and jerked her toward the sofa. "Damn it to hell, Lydia, do you know what the Ripper did to his last victim? Do you?"

"No, not exactly, but it doesn't matter."

John Lloyd let go of her arm to pick up the book he'd given Schroder and flip through the pages. Jenner knew what he was looking for and took a step forward to stop him. Schroder shook his head. "Leave it alone, son," he said softly.

John Lloyd thrust the book in Lydia's face. "That's a picture of Mary Kelly after the Ripper finished with her. Don't close your eyes, damn you, look at it! Know what you're facing. This is reality. This is evil. But you don't believe in evil, do you? You believe in psychology and psychiatry and sociology. Whether he kills you as a symbol of goodness and thus the reversal of himself, or because he hates his mother, or because he received sexual satisfaction, you will be just as dead. The social sciences will not help you because all the symbolic trappings are just another masquerade. Beneath the mask is the face of evil. He will kill you because it is in his nature.''

He closed the book and dropped it. ''Knowing the possible consequences, do you still choose to face him?''

She straightened her shoulders and raised her chin. ''Yes.''

Jenner thought Lydia Fairchild was the bravest person he'd ever met. Also the stupidest. But then so was he because he was going back to the Boulevard with her. She needed more than courage. She needed luck—and didn't Schroder call him the luckiest son of a bitch alive?

CHAPTER
TWENTY-FOUR

Amarillo Boulevard—September 16

LYDIA STARED THROUGH THE WINDSHIELD OF JOHN LLOYD'S big Lincoln. Even at nearly 1:30 in the morning there was life of a sort on Amarillo Boulevard, but then to those who only came out at night it was the middle of the day. Still, there was a panicked furtiveness about those who scuttled, lingered, meandered, or staggered along its length that Lydia hadn't noticed last night, and a tendency to clump together in groups, like blood cells under a microscope when the lab technician adds a clotting agent. The Butcher's double event had congealed the loners, the winos, the hookers into small milling groups who huddled together for survival.

But that was a tactic she could not and should not use.

"Miss Fairchild, have you lost your tongue?" John Lloyd asked. "You have not said a word since leaving Canadian, a period of silence that constituted a record of sorts for you."

"Maybe it's shock. Did you ever think of that? When you calmly announced to Schroder that of course you would be accompanying me on my—how did you put it?—'ill-advised crusade,' you left me too shocked to say anything. Except something very, very filthy, and I didn't feel up to listening to a lecture from you on inappropriate language. Damn it, John Lloyd, you and Mrs. Dinwittie are going to ruin everything. The Butcher will know he's being set up.'' Lydia unbuckled her seat belt and tugged at the bodice of her dress. She should have never let Mrs. Dinwittie rummage through that trunk in John Lloyd's attic unsupervised. The scarlet taffeta dress she'd selected for Lydia might have looked fine on John Lloyd's grandmother in 1903, but it barely covered the situation tonight. Or maybe she just had more situation to cover than John Lloyd's grandmother.

''If he is as intelligent as I believe he is, and if his sources are as good as the police believe they are, he knows already, Miss Fairchild. If I cannot dissuade you from risking your life, then I will at least accompany you to insure you survive the evening with your appendages intact.''

''My appendages won't be at risk because he won't come near me with you around. Schroder should have thrown you in jail when I asked him to.''

''I told him I would sue and he believed me. Sergeant Schroder is a very wise man.''

''Schroder is a weenie or he wouldn't have let you intimidate him.''

''What a disrespectful remark, Miss Fairchild.''

''Stuff it, John Lloyd. You got your way. You get to play macho male and guard me while the Butcher laughs and kills someone else. Your act won't fool him. He knows you're not a pimp, and he knows I'm not really a prostitute. I don't see the reason for this charade.''

''My function is not to guard you, although I will, and not to fool the Butcher, but to create a diversion. Miss Lydia Fairchild in the Bimbo would be a magnet to every kind of diseased, perverse predator that makes that establishment his den. Blondie is less likely to attract unwelcome attention, although I, as your vicious pimp, intend to attract a good deal of it.''

''How?'' Lydia asked skeptically.

He gestured nonchalantly with one hand. ''I shall improvise. While the attention of all the other predators is focused on me, the Butcher is free to make his approach unhampered by the less deadly competition. His ego will not allow him to resist the challenge.''

"Let's hope your plan works, or I'll never forgive you for interfering.''

"My part of the plan will work. It is Sergeant Schroder's part that worries me.''

"What a distrustful remark, John Lloyd," she said, leaning over to ease her feet back into her spike heels.

He glanced at her and made a choking sound. "Mrs. Dinwittie," he said in a hoarse voice to his secretary sitting happily eavesdropping in the backseat, "I believe this dress originally had a feather boa sewn around the neckline.''

Mrs. Dinwittie, looking like a 1920s flapper in a blue-beaded dress with matching headband, leaned over the front seat. "It did, Mr. Branson, but it was tacky-looking, and we couldn't have Miss Fairchild looking tacky." Lydia swore the secretary twittered.

John Lloyd glanced at Lydia's nearly bare chest. "Better tacky"—he grimaced as he pronounced the word—"than risk indecent exposure.''

"John Lloyd, we're going to the Bimbo. Every exposure is indecent there.''

"Perhaps you could wear my cape.''

"If you're going to play my pimp, get in character. Pimps don't worry about their bitches' modesty. Besides, you look soooo adorable in that cape. Just like Zorro ready to leap from a balcony ''

"Watch your language, please, Miss Fairchild. There is no need to adopt the vernacular of your assumed profession.''

"Don't lecture me. Your own language earlier this evening was as colorful as any I've ever used.''

"I was overwrought, a condition that has recently threatened to become chronic, and since you mentioned pimps, I have not forgotten that you had the audacity to attribute my physical characteristics to your mythical pimp.''

"I needed someone big and mean and strong and awe-inspiring and fearsome and handsome. Besides, you were the only man I could think of.''

"I am not mean.''

"I think you make a wonderful pimp, Mr. Branson," said Mrs. Dinwittie, and twittered again.

He clutched the steering wheel. "God help me," Lydia heard him mutter.

Lydia tugged her bodice an inch higher, took a breath, felt it slither down again, and gave up. There was nothing inherently indecent about cleavage—as long as she remembered not to lean over.

"Did your grandmother really wear this dress, John Lloyd, and did she really own a saloon in Canadian until the temperance movement closed her down?"

"I see Mrs. Dinwittie has been telling tales." He sighed. "Yes, to both questions."

"Tell me about her," urged Lydia.

"My grandmother is not a subject I wish to discuss."

"Then tell me who Theodore is."

John Lloyd slammed on the brakes and the big Lincoln skidded to a stop in front of the Bimbo. "That is not a subject I wish to discuss either, not now, nor in the future." His voice was several degrees below freezing.

"Then what do you want to discuss?"

He twisted around in the seat to face her. His eyes seemed to glitter even in the car's dark interior. "This," he said, gesturing toward the Bimbo and the surrounding darkness. "You, in a scarlet dress and that ridiculous hat—"

"What's wrong with this hat? It's perfect. The brim is so wide it shadows my face. I can watch people without their knowing it, and it's a wonderful defensive weapon."

"Unless you plan to vulgar someone to death, I cannot imagine that hat as a weapon."

"Hat pins. These old picture hats required hat pins to hold them on. Mrs. Dinwittie found two beautiful ones, long and sharp and carved on one end. See"—she bent her head—"they're sticking out on either side of the crown." She raised her head and smiled. "All proper young ladies in the nineteenth century depended on their hat pins to ward off advances."

"You're right as rain, Miss Fairchild. My grandmother always told me to be sure to keep a hat pin handy," said Mrs. Dinwittie.

"This is not parlor game, ladies! It is not the nineteenth century, and a hat pin will not frighten the Butcher." John Lloyd's voice was loud enough to be heard a block away.

"I think I'll just wait in front of the Bimbo," said Mrs. Dinwittie hastily. Lydia always knew the secretary was more intelligent than her dithery actions led one to believe. She was smart enough to leave the scene before a brawl.

John Lloyd wiped his face on his cape. "How do you manage to distract me so easily, Miss Fairchild? I had intended to say that this whole idea is ludicrous and dangerous and that you should reconsider. Instead I become embroiled in a discussion of fashion."

"You've already said it—several times, so there's no point in saying it again." She opened the car door and slid out. "It's time, John Lloyd, and please remember my name is Blondie." She started toward the Bimbo.

"Lydia!"

She stopped, but didn't turn around. Suddenly she didn't trust herself to look at him without crying. If she died, she would never know what might have been. She had always thought *might have been* were the three saddest words in the English language.

"Lydia, you have the gun?"

She nodded and patted her beaded purse. "In here. But, John Lloyd, I still don't want to take it. I don't like guns, I'm not familiar with them, I'll probably shoot myself in the foot. I'd rather have my brick."

"You have to be within arm's length to use your, uh, brick, Miss Fairchild. Arm's length is too close."

"But I trust Schroder. He'll have men staked out around the Bimbo."

"Do not trust anyone, Miss Fairchild, excepting myself and Mrs. Dinwittie."

"Come on, John Lloyd, what can a middle-aged secretary do?"

"Mr. Dinwittie doubted Mrs. Dinwittie also, much to his regret."

"Unless she brought an ax along, I don't think she'll be very helpful."

"The secret to successfully accomplishing a clandestine operation is the ability to improvise, Miss Fairchild."

"I'm not James Bond. I'll trust the cops. There's no way the Butcher can carry me off without all those cops seeing him. Besides, he'd better be a big man or all he'll get from the attempt is a hernia."

"Miss Fairchild, *I* do *not* trust the sergeant's plan. I *do*, however, trust the Butcher to have a strategy for evading arrest. If you do find yourself alone with him, remember that your gun is a double-action automatic. Pull the trigger once to load the chamber, pull the trigger again to fire. Do not try to wound him in the leg or arm. Only a marksman can do that, and you are not a marksman. Body shots, Lydia, as Sergeant Schroder told you."

"I remember," she said, and wondered if she could ever really shoot a man.

"The Ripper murdered Mary Kelly in a room, the only one of his victims not killed in the street. I believe the Butcher has a lair near the Boulevard. Do not enter a building that is not filled with people."

"I won't," she promised.

"Turn around and look at me," he said, his voice soft.

"Why?"

"Because I want to look at you."

"One last time, like viewing the corpse before burial?" she asked as she turned. The moon was over his left shoulder, shining in her face and leaving his in shadow.

"Don't," he said, hooking his cane over his arm and stepping close to her to grasp her shoulders. "Don't think about dying. Think about all the reasons you have for living. Think of poor Mrs. Dinwittie without you to listen to her homilies. Think of Sergeant Jenner without you to build his romantic fantasies around. Think of me withering away into old age, growing more and more eccentric without you to tease me and exasperate me and vex me until I lose my composure."

"I can't let you wither, can I?"

"You would never forgive yourself."

CHAPTER
TWENTY-FIVE

JENNER SURREPTITIOUSLY GLANCED AT HIS WATCH. WHERE the hell were they? It was 1:30, time the performance started.

"Patience, my boy," said Theodore, pouring a finger of the Bimbo's house brand of Scotch in his glass, a noxious liquid Jenner knew would prove to be carcinogenic if the government ever found any rats dumb enough to drink it.

"John Lloyd never fails to do what he promises, and I believe he promised you he would have Miss Fairchild here. His dependability used to be one of his most irritating habits, particularly since I never claimed that virtue. I felt guilty, and no one likes to feel guilty."

"So you were one of Branson's teachers, Theodore," said Jenner.

"In a manner of speaking."

"Was he any different then? When he was younger?"

"That is an impossible question, Larry. I don't know what kind of person he is now, so I can't compare and contrast."

"He's kind of a Victorian stuffed shirt, never gives anything away, never talks about himself. At the same time, he's intense, passionate, I guess, if you know what I mean. I once saw him hold off the police to give a murderer a chance to commit suicide because he believed that was the most just

211

solution. His idea of justice is different, and I think it's ruthless."

Theodore swirled his liquor around with his finger. "Interesting," he said.

Jenner frowned. Theodore was nearly as closemouthed as John Lloyd. "He seemed surprised to see you last night."

"Our paths haven't crossed in a number of years." He sipped his drink without grimacing, a superhuman feat in Jenner's estimation. "Maude, Preacher, and I want to thank you, Larry, for confiding in us about Miss Fairchild."

"It was Sergeant Schroder's idea."

Actually, Jenner thought resentfully, Schroder had wanted to throw all three in jail while Lydia was playing the tethered goat, but had decided it might look suspicious if none of the regulars showed up. Then the fat slob assigned him to make sure they kept quieter than a dead earthworm in a bass's stomach.

"Nervous, Jenner?" asked Bryant.

Jenner looked at the reporter slouched in a chair at the end of the booth, appearing both comfortable and watchful. "And I suppose you're not?"

"I'm not the one waiting to meet the Butcher."

"Scarlet woman!" exclaimed Preacher, looking as if his eyes were bulging out of his head.

Jenner looked toward the doorway and choked on his drink. Lydia stood in the open door looking like everyman's sexual fantasy; better, in fact, since most men couldn't fantasize that well without blowing all their sexual circuits. Besides, most men's fantasies wouldn't include that huge, feathered, plumed, ribbon-bedecked hat, and a taffeta dress that swished and cracked every time Lydia moved. He was surprised John Lloyd let her out of his house dressed like that.

On the other hand, John Lloyd was nearly as startling. Dressed in black slacks, black leather vest hanging open, white silk shirt unbuttoned to his navel, and a black cape lined in red silk, the attorney looked like Dracula slumming. Jenner watched to see if bats would fly through the door after him. There was no way to listen for wolves howling; the human variety were making too much noise slobbering over Lydia.

Standing next to John Lloyd and Lydia, Mrs. Dinwittie looked almost staid—staid and twenty years past her prime, if she'd ever had any prime. He wondered if she had a collapsible ax in her purse.

"My goodness," gasped Maude as she stared at the trio. "The Bimbo's never seen anything like that."

Lydia sauntered to the bar with a hip-rolling motion that sent Preacher into a tirade of quiet mutterings and the crowd into a chorus of lip-smacking. Propping an elbow on the bar, she beckoned to the tattooed bartender. "A Bourbon, please, and make sure you wash the glass first."

The bartender folded his arms, tattoos rippling. "Ain't you the hooker I tossed out last night?"

"Yes, and my pimp didn't think you were very polite."

The bartender looked at John Lloyd. "The phantom of the opera here your pimp?"

John Lloyd prodded the man's belly with the tip of his cane. "No one knocks my bitches around except me," he said, his voice low and harsh.

Jenner's mouth fell open.

The bartender pushed away the cane. "Fuck with me, and I'll chase your skinny ass out the door."

Jenner never saw John Lloyd's next movements except as a blur, but he heard the two loud claps as the lawyer backhanded the bartender across both cheeks, then jerked him across the bar by his shirt and dropped him face down on the floor.

"He shall chastise the wicked," intoned Preacher.

"Holy shit!" yelled someone in the watching crowd.

John Lloyd whipped off one end of his cane to reveal an eight-inch sword, placed the toe of his boot under the bartender's ribs, and heaved him over onto his back. "You need to clean up your mouth and learn to respect others, but first you need to clean up your slovenly self." With that comment, he laid his blade against the bartender's left cheek.

Jenner gulped and leapt out of the booth, banging his knees on the table. "Jesus!" he breathed.

"And smite the Philistines," continued Preacher as

John Lloyd drew his blade down the bartender's whisker-stubbled face, leaving a clean-shaven swath of skin behind.

Louis Bryant picked up his drink. "Believe I'll get a ringside seat."

"His enemies shall fall before him," said Preacher as John Lloyd switched cheeks. Jenner wondered if Preacher was talking about God or John Lloyd, or if he could tell the difference.

Chairs were pushed back and glasses tipped over as the Bimbo's patrons abandoned their drinks in favor of the floor show. Jenner climbed up on the table to see over the heads of the crowd. He could see Lydia leaning against the bar looking at John Lloyd as if he had suddenly sprouted horns and a tail. Mrs. Dinwittie was on Lydia's right, hanging on to the younger woman's arm and squealing. The crowd began stomping and clapping.

"Shave and a haircut—six bits," sang a young punk with terminal acne.

John Lloyd glanced at him. "An excellent suggestion, young man." He leaned down, jerked the cowering bartender up, and with a few flicks of his sword burred the man's head.

After wiping his blade across the front of the bartender's shirt, he sheathed it and walked casually over to the bar. He snapped his fingers. "Pour Blondie and me some Bourbon. Good Bourbon, not any of your usual poison."

The bartender scuttled behind the bar. "Yes, sir."

John Lloyd rested one hand on his hip and twirled his cane with the other. "I'm known as the Undertaker, but everybody can call me *sir*."

"Yes, sir," chorused the spectators.

Jenner scanned the crowd, but nobody seemed to be moving toward Lydia or even acting as if they wanted to. Maybe they didn't want John Lloyd to think they were impolite.

He noticed Louis Bryant standing at one end of the bar, making notes in his spiral. The man would make notes during the Second Coming, hoping to make the last edition before the world ended.

Theodore nudged Jenner's foot. "He must care for her to make such a spectacle of himself."

Jenner nodded. "Yeah, I guess he does. Nearly went berserk when she agreed to do this, but he let her make the choice."

Theodore took another drink. "He always was a noble fool, young John Lloyd, full of self-sacrifice and gallantry."

Jenner wasn't sure what being noble and gallantry had to do with whipping the Bimbo's surly bartender, but then he wasn't a professor. The few he'd met always seemed to take the long way around to say anything.

Theodore set his drink down. "He was born too late, Larry. He would have made a magnificent Confederate officer, the kind who charged the Union troops armed with only a saber. Perhaps an even better analogy would be Sydney Carton sacrificing himself on the guillotine in *A Tale of Two Cities*."

"I think I saw the movie," said Jenner.

"Think of his conflict, Larry. He can't die in her stead because he's not a woman, yet he won't stop her because he believes in every man, or woman, making his or her own choices. What do you suppose he'll do if she dies?"

Jenner set his glass down abruptly. He didn't want to think about Lydia dying, and he didn't want to think about John Lloyd's grief if she did. "He'd turn to stone," he replied, and was surprised to discover that idea made him sad.

Preacher leaned across the table and grasped Theodore's arm. "He's a good man. We'll protect her for him."

Jenner scrambled off the table. "Listen, you three stay out of this. It's not safe for one reason, and for another, you'll just get in the way. If you do get in the way, I'll—" He never finished his threat because the door burst open and all hell broke loose. Actually he saw it was Big Bill Elliot, but hell would have been preferable.

"We're here to close this place down," Elliot announced as his supporters poured through the door, carrying baseball bats and cattle prods. "The police ignore this eyesore, this filthy cesspool, this breeding ground for scum who spread corruption through this city, but decent citizens cannot and will not." Jenner decided Elliot must be trying out a new speech writer, because his rhetoric sounded grammatical for a change.

"Hypocrite!" shouted Preacher.

Theodore leaned closer to Jenner. "Elliot once tried to have Preacher arrested for being a public nuisance. Preacher decided even Christian forbearance has limits, and he hit Elliot over the head with his leather Bible. Preacher spent a month in the Potter County Correctional Facility until the other prisoners petitioned the court to commute the rest of his sentence. He was preaching a sermon every morning after cell check. The inmates didn't appreciate his eloquence."

"All right, boys, let's rid this place of vermin," shouted Elliot. That convinced Jenner. Elliot definitely had a speech writer; on his own, the mayoral candidate couldn't pronounce *vermin*.

"Get out, you damn fool, and take these misguided disciples with you!" commanded John Lloyd, tossing his cape back over his shoulders and seizing his cane in both hands.

"Oh, shit!" exclaimed Jenner, and started toward John Lloyd. Somebody had to stop him before he skewered Elliot and ended up in jail.

Mrs. Dinwittie must have had the same idea because she picked up a bar stool and rammed it into Elliot's overhanging belly. "Remember the Alamo!" she shouted.

Jenner didn't see any comparison between Big Bill Elliot and Santa Anna, but he guessed the Bimbo was as much a symbol of freedom to the misfits on the Boulevard as the Alamo was to early Texans. At any rate the crowd thought so because it took up the cry in unison as it swayed as one body toward Elliot's followers. Someone kicked Jenner's knee, the same one the screaming blonde had attempted to dislocate, and Jenner went down, covering his head with his arms.

"Police!" yelled a voice.

"It's the fucking Mexican Army! Let's kick ass!" screamed the kid with acne. Jenner didn't think that was a direct quote from Buck Travis when the Mexicans broke through the walls, but it was just as effective. The crowd howled as it shoved and kicked and punched its way in the direction of the door. Bodies were beginning to stack up around John Lloyd and Mrs. Dinwittie as they stood back-to-back, as some accounts say the last defenders at the Alamo did. Jenner saw Theodore using a chair to bludgeon his way through the punching, spitting, cursing, shouting mass of mostly smelly humanity.

That was the last thing he remembered until somebody poured what seemed to be an entire cattle tank of water over his face.

"Wake up, you careless bastard!"

Jenner heard the words, decided somebody was pissed pea green and purple, and opened his eyes. "Who won, John Lloyd?" he asked, noticing the lawyer's swollen eye and split lip.

"Where's Lydia?"

Jenner thought for a minute he would lose control of his bladder for the first time in his ten years as a cop. But then he'd never been so scared in all those ten years. "She's not by the bar?"

"There is nothing at the bar but her handbag with this tucked under it!" he shouted, and waved one of the Butcher's invitations in Jenner's face.

CHAPTER
TWENTY-SIX

LYDIA SCRAMBLED AROUND THE CORNER OF THE BAR AND crouched next to the shorn bartender. "You've got to throw that bastard out of here!" she hissed.

The bartender rubbed the stubble on top his head. "Get that crazy pimp of yours to do it."

"The last time I saw him, he was fighting three men carrying baseball bats."

"I hope they scramble his brains and bust his balls."

"You're a sore loser."

"I'll get this one!" yelled a huge man as he lumbered behind the bar and reached for Lydia.

"Go to hell!" she yelled, and scooted backward into the bartender.

"Take her! She's more trouble than a boil on a jockey's behind," said the bartender as he pinioned Lydia's arms.

"John Lloyd'll kill you!" she yelled as he passed her to Elliot's man who grabbed her hands and ankles and heaved her around his shoulders like a muffler.

"Shut up!" said the man as he headed toward the wall at the end of the bar.

"Where are you taking me, you sanctimonious cretin?"

demanded Lydia, debating whether or not she should bite him. She wondered if he'd ever been tested for AIDS.

Her captor kicked the wall and a door flew open. Lydia didn't know the Bimbo had more than one door, and wondered uneasily if Schroder and Green knew.

"We're gonna take you women and your pimps to the county line and dump you. We don't want you back in Amarillo neither," he said as he jumped through the door and started jogging northwest away from the Bimbo.

"John Lloyd! Schroder! Jenner! Help!" screamed Lydia.

The man rolled her over his head and dropped her on the ground on her back. "Hush up, now," he said as he pulled a piece of rope out of his pocket. "I'm not going to hurt you none, just tie your hands together."

Lydia lay on the ground and hugged herself, trying desperately to draw air into her lungs. She'd never realized how incapacitating it was to have your breath knocked out.

As the man leaned down to tie her hands, there was a tinkle of glass breaking against a hard object, and he toppled over to land with a resounding thud next to her.

"I hate to waste good Scotch on such an inferior brand of human being, but fortunately, this wasn't very good Scotch."

Lydia finally drew a cold, dusty breath of air into her empty chest. "Theodore," she croaked, peering through the darkness.

He tossed a broken whiskey bottle aside and helped her up. "Are you all right, Miss Fairchild? He didn't harm you at all?"

She adjusted her hat and tugged up her bodice. "No, but I hope you harmed him. Can you imagine the gall of that Elliot sending out a citizens' goon squad?"

"Tonight's demonstration was a little too imaginative for Bill Elliot. I wonder whose idea it was?" mused Theodore.

"Oh, my God!" gasped Lydia. "It was a diversion!" She grabbed his hand. "Come on, Theodore. I have to find John Lloyd."

Theodore didn't budge. "I think you had better hide, Miss Fairchild. The situation in the Bimbo is, shall we say, in a state of flux. The defenders are fighting both Elliot's followers and the police, as well as occasionally one another by mistake. What with the dim interior and the fact the crowd has to stand belly to belly to fight, it's only natural to make a few mistakes. Larry is a casualty by mistake, not serious, I'm sure, but he was unconscious the last time I saw him. As for John Lloyd, well, he was holding his own, laying about with that cane of his like a mad schoolmaster, but it'll take him a while to fight his way to the door. I don't think you would be safe back there. Too much of a chance you'd be abducted again, and this time your captor might be the Butcher.''

''I know it, but I have to be abducted again. That's the only way to catch the Butcher. But the police have to see me being abducted so they can follow, or otherwise I might be dead. Never mind, it's too complicated to explain.'' She rubbed her forehead and tried to think. Reversals again, she thought. The Butcher reversed their plan and used his own diversion. ''I'll find Schroder, then. He's in a van parked on the Boulevard a half a block from the Bimbo.''

''We'll have to circle around,'' said Theodore in a heavy, breathy voice. ''There is a crowd milling around outside the Bimbo as well as inside.''

Lydia looked toward the Bimbo. Theodore was right; there were people scattered all around the building. Some of them must be cops, but in plainclothes, working undercover, how was she to know who was a cop and who was a goon or worse. And she couldn't risk being taken without witnesses. And it was so dark, with only the lights of the Boulevard, now more than a block away, to relieve the blackness, that she could hardly see anyone. Even Theodore was just a black shape with only his voice to identify him.

He tugged at her hand. ''Come along, Lydia.''

She let herself be pulled after him. ''You called me Lydia.''

''I'm sorry, I didn't mean to be so informal.''

She giggled, heard a note of hysteria in her voice, and sobered. ''I guess anybody who rescues me can call me Lydia.''

Theodore let go of her hand, and Lydia sensed more than saw him slump over. ''I'm afraid I'm not a very good rescuer, Lydia. I have to leave you. Chest pains, I'm afraid. One of the unpleasant things about growing old. You walk straight ahead to that unpaved street and follow it back to the Boulevard.''

"I can't leave you."

"I'll be all right. I have some pills in my room. I'll just walk home and take one. It's only another block." He took a step and stumbled, catching himself before he fell.

Lydia grasped his arm, thinking how much smaller he seemed hunched over in pain. "No, I'll come with you and call the paramedics. It won't take long, and I can make it back to the Bimbo in time to be abducted again. I suspect the Butcher won't mind waiting."

"Thank you, Lydia," said Theodore, a note of relief in his voice.

Theodore's room was the smallest, most barren Lydia had ever seen, she thought as she walked in and Theodore flipped on the lights. It was no more than twelve by twelve with a single bed flush against one wall, an old wooden bedside table next to it. On the wall opposite the bed was a fireplace, one of the freestanding kinds, and a small round table and chair. There were no other furnishings except pictures that covered the back wall by the bed.

She walked over and braced one knee on the bed to examine the photographs. She gasped and grabbed the wooden headboard. All the photos were of bodies. All the Butcher's victims stared at her from dead eyes—and in living color. "Where did you get these, Theodore?"

There was a chuckle from the man standing behind her. "Why, Miss Fairchild, I took them, of course. I had to have a way to keep score in my game."

Lydia felt the cold spot in the middle of her back, felt it spreading until her whole body was chilled. She recognized the room now; it was a duplicate of the one in the photograph John Lloyd had forced her to look at. It was Mary Kelly's room!

"Don't you like my pictures, Lydia?"

The voice was different, higher, yet more raspy, and Lydia's chill spread inward to freeze her heart. Awkwardly she turned around. "You!" she exclaimed.

"Did I really fool you, Lydia?" asked Louis Bryant.

CHAPTER
TWENTY-SEVEN

JOHN LLOYD LIFTED THE UNCONSCIOUS BARTENDER OFF THE floor and propped him against the wall. Grabbing a bottle of whiskey from the shelf, he splashed half of it in the man's face. The bartender came awake groaning and scrubbing at his face. "Goddamn it, that stings!"

"You should've used water, Branson," said Jenner. "The Bimbo's whiskey is the closest thing to paint remover I've ever tasted. His face will probably peel off and drop on the floor by tomorrow."

"That would only improve his appearance," answered John Lloyd. "Wake up, you worthless miscreant!"

The bartender turned his bleary eyes toward John Lloyd. "Ah, shit, it's you. Listen, I didn't have no choice. That big guy was going to take her out of here whether I liked it or not."

"You allowed Lydia, er, Blondie to be kidnapped?" asked John Lloyd quietly. Jenner distrusted his tone of voice. He'd heard a district judge pass the death sentence on a murderer in exactly that same kind of voice.

"What was I supposed to do?" asked the bartender belligerently. "The guy outweighed me by a hundred pounds."

222

"You could have defended her," the lawyer replied in that same quiet tone of voice. "Which way did he take her?"

The bartender pointed. "Out the back door."

"If you saw them leave, then who knocked you out?" asked Jenner.

"Hell, I don't know. Whoever left after Theodore, I guess. Theodore asked the same questions you did, punched me in the jaw, and lit out the back door, taking a full bottle of Scotch with him. I tell you, I'm tired of being knocked around. If Theodore didn't buy enough booze every night to fill up Lake Meredith, I'd have beat him up and thrown him out the door. But Jo-Jo don't want the regulars bothered." The man suddenly covered his face and rocked back and forth. "Jo-Jo! He's gonna bust my ass when he gets out of jail and sees this place."

"I do not believe you will have to worry about Jo-Jo," said John Lloyd as he pulled the bartender to his feet. Carefully tilting the man's chin until it was exactly parallel to the floor he drew back his fist and landed an uppercut on the man's chin that lifted him several inches off the floor.

"Hurry, Jenner," said the lawyer, stepping over the bartender's prone figure and leaping out the back door, stumbling when he landed.

Jenner saw him grip his cane and lean over to rub his knee. It was the first time he'd ever seen John Lloyd nearly fall. He wondered just how bad the lawyer's knee really was. Most of all, he wondered how he injured it.

Looking wildly from side to side, John Lloyd pointed northwest. "He took her this way. It is the only direction in which there are no witnesses." He began running through the darkness, his limp very pronounced.

"Wait up!" called Jenner, puffing after him and wondering how a man six or seven years older and semihandicapped could outrun him. He saw the lawyer's black silhouette bend over suddenly and decided the stubborn bastard had probably torn up whatever was left of that knee.

"Hey, John Lloyd, you okay?" he panted when he finally reached the hunched figure.

"I am perfectly fine," snapped John Lloyd. "However, Theodore is not."

Jenner knelt down. It was black, moonless, and impossible to see more than a blur of a face on the ground. He leaned over and caught a whiff of Theodore's breath and recognized the smell of the Bimbo's house brand of Scotch. "Theodore, what happened?" He put his hand on the old man's face and felt the warm, thick liquid trickling from Theodore's mouth.

"I feel certain it's a knife wound to the lung," said John Lloyd. "Bleeding from the mouth is usually a symptom."

Theodore grabbed John Lloyd's cape. "I never saw who did it, but he was chasing Lydia. I was trying to keep her safe for you." He coughed, and Jenner heard the bubbling sound of air filtering through liquid. "It's ironic, isn't it, that the one time in my life I take responsibility, I get killed. I always knew being irresponsible was more pleasant. I'm too old to begin acting like an adult, John Lloyd, but I did try for you. But it's too late, isn't it?"

John Lloyd didn't answer, and Jenner elbowed him. "Say something, you cold-blooded son of a bitch. The man's dying."

"I wish," began John Lloyd in an odd voice, then he broke off his sentence, and Jenner knew whatever he had intended saying, he had changed his mind. "I do thank you for Lydia's sake. As for the other matter between us, I cannot forgive you."

"I never asked you to."

"We let it stand?" asked John Lloyd, some emotion Jenner couldn't identify making his voice hoarse.

"We always have."

There was a silence, then John Lloyd stood up and peered into the darkness. "It is useless to continue, Sergeant Jenner. She has disappeared, and we must contact Sergeant Schroder."

"What about Theodore? We can't leave him bleeding in the dirt."

John Lloyd knelt down, picked the old man up in his arms, and began loping back toward the Bimbo, his cane hooked over his arm.

"I'll radio for an ambulance," said Jenner, jogging beside the taller man with his injured burden.

"He is dead," said John Lloyd abruptly as he entered the

Bimbo's back door. Laying Theodore on the bar, John Lloyd covered the body and face with his cape.

"This isn't very respectable," said Jenner uneasily. "And we fucked up a murder scene by moving the body."

John Lloyd stared at Theodore's body. "He would find a wake with the body laid out on the bar very appropriate. Tell Mrs. Dinwittie to contact the proper authorities." He turned and was gone.

Jenner caught up with John Lloyd as the lawyer jerked open the back door of the unmarked van and vaulted in, quite an athletic feat for a man with a bad leg, Jenner thought. But then so was carrying a dead body across a vacant lot.

"Schroder!" roared John Lloyd as he grabbed the homicide detective by his lapels and jerked him off the folding camp stool he had been sitting on. "She's gone, Schroder. I can't find her in that crowd of subhumans around the Bimbo. I want you to get your men out of that hellhole of a bar and send them out to kick down every door in every block on this godforsaken street until she's found. And if she's dead, I will personally exact retribution from every police officer who allowed himself to be distracted, every piece of offal in that bar who walks upright, and every sanctimonious hypocrite who held a bat or cattle prod and interfered with me beginning with that lunatic Elliot, and then I will come after you and your ineffectual cohorts!"

Jenner though John Lloyd's threats sounded pretty frightening even if the lawyer had delivered them bent over in the back of a van. He didn't know about Schroder and the rest of the department, but personally, he, Sergeant Larry Jenner, was putting his kicking shoes on.

"Calm down, Branson!" said Schroder, and waved a handful of papers in the lawyer's face. "I need you to think, goddamn it, instead of running off at the mouth. You're the only person I know who takes so many words to say you're gonna castrate everybody who fucked this investigation up."

"Beginning with you."

"Listen to Schroder," said Green, bouncing around on the floor of the van like a chimpanzee. "He's got a list of utility hookups for an area three blocks on either side of the Boulevard and from one end of it to the other!"

John Lloyd dropped Schroder. "What have you found?"

"Since you figured the Butcher had a room close to the Boulevard, Green and I rousted out the computer department at the gas and electric company and got a printout of everybody who ordered utilities hooked up in the last six months."

John Lloyd waved his hand. "You can delay the explanations for a more convenient time. I do compliment you for original thinking, however. It is unfortunate for Miss Fairchild that you did not do more of it sooner."

Jenner decided John Lloyd had calmed down since the lawyer had stopped using contractions and was calling Lydia Miss Fairchild again.

"What have you found, Sergeant, or rather, who have you found?" asked John Lloyd again.

"Nothing and nobody," said Green glumly.

"First, Green and I checked everybody's name in the department against this list in case the Butcher is a cop. No matches. Then we checked everybody's name who's been involved in the investigation including secretaries. No matches. Then we checked the department's list of sex offenders, murderers, et cetera. No matches. Now we're sitting here going down the names on the off-chance we recognize somebody. I don't know what the hell else to do, Branson. I've already called in everybody, and I mean everybody, including the chief, to start kicking in doors, but that could take hours, and I don't think we've got hours."

"We have almost no time at all, Sergeant Schroder. Not if the Butcher stays with the Ripper's pattern. Mary Kelly died between three-thirty and four A.M. It is now three-twenty-five. Miss Fairchild"—his voice cracked and he stopped—"Lydia has between five and thirty minutes to live."

CHAPTER
TWENTY-EIGHT

From Hell

"YES, YOU FOOLED ME," SAID LYDIA, SWALLOWING AND trying to convince herself she was wrong, that Louis Bryant had a quirk about crime-scene photographs, that she had misunderstood his remarks. He was referring to a different kind of game than the one John Lloyd and Schroder were playing with a serial killer.

She tried to convince herself, but it wasn't working. She vowed to learn better methods of self-persuasion when she got back to Dallas.

If she got back to Dallas. The prospects of getting out of this room were not good, and she wouldn't make it to Dallas if she couldn't get out of this room.

"I'm very good at impersonations. Would you like to hear one of your boss? We have some time to spare. You must die in the next thirty minutes but I'm free until then. After that, I'll be very busy, and you won't be able to enjoy my talents."

"No, I don't think so. I'm tired of playacting," she said, raking her teeth over her lower lip and glancing around the room. The Butcher was standing within an arm's length of her, and she was trapped. She could feel the edge of the bed against the backs of her knees, and the Butcher stood between her and the door. She scooted her feet sideways toward the head of the bed and suddenly grabbed the small bedside table, swinging it up like a shield to cover her torso. God, but she couldn't stand the idea of a knife ripping her open. She'd always hated knives.

But the Butcher wasn't holding a knife; he held a long silk scarf. Red, Lydia noticed over her rising panic. She lifted her head to stare at him. His eyes were bright glowing blue, yet at the same time opaque. She noticed the contradiction, but dismissed it from her mind. She really didn't have the time and energy to spare for worrying about why the Butcher's eyes appeared both animated and dead at the same time.

"Lydia"—he savored her name—"Lydia, you are not supposed to struggle. None of the others struggled."

Lydia took a deep breath. Her heart was beating so hard it seemed to shake her whole body. It also seemed to have moved from her chest to her throat and lodged there. "Why didn't they struggle, Bryant?"

He whipped the ends of the scarf around his hands. He had on gloves, Lydia noticed, heavy work gloves. He must have put them on while she was staring at the photographs. "Didn't your clever boss come up with a theory? He certainly had no shortage of theories for my other activities."

"No, he didn't," she replied. Keep him talking, she thought; as long as he's talking, he's not killing me.

"Maybe I mesmerized them with my eyes. Did you ever notice that the greatest of us have unusual eyes?"

"The greatest of whom?" she asked, watching him jerk the scarf taut. Each time he did, the scarf made a snapping sound.

"Of those like me. Rasputin and Manson—and Jack the Ripper. The only witnesses who saw me in Whitechapel mentioned my eyes."

"Me?" She swallowed. He was not only crazy, he was *crazy*! "You are not Jack the Ripper," she enunciated slowly and clearly. "You are Louis Bryant, a journalist in Amarillo, Texas, and you are emotionally disturbed. You need help."

He laughed—and Lydia cringed from the sound. Not because it was maniacal, but because it wasn't. He laughed as would a normal person laugh at a joke. "Your boss was right. You don't believe in evil."

"Not in the same way he does, no. Old Testament fire and brimstone, the serpent and the apple, that sort of thing, is a little too metaphysical for me."

He snapped the scarf taut again. "You're wrong. I *am* Jack the Ripper."

"He's dead!" cried Lydia desperately, shifting the table to get a better grip. The little square table was heavy and awkward, and her arms ached from holding it. "He's got to be dead! It's been over a hundred years!"

The Butcher laughed again. "Poor Lydia. You just don't understand. Jack the Ripper was evil and I'm evil. We are the same kind. Evil doesn't die. It's immortal."

"He was mad!" shouted Lydia.

"No, he wasn't!" retorted the Butcher, beginning to twist the scarf as if wringing a chicken's neck.

Brilliant, Lydia, she thought. You made him angry. Caught in the same room with a serial killer and you have to start an argument with him.

"You can't believe that some of us choose to be evil. We are the other inhabitants of this planet, and it belongs to us as much as to your kind. Good and evil, light and darkness."

"I told you, I'm not big on metaphysics. Maybe you should go back to the Bimbo and debate with John Lloyd. He sees things on a cosmic scale."

"We have evolved beyond your pitiful species, and you're of no use to us except as a game," he continued, ignoring her interruption.

"And this is a game to you?" she asked, wondering exactly what kind of insanity he suffered. In her position, on the other side of a wooden table, the diagnosis wasn't really important.

He smiled, or at least his lips moved. She licked her own lips and wondered if she were the one who was insane—because he looked different than he had a moment ago. His face had metamorphosed into something else. But that was impossible. His features were the same, his size, coloring, hair, were all the same. Yet he was different. He even smelled different. He smelled—hot. But his odor wasn't the musky, sweaty hot of a normal man; it was the acrid, sulfurous smell of— She rejected her impression; no one smelled of brimstone. It was the fireplace, which she only now noticed was burning, adding to the unbearable heat of the room.

"It amuses me to kill you," he said in a conversational tone as if they were speaking of the weather. "I bore easily and playing this game isn't boring, not yet anyway. The difficulty was finding opponents to play with me. That's why I was excited when I discovered who you were. John Lloyd Branson was perfect. And he believes in me. For a while, he was a challenge. I enjoyed his observations this afternoon. But in the end, I beat him."

Ego, Lydia reminded herself. His ego is his Achilles heel. "Did you?" she asked.

"I have you," the Butcher pointed out. "The thing he values most."

"In the first place, I'm not a thing, I'm a person. In the second place, your game is pitiful. I'm surprised John Lloyd agreed to play at all. The game has no originality, none at all. John Lloyd saw through your game almost immediately and was able to anticipate your moves. He knew you would come for me. He even told me to stay out of rooms and buildings unless they were full of people. All you won was a chance to kill me. He won the game. If I had listened to him, I would never have come this far with you no matter what you told me, or who I thought you were. Your controlling me has nothing to do with John Lloyd. Because I'm human, too, not an object. I'm playing in this game, and I think it's boring. Jack already played it a hundred years ago and won because he was never caught. Since John Lloyd knows who you are masquerading as, he'll soon discover which boring, banal little man is behind the mask."

He hissed, actually hissed, as he tried to circle around her, but Lydia kept turning with him, always keeping the table between them as a shield.

"Don't call me names, slut!"

"You deserve them," taunted Lydia. "You're a banal little man who can't get it up like a *real* man. Like John Lloyd Branson!" she finished in a shout.

With a harsh, reverberating cry, he rushed her. "Bitch, bitch, bitch!"

Using the table like a battering ram, she pushed him back, watched him stumble backward against the door. "Unoriginal again," she panted her arms trembling with the effort required to continue holding the table. "Preacher can make up a better list of synonyms. How many names does a hooker have? Ask Preacher. He invented that game. You're copying again."

With that same harsh shriek, he pushed himself away from the door and rushed her again, dodging the table legs to loop the scarf over her head and jerk it tight around her neck. "You have to die!"

She felt her breath cut off, and desperately heaved the table up to slam its edge into his arms. With a wounded scream, he let go of the scarf as her blow temporarily paralyzed the nerves in his arms.

"No, I won't die," she screamed back at him, dropping the table to rip the scarf off her neck. She darted across the tiny room and threw it in the fireplace. "The pattern's broken. You can't strangle me."

"No!" he howled, and shoved her aside to retrieve the scarf. But the fragile material disappeared in a burst of flame even as he tried to force his numbed hand to function.

Lydia scrambled for the door. Just as she closed her fingers around the lock, he leapt upon her back.

"I'll kill you this way!" he screamed in her ear, his fetid breath heating her cheeks under the broad-brimmed hat she still wore. He fastened his hands around her throat. "No one could tell how I killed Mary Kelly. I didn't leave enough of her flesh on her bones for the postmortem to determine cause of death. As long as I slit your throat, it doesn't matter if the strangulation is ligature or manual."

Lydia tottered backward on her spike heels and lost her balance, falling over backward onto the floor. She heard the crack as the Butcher's skull hit the floor and felt his hands loosen. She grabbed his little finger and ring finger and viciously bent them backward until she heard them crack. The Butcher screamed again and jerked his hands away.

She rolled away and crawled toward the table she'd dropped. She was going to have to beat him senseless before she could escape. Scrambling to her feet, she lifted the table and whirled around to see him standing unsteadily in front of the door and pulling something from his pocket.

She screamed; she couldn't help it.

The Butcher's left hand hung uselessly by his side, but in his right hand he held a vicious knife with a blade Lydia was sure had to be at least ten inches long. He looked at her, his eyes glowing in that strange way, as if flames burned behind those opaque orbs. "Look at me," he crooned in a soft musical voice that held a hint of melancholy. "I am Jack," he continued in that same soft voice so unlike his normal one.

Lydia felt her heart slam against her chest as the final horror began. The Butcher spoke with a pronounced British accent. For a moment she smelled the choking fumes of a city heated by coal in a time before pollution was more than a word, smelled also the stench of thousands of unwashed bodies, malnourished bodies sharing a too-small space, felt the dampish chill of a colder, more humid climate. She shook her head and resolutely looked away from his eyes. She understood now why the others didn't struggle. He used that hypnotic voice and those eyes to lull them, then before their wretched, drug-dazed minds comprehended their danger, the Ripper strangled them, all the while talking, talking, talking in that soft voice.

The Ripper?

She had called him the Ripper!

He wasn't; of course he wasn't, but it didn't make any difference whether she was losing her sanity or sharing his illusion, she would be just as dead.

The Butcher walked toward her, one graceful step at a time, his eyes fixed, a smile on his lips, and Lydia tried to sense the mind behind those eyes. Her only weapons were a table and her reason. If she could reason with him, touch his mind, find some frame of reference, she might survive after all.

"Louis," she said. "Louis, don't do this."

He didn't answer.

Because Louis wasn't there, had never been there.

"John Lloyd!" she screamed. "Help me."

CHAPTER
TWENTY-NINE

JENNER FELT JOHN LLOYD'S PANIC AS THE LAWYER ANnounced the countdown on Lydia's life. He thought he detected the sound of a choked sob before the lawyer asked Green a question. "Are the lists in alphabetical order?" he asked.

Green nodded, his face a gray-green color in the van's interior lights. "The gas company gave us two lists: one by address and one alphabetical by last name."

"Give it to me," commanded John Lloyd.

"Here's half," said Green. "I'm checking the other half."

"I'll take both," said John Lloyd. "Since a thorough study of historic crimes does not seem to be included in the curriculum at the police academy, I am the only one familiar with all the suspects in the Ripper case."

"We ain't looking for suspects in the Ripper case, Branson. We're looking for suspects in the Butcher case," protested Green. "You got the Ripper on the brain."

"It is not my brain we are concerned with," said John Lloyd. "It is the Butcher's brain, and he believes he is the Ripper. Taking that as our point of reference, then it is logical to assume that on the Boulevard he uses the persona of one of the suspects in the Ripper case. The only question is which

233

suspect, and since I have no way of knowing or guessing which of the various theories as to the identity of the Ripper our murderer subscribes to, I shall have to check the list in its entirety."

"Give him the list, Green, and cross your fingers," said Schroder.

Jenner could still hear shouts and curses from the crowd at the Bimbo. With all the cops off kicking in doors, the riot at the Bimbo had evolved into a free-for-all. He hoped Bill Elliot was getting the shit kicked out of him.

John Lloyd tapped his finger on the list. "Here is the name. I was hoping our Ripper subscribed to the same belief in the real identity as I did." He tore the sheet off the printout and handed it to Schroder. "Call your men, those you can reach by radio, and send them to that address. And hurry!"

Schroder took a quick look at the address and passed the sheet to Green. "Get on the radio, tell the dispatcher it's an officer in need of assistance. That address is only about three blocks away. Jenner, Branson, and I are getting our tails over there now."

Schroder crawled over the seat and started the van while Green grabbed the microphone. "How'd you know the Butcher would pick this guy, Branson?"

"Logic, Sergeant," he answered, clutching the driver's seat as Schroder swung the big van away from the curb and floorboarded the gas pedal. "Montague John Druitt was a barrister who earned his living as a schoolmaster and was dismissed from his post for erratic behavior. What kind was not recorded. His mother was confined to a mental institution in July of 1888, a little more than a month before the murders began. He was last seen alive on December 3, 1888, and his body was pulled out of the Thames on December 31, 1888 in an advanced state of decomposition. There were no more murders after his suicide, and the investigation into the case was disbanded shortly after his body was discovered. Some accounts say Druitt's family approached the police with proof of his guilt. If that is true, none of those involved saw fit to say so in their memoirs. However, these memoirs are written by Victorian gentlemen who had a horror of scandal and could very well not have mentioned Druitt's name out of respect for his family. As for empirical evidence, we have independent proof that he was in London playing cricket on the days of at least two of the murders. He bears an uncanny resemblance to the Duke of Clarence who had been accused by some crime writers of being the Ripper. His physical description matches those of the few witnesses who admitted seeing anyone.''

John Lloyd swayed against Jenner as Schroder took a sharp right turn onto an unpaved street. ''Druitt's father, grandfather, brother, and nephew were physicians, thus providing him with at least some medical background as well as access to medical instruments. While the pathologists of the time didn't agree on the extent of the Ripper's anatomical knowledge, their opinions ranging from none to at least some familiarity with human or animal anatomy, I believe that the Ripper had to have some knowledge. The human kidney is hidden by a membrane and I doubt a layman completely ignorant of anatomy could find it. Druitt was the only recorded suspect who had any background knowledge other than Dr. Gull, the queen's physician, who was an elderly man and a stroke victim at the time of the murders. The most telling evidence against Druitt to me is psychological. The murders began soon after Druitt's mother was declared insane. Given the tangled, often unhappy relationship serial murderers have with their mothers, that confinement could have been the impetus to push Druitt into his own nightmare. The murder of Mary Kelly with its surfeit of cruelty could have provided the psychological shock necessary to cause him to take his own life less than a month later.''

''So you're saying the real Ripper was insane?'' asked Schroder.

''If I had been his attorney, I would have most certainly argued that he was insane. Our own Ripper, however, is not. By deliberately duplicating the Ripper, he is making a conscious choice. Our Ripper is completely evil, beyond mercy and beyond redemption.''

Schroder slammed on the brakes, nearly sending Jenner over the seat into Green's lap. ''Here it is, third little cabin.''

Jenner followed John Lloyd out the van's back door. They were parked in what fifty years ago had been a tourist court.

Each of the cabins had been converted into individual dwellings—if one was poor enough or desperate enough to rent one of the peak-roofed, unpainted, sagging, narrow little units.

John Lloyd ran at the door and hit it with all the force of his lean body. When the door buckled but did not open, he lawyer pulled his 1873 antique Colt out of a holster Jenner assumed he must have had clipped to his belt, and fired two rounds through the lock. There was a thin, wavering scream from inside the cabin.

"Lydia!" screamed John Lloyd, and kicked the door off its hinges.

Jenner followed him through the door.

And froze.

The room was a charnel house of blood. Droplets of blood were splashed on the walls, the floor, the baseboards. The bed was soaked with it while the wall at the head of the bed showed the unmistakable signs of an arterial blood spray. The body lying on the bed showed surprisingly few signs of violence. If one discounted the long needlelike object with the fancy carving on one end sticking out of Lo iis Bryant's jugular vein.

CHAPTER
THIRTY

LYDIA SCREAMED AS SHOTS EXPLODED THROUGH THE DOOR but couldn't summon the energy to do anything more. Since she'd killed the thing on the bed, she hadn't been able to summon any energy to do more than crawl to this chair. How long ago had that been? Two minutes? Five minutes? Probably no longer, but she couldn't remember. She remembered tearing a huge strip from the skirt of John Lloyd's grandmother's dress and wrapping it around her arm to stop the bleeding. She supposed she'd have to have stitches to close the several gashes made by the Ripper's knife. Defensive cuts they were called, a medical or legal term, she didn't know which. It was a very descriptive term though; when you throw up your arms to defend your face, you get cuts on your arms and the sides of your hands. Nasty things, defensive cuts; they bleed a lot.

The door flew off its hinges, and she looked up to see John Lloyd burst into the room, look first at the bed, then around the room until he saw her. His face blanched and he swayed, but he stumbled the few feet separating them and leaned over her.

His right eye was swollen almost shut and his lower lip cut and puffy. She lifted her right hand, the one that wasn't cut so badly, to gently touch his lip. "John Lloyd, have you been fighting again?" she asked.

He reached out and gathered her into his arms, holding her against him. "Thank God, Lydia, thank God."

He pressed his face against her bare shoulder, and she felt something hot and wet falling on her skin. She lifted her right hand again to stroke the back of his neck. He was so warm and he smelled of bay rum and man. Odd how he smelled differently from her even without after-shave and talcum powder. He had a scent to his skin, like the smell of the soil after a rain shower, clean, pure, primitive like the earth at its beginning.

John Lloyd smelled nothing like the thing on the bed.

She looked over his shoulder at Jenner and Schroder and Green who were staring at the creature.

"I never thought of Bryant," said Green, scratching his head. "No wonder we couldn't get anywhere. He knew everything we were doing, and what we didn't tell him he picked up at the station from some of his undisclosed sources."

"I never liked his eyes. They always seemed to absorb the light without reflecting any back," said Schroder. "He was a smart son of a bitch, though. He took us all on and nearly won. Had us so twisted up trying to figure him out, we missed the obvious."

The burly detective turned to face Lydia. "Miss Fairchild, you did the right thing even though we didn't know it at the time, because the Butcher was going to kill a woman tonight if you hadn't stopped him. See, last week when he brought that letter to Special Crimes, he heard me tell Green that the D.A.'s office was gonna close down the motels on the Boulevard that catered to the hookers. He knew he had to do his killing this weekend, or he wouldn't have good pickings. So you don't have to feel guilty. He didn't start killing faster just because you were on the Boulevard like John Lloyd figured."

"No," replied Lydia. "Maybe beating your deadline was his original intention, but when he found me, all he could think of was drawing John Lloyd into his game."

Schroder scratched his head. "As I see it, the Butcher just made one mistake when he was playing his game."

"What was that, Sergeant?" she asked.

"He figured you for a bust hand instead of a straight flush."

She nodded at the detective and rested her chin on John Lloyd's shoulder. Schroder could believe what he wished, but she knew she had been the touch of death for Cowgirl.

"What the hell is that thing?" she heard Jenner ask the older sergeant.

"It's a hat pin, son."

Green tilted his head to look more closely. "A hat pin? She killed the Boulevard Butcher with a hat pin?" he asked.

"Don't you dare laugh!" screamed Lydia, pushing John Lloyd away and advancing on Green.

John Lloyd caught her by the waist and gathered her into his arms again. "No one will laugh, my dear," he said softly, picking her up and sitting down in the chair to hold her on his lap. He began wiping the blood off her face and shoulders with his handkerchief.

"What happened, Miss Fairchild?" asked Schroder, coming over to squat down beside the chair.

"Not now, Sergeant!" John Lloyd's deep voice seemed to bounce against the walls.

"No, John Lloyd, I've got to talk about it now, while I still remember most of it."

Schroder pulled a notebook out of his pocket. "Whenever you're ready, Miss Fairchild."

"I thought he was Theodore. It was so dark I couldn't really see him, and he mimicked Theodore so well."

"John Lloyd and I found Theodore outside the Bimbo's back door," said Jenner. "He's dead, Lydia, stabbed. He was going after you when Bryant caught him. He told us he was going to protect you. I'm sorry, John Lloyd. Maybe it's none of my business, but I figure he was something to you even if you and he didn't seem to like one another too well."

John Lloyd's face was stiff, like a man trying not to scream. "As you said, Sergeant, it is none of your business."

"Keep your nose out of Branson's business," said Schroder. "Go on, Miss Fairchild."

Lydia laid her head against John Lloyd's chest. She knew whoever Theodore had been and whatever he had done, he had wounded John Lloyd almost beyond healing. She wasn't going to argue in favor of forgiving and forgetting. Maybe not everybody deserved forgiveness.

"When I walked in this room and saw the pictures, I knew the man standing behind me was the Butcher, and that he was worse than even John Lloyd tried to tell me. I don't know if you noticed or not, but he had before and after shots. He took photographs of his victims before he killed them. He had that one of me in the Bimbo. Cowgirl's was odd, though. It was a profile shot and she looked terrified."

"Flashbulb!" exclaimed Jenner. "That night when Cowgirl jumped in front of my squad car, her face was white and I knew it wasn't my headlights because the angle was wrong. It was Bryant's flashbulb."

"So she did see the Butcher?" said Green.

"If she did, she didn't remember him," said Jenner, scooting closer to Lydia's chair. The Special Crimes Unit was coming in now, and the room was getting crowded. He could hear other voices outside, other officers holding back the spectators. Even though no one in this room had talked to anyone else, word had gotten out on the Boulevard: the Butcher was dead.

"Jo-Jo explained how hookers don't remember faces. He told me something else Cowgirl did, too. When she was working, picking up men and so forth, she always wore rubber gloves so she wouldn't have to touch them. People are funny, aren't they? They'll do damn near anything to keep from thinking about what they really are."

"Not the Butcher," said Lydia grimly. "He thought about it all the time. He reveled in what he was. He only existed when he committed some evil act. He was like a man locked up in a glass box. You could see him, hear him, but you couldn't touch him because there was no one in the box. Just a void where a person was supposed to be. I kept trying to sense what he was feeling and what he was thinking so I could persuade him not to kill me, but there was nothing there. He thought of me, of women, of all of you, as things, as objects, when all the time that's what he was: just an object with nothing inside."

EPILOGUE

IT WAS OVER, THE STATEMENTS, THE CAMERAS THRUST IN her face whenever she stepped outside John Lloyd's house, the appearance before the grand jury when they ruled that Lydia Fairchild had acted in self-defense, the press conferences, even the nightmares were occurring less frequently. John Lloyd had considerably expedited both the legal procedure and the media interest. He had issued hundreds of press statements until as he said the market was glutted, and even the *National Enquirer* hadn't called recently.

Her stitches had been removed and her healing flesh only hurt occasionally. She'd have scars, but only faint hairline ones since John Lloyd had called in the finest plastic surgeon in the state to sew up her arm. He had also stood guard in her hospital room, questioned the nurses about every pill and every procedure until three had threatened to quit. He had taken her home with him and coddled and spoiled her until she felt like screaming.

Lydia glanced at John Lloyd, who was staring out the glass wall of the airport waiting room. John Lloyd had been wonderfully caring, supportive, and tender. Almost maternal.

But she didn't need a mother; she already had one.

"Is your arm hurting, Miss Fairchild?" asked John Lloyd.

Lydia thought she might hit him if he didn't stop acting so solicitous. "No, it's fine."

"Do you have your ticket?"

"Yes."

"Do you have your claim checks for your luggage?"

"Yes, and I have on clean underwear and I've been to the bathroom and I drank my milk at breakfast. John Lloyd, you are treating me like a child and it's driving me crazy."

"Never having had a daughter, Miss Fairchild, perhaps I am being a trifle overprotective."

"I am not your daughter, and I won't let you hide from me behind a façade of paternal interest."

"I am not hiding."

"John Lloyd, I don't blame you for what happened to me. You don't have to feel guilty. It was my choice. I faced the consequences and they were horrible. I doubt that I'll ever be quite the same again."

She looked down at her hands. "You were right, you know. About the Ripper."

"In what way, Miss Fairchild?" She noticed he didn't correct her when she said Ripper instead of Butcher.

"He was evil, but he was such an unoriginal, banal man I didn't recognize it until it was almost too late. Even so, for a moment, for several moments, I believed I was really facing Jack the Ripper."

"I am not surprised."

"What!"

"Evil never changes. It only takes different forms."

Lydia shivered and changed the subject. "Schroder told me the Boulevard is calling Bill Elliot's demonstration the Battle of the Bimbo Bar."

"It seems an apt name."

Lydia took a deep breath. There was no point putting it off any longer. "Will you let me hold you while you heal?"

"I have no idea what you are talking about, Miss Fairchild."

"Theodore."

He stared out the window. "A man's life is often a dark and secret thing. Sometimes those secrets cannot be shared."

"Quit protecting him, John Lloyd. Theodore was charming and funny and very polite to me, but probably the only really decent thing he ever did in his life was try to save me. He was a drunk and an unrepentant one, and those invitations that he made for Preacher were ugly, frightening things. Remember he said at the police station that he wanted expiation? That is marvelous, that is commendable, but in Theodore's case it was self-indulgent. He was an old man. Why didn't he try to earn your forgiveness before now?"

She rubbed her healing arm. Sometimes it still ached, ached as much as John Lloyd's heart must be aching. "I remember something else about his tirade at the police station. He absolutely railed at you for not protecting me. That's why you're walking around in an invisible hair shirt feeling guilty. I'm surprised you don't buy a whip and scourge yourself."

"Miss Fairchild!" His eyes were blazing with fury, and Lydia was ecstatic. At least he was showing some emotion besides protectiveness. "Miss Fairchild, you are trespassing where you are not wanted."

"Don't kid yourself. I'm wanted, John Lloyd, that's why you feel so damn guilty. You want me and I don't mean for a little hand holding or an interesting predicament on occasion. I mean you want me with every bit of that earthy, aggressive virility that you try to sublimate or ignore."

"That is enough, Miss Fairchild!"

"No, it's not. I'm just getting started. You don't owe Theodore anything—"

"His name was Theodore Branson. I saw him when I was three, when I was seven, when I was twelve; and when I was eighteen, we had a difference of opinion. As you have observed, Miss Fairchild, I am very Victorian, and like the Victorians, I do not like family scandal. I had not seen him for eighteen years until that night at the police station."

"What was the difference of opinion?" asked Lydia.

"It is unimportant."

"I don't think so. I think that it has something to do with why you are acting the way you are. I think that it will explain why you didn't stop me from doing something so obviously dangerous. If you don't tell me, I shall embarrass you down to the toes of your custom-made boots in front of all these people, and you won't be able to stop me short of physically manhandling me and you won't do that because I'm still— unwell.''

He turned his head to look at her, a glint of humor in his black eyes. ''What nefarious action are you contemplating, Miss Fairchild, that could possibly intimidate me?''

''I'm going to feel you up,'' she replied, and laughed when he looked stunned.

He sighed. ''We disagreed over my draft card.''

''What?''

''Among the many barriers to a more personal relationship between us, Miss Fairchild, is age. I reached draft age at the very end of the Vietnam War. My number was called, and I refused to get a deferment.''

''Why, for God's sake?''

''Because the next number after mine belonged to a young man with a very pregnant wife. He was not college material, I believe the term is. He did not attempt to set himself up as a minister of some self-proclaimed church, did not work in a defense industry: in short, he was ineligible for a deferment. My situation was very much like yours. I could have avoided what I saw as my responsibility, and another man could have died in my place. I did not choose to do that.''

''Theodore disagreed?''

''He seemed to think I was more worthy than the other young man.''

''So he shot you?''

John Lloyd looked stunned again. ''Miss Fairchild, wherever did you get an idea like that?''

''Well, the dean said an old reprobate shot you, and you wouldn't talk about Theodore just like you won't talk about your leg, and Theodore was a reprobate, and I concluded—''

''As usual, you jumped to your conclusion. He did not shoot me. As a means of protecting me, he took away my choice.''

''How?''

''He managed an appointment to my local draft board, a very suspicious appointment since he was only temporarily in Canadian and only temporarily sober. He filed papers for my deferment himself in secret and sent the other boy his notice. By the time I asked where my orders were, it was too late."

"So you went to college."

"Of course not. I enlisted. I had a responsibility not to continue my life without interruption at the expense of another. I spent my enlistment at Fort Benning, Georgia. By the way, Miss Fairchild, I don't recommend Fort Benning as the most desirable place to spend the tag end of one's youth. I never got to Vietnam in spite of requesting duty there."

"What happened to the other man?"

John Lloyd's hands twisted over the top of his cane. "He was the last casualty of the Vietnam War."

"Oh, God, I'm sorry. So you really did understand why I made my choice even though you tried to persuade me against it. I put you through a ghoulish evening, didn't I? You wanted to protect me, and you couldn't without taking away my choice. If you had done that, and another woman had died in my place, I would have hated you."

"Your summation is accurate," he replied.

"You said family scandal," said Lydia, clasping her hands together and deciding she hadn't learned much on the Boulevard after all. She still didn't know how to remain silent.

John Lloyd's mouth twisted. "You leave me no privacy at all."

"I've killed a man, John Lloyd. You know the worst there is to know of me."

"He was my father."

She groped for his hand and held it. "I'm sorry, John Lloyd."

"The dead are buried, both the innocent and the guilty. It is time to get on with our lives."

"Not quite yet, John Lloyd. Who shot you?"

He smiled, his eyes totally implacable. "That is not a subject I intend to discuss. You discovered my father's identity. I believe that is enough for now."

"But—"

"Leave it, Miss Fairchild, for another time."

She gave up then. There was always Thanksgiving, which she planned to spend with him and Mrs. Dinwittie.

He squeezed her hand. "All the loose ends tied up, Miss

Fairchild? Nothing else disturbing your curiosity or sense of justice?''

"There is one thing," she said slowly. "You know what makes me really angry, John Lloyd?"

"When your mother refers to your nightmare with the Butcher as *your little accident*?" he asked, the shadows clearing from his eyes.

"That's second on my list," she said, grimacing. "No, it's that with so many dead and so many lives changed, Jo-Jo Jefferson is still on the Boulevard to prey on women."

John Lloyd chuckled, the first time he'd laughed since, well, since her little accident. "I have taken steps, Miss Fairchild, to guarantee that Mr. Jules 'Jo-Jo' Jefferson finds freedom a temporary condition."

"How?" asked Lydia. "You and Sergeant Schroder said nothing could be proved against him. He can go on being the drug and prostitute entrepreneur of North Amarillo until someone agrees to testify against him, and you both agreed that probably wouldn't happen. So what are you going to do, hire a hit man?"

"Actually, it was your idea, Miss Fairchild," replied John Lloyd, stroking the silver head on his cane, a self-satisfied expression on his face.

"What was my idea?"

"I reported him to the IRS for tax evasion. A little matter of not paying withholding taxes on his employees."

About the Author

D. R. MEREDITH's first John Lloyd Branson mystery novel, MURDER BY IMPULSE, was published by Ballantine Books in 1988. This series debut brought renewed acclaim to Ms. Meredith, whose celebrated Panhandle thrillers featuring Sheriff Charles Matthews are also popular. John Lloyd Branson reappeared in MURDER BY DECEPTION (1989) and, now for the third time, in MURDER BY MASQUERADE. Ms. Meredith lives in Amarillo, Texas, with her husband and their two children.